- Ded

Love is the most beautiful thin
and the most p

We here at Breaking Rules Publishing would like to dedicate this first issue of the Love Is Love Anthology to all of those who have experienced love, even for just the slightest moment. For they have realized that life is worth very little without it.

We are also proud to have such a variety of stories from authors all around the world. To the authors within this book we say -

Thank You And Well Done!

Authors Table

A Love So Madly

by Marlon Martinez

New York

So now everyone at the party is looking at us. She continues to yell while the drink she threw on me loiters and leaks off the focal points of my face. They go *drip, drip,* a slight pause then *drip* again. Her words have become the rhetoric news anchors recite: *The World this, and the World that. Another mass shooting and this causes cancer.* The diarrhetic verbiage she uses is so processed, so heard often by me, it falls limp on the reaction it was suppose to catalyze. They're things I've heard before. Things I'll hear again. . .

Long ago, she walked into a room. I was sitting on a bean bag below the plume of pot and cigarette smoke that clung to the dorm's ceiling. Her scent reached me before I knew her name. She walked toward my direction, displacing the blue smoke the closer she came. My capacity to move was stymied by the prospect of being near something that beautiful. To this day I'm unsure if it was the haze of controlled substance or the simple attraction that caused my hysterical atrophy. I was barely able to gain my composure when we were introduced. Her name was Nina- - and then we spoke.

. . . So lately, biting my tongue was the strategy I used when dealing with Nina during these sort of public out bursts. My past disposition is a hard thing to shake because the look everyone gives me when she says what she said about my mother tested this new battle plan of mine to its threshold. The longer our relationship stretched, the more like tracing paper it became. Nina saw through every defense or tactic. She knew exactly what to say and when to say it. Nina was an artist and my temperament was her paint. . .

The particulars of our first fight get lost on me. That argument set the tempo of our relationship. Over the years, like any great pugilistic rivalry, Nina and I learned one another's weaknesses. A detail that I distinctly recall from that first contest was her intoxicating aroma. I remember her *bouquet* being louder than our shouting. It was too much of what I wanted when I didn't have it. Nina never forgot this morsel of information and would use it to devastating effects in future fights. With awing precision, she'd use her smell to get
me to do the things I said I wouldn't.

. . . So then we're outside, and I grab the back of her arm where there's enough *pudge* to remind me that I'm still very attracted to her. I spin Nina around as if mid *tango* and her whipping eyes settle on mine. We almost kiss before the screaming starts up again. The pedestrians that are watching our show can't distinguish if it's passion or hate we're displaying. She gets in a cab and I go back thirteen flights to pick up the pieces at the party. The only thing that ever seems *brand new* after a public quarrel is the awkward anxiety of apologizing to your friends and family. . .

Once, Nina slapped me. I was wearing my favorite T-shirt while we were lounging out like dueling house cats. It was a playful accident but her claws tore a hole in the fabric. The shirt was from a vintage era that Nina was not a part of. I flew off the handle and in doing so I touched on the unnecessary by bringing up the abortion she had the year prior. The sound of her hand connecting with my face rang of meat being thrown down on a butcher's slab. It stilled me, as it did Nina. She knew I would've never struck her back, and that's what killed us. We made up that day and never spoke of it again.

. . . So in a few years, when I retell tonight, after it's a memory, I'll start at the beginning before jumping ahead to the *weighted* walk up the stairs to our apartment. I'll acknowledge Nina's fragrance the more about my key got to its burrows. I'll remember how mindful I was not to wake her when I opened the door slowly in the event that she was sleeping. I'll walk in to the apartment and see Nina on the couch stoically crying with *tiny crumpled clouds* scattered all around her. She'll remind me of a painting I saw somewhere of a floating Greek goddess in a half-shell, wearing a T-shirt I have. The one with the *hole* in it. I won't look at her long in that state before I'll head into the kitchen. When I open the refrigerator, all the cold escaping light will guide Nina's way. My back will be towards her when she places unstable fingers in the small of my hand. I'll recognize her touch the way my tongue knows every *out of place* bud, bump, or crevice in my mouth. Nina will turn me, with our hands clasped, and she'll say things I've heard before. The things I'll hear again.

Farewell

by Christopher T. Dabrowski

Poland

The time of farewell has come. They did not want to break up but they had no choice. Force majeure. When they looked into each other eyes the memories came alive. Whole common life like a film run on the mental screen. They know each other very well, they had so many experiences that essentially they were unity. Unity of souls and fleshes. The second one needn't say anything to know about what the first one is thinking. They hugged each other once again. Strongly, the last time. Tears came to their eyes.

What will be then? Will they be together? Will they meet find each other?

They were not afraid of death. They were only afraid of the fact that it divide them.

In the blink of an eye they evaporated... Carried away by the wave of atomic bomb.

SIMON

by Richard Natale
California

Standing in the doorway of Ty's, Simon considered hailing a taxi and heading home. The bar was crowded for a Monday. A rag-tag assortment of solitary poseurs; men wearing plaid flannel shirts over Wrangler's tucked into Tony Lama boots; a mustachioed denim and leather clad bartender dispensing beer bottles with both hands while the cub-like, bare-chested bar back refilled empty cases with the discards and hauled them down to the basement. Despite being cheek by jowl, the men seemed aloof, distracted, as if they'd wandered into the bar by mistake and were not sure what to do now.

The night air was raw with periods of rain; large intermittent drops that popped when they hit the sidewalk. Simon reconsidered. An instinct to get out of the cold, overrode his hesitance. Pushing open the door, he deposited his brolly in a receptacle just inside. He removed his lined-leather gloves and loosened his scarf and prepared to order a whiskey.

It was a whiskey kind of night.

Earlier, in an under-heated movie house on West Thirteenth, Simon had shivered through a faded print of Altman's new film, "The Long Goodbye." His third viewing actually, the other two under more favorable circumstances back in Manchester while visiting the family. The film's determinedly syrupy theme was still stuck in his head and he hummed it absentmindedly.

The foul weather reminded him of home, fondly so. During his harried internship at Bellevue, he'd had little time to scratch the nostalgia itch. With his days now more structured, he'd been plagued by visits from the homesickness hound baying outside his window. He missed the folks and also Dwight, the closeted man who'd brought him out and had sworn to commit suicide if Simon emigrated to the U.S. At Christmas, Dwight had sent a card and inserted a photo of himself beside an adoring young man, his after-life boyfriend no doubt.

Spiteful bugger.

Though the American Psychiatric Association had finally declassified homosexuality as a mental disorder the previous year, most of Dwight's Bellevue colleagues were more comfortable treating certifiable lunatics than depressed queers. Consequently, gays and lesbians who'd tried to kill themselves (and not merely indulged in extortion like Dwight), were routed to Simon. While not remotely out at work, he was regarded as "sympathetic."

Probably his accent. Brits. Queers. Same difference. An assumption that went hand in hand with the generalization that all Englishmen were whip smart and could quote Shakespeare and Keats on command. Only other ex-pats picked up on Simon's regional accent, which, despite his efforts at university to erase it, resurfaced, especially when he was fatigued. "You sound like John Lennon," one fellow medic mentioned. Liverpool. But close enough.

"Another?" the bartender asked, pointing to Simon's empty glass.

"For the road," Simon nodded. Since he had little experience in the etiquette of cruising – how to look, how to be looked at – he'd already grown restless and bored. "Going to the toilet. Be right back," he told the bartender, slapping down some bills.

As he relieved himself at the urinal, a blinding flash went off in the stall nearby. Then another. Simon rapped on the stall door. "Is everything all right in there?" he inquired.

"Yeah," said a voice from within. "Just trying to get a good shot of my stuff."

"Come again?" Simon said.

The door swung open: A young man was sitting on the toilet, a zoom lens bearing down on his crotch. The flash clicked several times. Then the man whipped the camera strap over his shoulder, rose to his feet and zipped up. He smiled at Simon who thought him unnaturally beautiful – if possibly deranged.

"Hi. I'm Titus. I notice that you're uncircumcised," he said, hovering over Simon who was still in mid-stream. "Would you mind if I took a few shots while you have it out?"

"Yes, I think I would," he said, shuddering.

"Just so you know, I'm not a perv. I'm a professional photographer. I've had an exhibition."

"At the dirty bookstore on Hudson?" Simon scoffed.

"No. At a real gallery in Soho. Last year. Got good reviews too. Even sold a few prints," Titus said, digging into his jeans. He pulled out an embossed business card with an artful photo of two women folding laundry in one corner, and flashed it at Simon. "What I'm working on now isn't porn. They're abstracts. I zoom in so close that they look like anything but genitals. It's freaky."

"I've no doubt. Just the same, thank you, no."

"Please," he said, tilting his adorable kinky-haired head to one side. "I don't have many uncut men. This is America. Foreskin is forbidden."

Simon couldn't help but be amused by Titus' affectless delivery, which only reinforced his angelic bad boy aura.

"Very well, but let's be quick about it before someone comes in."

"No prob. I can get off a dozen shots in a flash," Titus said. "Now face me and would you mind taking out your nuts too? I need the whole package."

Simon reached into his trousers and struggled to retrieve his testicles. *Why am I doing this, he asked himself. Me, the poster child for British propriety.*

"And I need for you to be flaccid," Titus said as he fiddled with the zoom lens.

"I am," Simon said, sternly.

"Oh. Well, congratulations," Titus said as a series of blinding flashes went off in rapid succession.

"This is quite uncomfortable," Simon remarked, certain that he'd lost his mind.

"Almost done," Titus said, the shutter rapidly clicking. The door opened behind them and Simon quickly packed up his equipment.

Titus jumped to his feet. "Thanks a heap, man. How about I buy you a drink?"

"I have one waiting for me, but I appreciate the offer," Simon said. As he opened the door, he added, "Perhaps you'd like to join me? I'm Simon, by the way."

"You're on, Simon," Titus said, bouncing on the balls of his feet ahead of him. Approaching the bar, he signaled to the bartender, "Hey, Billy. A Miller."

When Billy brought his drink, Titus said, "I just took a picture of his stuff. He's uncut."

"Must you?" Simon said, abashed.

"It's cool. I shot Billy last week. In the back room. Right?"

"Yup," Billy replied. "He showed me the pictures. Weird.

Never in a million years would you think that's what you were looking at."

"I threw a blue wash over them. They have this Georgia O'Keefe vibe."

"The woman who painted flowers that looked like vaginas?"

"Well aren't you the culture vulture?" Titus chortled. "By the way, I've also shot about a dozen vaginas. And a couple of them actually do look like flowers. Well, more like rose bushes. Did you know that pussies can look as different as dicks?"

"Can't say as I've had the pleasure," Simon said.

"Well, they do. I've done nipples too. But only on women. They're like moonscapes."

"How about buttholes?" Billy asked.

Titus shook his head. "Nah. I tried. Did mine and my roommate, George, while he was asleep. They're just not that interesting."

"Ears," Simon interrupted. "Have you tried ears? They can be quite diverse."

Titus brushed the hair away from Simon's right ear. "Hmm. It's a thought. Yours are nice, and so is your..."

Simon pushed his hair back into place, pretending to ignore the remark. Downing the last few drops in his glass, he turned up the collar on his mac. "Well, then. It's late. I should be in bed like a good boy."

"Thanks for doing that," Titus said. "I know it wasn't easy for someone as uptight as you. You want to see the pictures when they're done?"

"Thanks just the same," Simon said, bridling at Titus' observation. The only reason he'd cooperated was to prove that he wasn't uptight. Wasn't it?

"Too bad. I was hoping to see it again. And not to photograph," he said casually as if he'd asked Simon to tea.

"A tempting offer," Simon said. "I'm likely not the first person to say this, but you're quite fetching."

"No, you're not the first," Titus said. "Thanks, but I don't see it. I've done a few self-portraits. My features are small and flat. There's no real character in my face."

"You'll get no pity from me," Simon said. "And I disagree. You've plenty of character."

"Now that's a compliment I'll take," Titus said.

"Tell me, this fellow you mentioned, the roommate whose bunghole you photographed, is he your ....?"

"George? No, he belongs lock, stock and barrel to somebody who belongs to somebody else. But he lets me use his body from time to time."

"Is that another hobby of yours? Using men's bodies?"

"I told you already. Photography's not a hobby," Titus said, wrinkling his nose. "I plan to make a living at it someday. As for men's bodies, sometimes it takes the edge off being lonely."

"I shouldn't think that would be a problem for you. Whereas I...," he sighed. "You know, stranger in a big city."

Simon was caught up short. Displaying his privates seemed somehow less intimate than confessing to solitude. For the second time since meeting Titus, had done something completely out of character. Distressing. "Well, nice meeting you," he said, pulling on his gloves.

Titus leaned in and brushed his lips along Simon's cheek. "Take me with you?" he asked.

A simple request with no neediness. It would have been heartless for Simon to refuse.

* * *

They spent a cozy night together. The sex was tame. Felt more like payment for the privilege of sharing his bed on a chilly night. In the morning, Titus again offered to come by and show him the photos. He jotted down Simon's number, though he didn't expect to hear from Titus again.

He was wrong. A week later, Titus rang him up. He arrived at Simon's flat with a bottle of Merlot. The photos, they concluded, resembled the tip of an elephant's trunk sinking into a swirling pool of quicksand. Titus then unzipped Simon and blew him.

"That was great, thanks," Titus said with a wink, and kissed him for good measure. His directness and ease with sex seemed alien yet intoxicating. Simon was still coming to terms with his nature, which he continued to regard as somewhat aberrant despite years of psychiatric training. Studying Freud, Hirschfeld and Kinsey had done little to alleviate his internal struggle and he pursued his yearnings only when resistance proved intolerable.

While Dwight had forced him out of denial, this capricious

street urchin, who didn't seem to care a whit for social convention, threatened to drag him into the light of day. And he felt powerless to resist.

That Friday, they went out for a meal at a Polish restaurant on Second Avenue. Simon had argued against it. He was a boring eater, he said, strictly meat and potatoes. Titus assured him that the Poles served both. Simon ordered a goulash, which seemed safe, though he deemed the liberal use of paprika "exotic." Titus found it so funny, he almost gagged. Simon was seized by the urge to throw him on the ground and bugger him right there in the restaurant.

Troubling, he thought, especially when it dawned on him that he desired more than Titus' body. He wanted to osmose his freewheeling spirit.

After dinner, they went to Titus' apartment and perused his portfolio. Simon was impressed, particularly by the photos from his first exhibit, a montage of Greenwich Village – where Titus was raised – over the past decade. Titus told him about his rootless upbringing. His white mother, a writer, and his black father, a jazz musician. To Simon's ears it sounded almost romantic, until he mentioned that his mother had murdered his father. Accidentally, but nonetheless.

How had Simon missed the dark undercurrent in Titus' sang froid attitude and was only hearing it now when he spoke about his childhood? Clearly, his infatuation had muddied his psychological faculties.

Since Titus' roommate/sometimes bedmate, George, was in Atlanta visiting his children, Titus was free to, as he put it, "play music written in this century. Do you like Zeppelin?"

As the needle dropped on "When the Levee Breaks," Titus threw off his clothes and undid the buttons on Simon's shirt. He stretched out on the sofa and Simon sat on the floor beside him and caressed and kissed him. He forcefully masturbated Titus, and took immense pleasure in his rhythmic writhing and groans. Titus' release was so thrilling that Simon ejaculated without stimulation.

"How did you do that?" Titus marveled.

"Sorcery," Simon said. While his tone was playful, it was edged with truth. In Titus' presence, he felt possessed.

When the music ended, the silence was interrupted only by the occasional whirr of a distant siren. Titus asked him about Dwight. Did Simon love him? No. Would he have known if he had? Probably not. Simon in turn, was curious about George. "He's a great person. But tortured," Titus said. "He's been crazy in love with this guy, Donald. For years. And scared shitless about it the whole time. Then he ran away and by the time he came back, Donald had moved to Brooklyn to live with a cop who loved him as much as George did, except he didn't feel bad about it."

"Sad," Simon said. "How did you end up living with him?"

"Originally, I lived here with my mom's friend Terry, who got custody of me after she went to prison. Terry was walking past Donald's old apartment one day and found George sitting on a stoop across the street staring up at his window. Terry told George what had happened and he completely fell apart. Terry felt bad for him and let him stay with us for a while. Then Terry moved in with his boyfriend and George inherited the apartment. And me. He sleeps with me occasionally, and other guys too, but he's still stuck on Donald."

"I'm sure there are dozens of men who are "stuck" on you," Simon assured him.

"I don't know of any. Not that I care. Why? Are you stuck on me?"

"I don't think that would be a good idea," Simon said.

"The transistor radio is a good idea," Titus snapped. "Frozen food is a good idea. Love is never a good idea. I've seen what it does to people. Nope. Not for me."

* * *

They saw each other sporadically over the next several months. They went to hear Alberta Hunter at the Cookery on Eighth Street, saw Bob Fosse's astringent new musical, Chicago (but only because their first choice, A Chorus Line, was completely sold out), and a couple of films, Nashville and Jaws, which they enjoyed immensely if for different reasons. Simon was taken by the stories while Titus, true to form, was obsessed with the cinematography.

Then Simon's work schedule changed. His lease ended and he became preoccupied with finding a new apartment, finally settling on a doorman building on East Ninth off University Place. Titus traveled to Berlin for a vernissage, which included several photos of the abstract genitalia series. They didn't communicate for two months and got together only once, for a drink, after Titus returned from Europe. He quickly ran off citing a prior commitment. Simon assumed that Titus' infatuation had run its course and he had moved on. Now he needed to do likewise. A tall order.

With Dwight, he had felt safe. There'd been a line of demarcation which, by mutual agreement, they'd never breached. With Titus, boundaries had been crossed from the onset, and Simon felt himself being drawn into dangerous territory. He rang Titus several times and there was either no answer or George picked up and took a message. But Titus never called back.

Perhaps a little heartache would do him good, he reasoned. Better now than later. Titus was impermanent by nature, carefree to the point of carelessness. His opposite in almost every way.

One good thing came of it though. Titus had emboldened him. Given him confidence. He began dating a puckish young man named Darryl whom he'd met at John's Pizzeria on Bleecker, or rather made eye contact with and followed home hoping to be invited up. Which he was. He would never have dared such a bold move before he met Titus.

Darryl was taciturn but frolicsome in bed. One Friday evening several weeks after they met, Darryl popped by with his next door neighbor, Patrick, with whom he explained, he had an "on and off thing." Patrick, a sprightly, energetic bloke, was talkative and amusing. He had brought a joint and they passed it around. Simon only became aware that Patrick was to be included in the evening's entertainment when Darryl suggested Simon kiss him while he watched.

* * *

After a particularly trying day, which had included a grueling two-hour session with parents who were in deep denial about their daughter's sexuality and suicidal tendencies, Simon was at home finishing off two bangers (sorry, hot dogs) he'd bought at Gray's Papaya, when there was a knock at the door. Probably a neighbor he thought since, normally, the doorman announced all visitors.

"Well this is a pleasant surprise," Simon said to Titus who was standing in the doorway. "How did you get by the...?"

"He's probably on a cigarette break," Titus explained. "Can I come in?"

"Yes, yes, of course," Simon said, opening the door wide

and it struck him that he hadn't actually given Titus his new address. "How did you find me?"

"I called information," Titus replied. "Nice place," he added as he crossed into the dining area. "This wall needs something. You should come by some time and pick out one of my photos and hang it here. I won't charge you for it."

"What a lovely offer. Perhaps I shall," Simon said, noting that Titus was uncharacteristically on edge. "Would you like something to drink?"

Titus turned sharply and looked directly at him. "I got your messages," he said. "I didn't call you back because, well, the thing is, I think you may have gotten the wrong idea. I was looking for a fuck buddy, someone to hang out with and maybe spend the night. You know, something casual."

"Oh, I see," Simon said, blindsided. "And I made it complicated?"

"Kind of. I still like you though and if it's okay with you, we could try again," Titus said. "But just so we're clear. Fuck buddies, right?"

"Fuck buddies," he repeated, though he hated the vulgar term. But it if meant seeing Titus again, he would have agreed to assassinate the Archbishop of Canterbury.

"Great. And since I'm here, do you want to have sex?"

Simon nodded meekly.

"Good. How about you get down on your knees," Titus said, undoing his trousers.

When he had finished, Titus took Simon's hand and led him to the bedroom, where he straddled him, kissing him and gazing deeply into his eyes. Simon didn't want it to end. He resisted climaxing with all his might but he was no match for the sorcerer.

"That was fun, wasn't it?" Titus said, resting his head on Simon's chest.

"I should think the answer is self-evident," Simon said.

"See. We can do this."

"I'm afraid you'll have to be patient. I don't have much experience at this sort of thing."

"So how many guys have you slept with? More or less."

"More than five, fewer than ten," Simon admitted.

Titus lifted his head and stared straight at him. "Really? God. I've been with more men than that in the past month."

Titus probably hadn't meant to sound disparaging. If Simon hadn't been awash in post-coital bliss, he might have glossed over the comment. But at that moment, he was feeling particularly vulnerable and he was furious. He pushed Titus away and abruptly shifted to the other side of the bed. "You're a horrible boy. Put on your clothes and leave this instant."

Titus reacted as if he'd been struck. He dressed quickly and left without saying goodbye.

Simon regretted the words immediately. What did it matter how many men Titus was with so long as they could be together – even if only on a semi-regular basis? Surely that was preferable to losing him completely. He was rousted from his thoughts by the screech of tires outside. He ran to the window and saw Titus standing in front of taxi, which had missed hitting him by inches. He was pounding the hood of the yellow cab and swearing at the driver.

Simon opened the window and called out to him, "Are you all right?"

Titus glanced up four stories but didn't reply.

"I apologize for what I said," Simon blurted. "I can't help it that I'm in love with you."

"What?" Titus said as he walked away. Simon shut the window. What a damned fool thing to say. Hadn't he done enough damage for one evening?

Titus made no further attempts to reach him and Simon suffered through it as best he could, distracting himself with a holiday visit to Manchester. On New Year's Eve, he even fell back into bed with Dwight. For auld lang syne.

On a bitter cold night in February, Darryl invited him to go dancing at a private club called Flamingo on lower Broadway. An open space crammed with sweaty, attractive, shirtless men. The walls and floors vibrated from the relentless beat. They split a Quaalude and washed it down with chilled vodka and Simon enjoyed the sensation of being lithe and lively on the dance floor. If he looked ridiculous, so what of it? He was enjoying himself thoroughly.

While Darryl was in the loo, Simon's eyes wandered until they fell on a familiar face and he stopped breathing for a moment. Titus was being pasted against the wall by a handsome young man, his neck and chest covered in kisses. Simon gazed open-mouthed, pain shooting through his numbness. When Darryl returned, they resumed dancing but, later, he was not able to perform. He blamed it on the drugs.

That summer, Darryl invited him for the weekend at the house he was sharing on Fire Island. When Simon arrived, Darryl showed him to his room and explained that he would be away most of the time. He was "hot and heavy" with a boy who lived in a house on the bay. "I'd invite you along," he said, "But I'm not ready to share him just yet. Anyway, I think you and I are becoming more like friends, don't you?"

Simon was confounded by the fluidity of queer mating rituals. Hot and heavy, fuck buddies, friends, sisters. Arbitrary rules that changed as often as the players. Perhaps he should just head home on the late night ferry. The Village was pleasantly sparse and quiet on summer weekends. The gays headed off to Fire Island and the straights to the Hamptons, with some crossover.

But first he'd spend the day at the beach and inject some color into his pale, freckly skin. After a dip, he fell asleep on his towel. He woke from the nap, sat up and lit a cigarette. At that moment Titus wandered past and stopped at a blanket about twenty feet away. He was naked as was the young man beneath him, who appeared to have swallowed barbells that went directly to his biceps and pectorals.

Their eyes met. Simon threw himself back down on the towel and wished him away.

"What are you doing here?" Titus said, standing over him.

"I was invited out for the weekend," he replied, squeezing his eyes shut.

"By who?"

"I don't see how that's any of your concern," Simon said. He opened his eyes and tried to gauge Titus' reaction but his face was in shadow.

"Well goodie for you," Titus said. Then he crouched down and pointed to the naked man on the blanket.

"Hot, isn't he? He fucked me senseless last night. I don't think I've ever come so much in my life. Do you want to know why?"

"Not particularly," Simon said, angrily flicking his cigarette away.

"Because the only way I could get excited was by imagining that it was you," he said. "How screwed up is that?"

Without another word, Titus returned to the blanket. He bent down and kissed the man before running down to the water's edge and jumping in.

Simon hated Titus fiercely, in a way he recognized, that only reinforced how much he still cared for him. *Oh physician, heal thyself.*

Simon boarded the next boat for the mainland.

When, in mid-September, Titus once again snuck past the doorman and pounded on his door, Simon guessed it was him.

"You busy?" he said when Simon opened the door a crack.

"Yes, as a matter of fact. I'm entertaining," Simon replied, coldly.

"You are not. You came home alone. I know because I was taking pictures of you from the across the street," he said, pushing open the door. He ducked under Simon's arm and entered the room.

"You were photographing me? Why?"

"Part of a new series. I catch people going in and out of their buildings, like a private detective gathering incriminating shots of a criminal or an adulterer. The faces and bodies are a blur and they have this ghost-like quality. I think you'd like them."

"Yes. It does sound interesting," Simon conceded, noting that his heart had begun clocking at above average speed. *Control yourself, man.*

Without asking, Titus helped himself to a beer from the refrigerator. "Imported. Fancy," he said as he scrounged through the drawers for a church key. He took two long swigs and peered out the window and sighed.

"This has got to stop," Titus mumbled. "It's getting boring."

"Whatever do you mean?" Simon asked.

"That night at Flamingo. The way you looked at the guy I was with, it was like you wanted to tear him apart. Where do you get off?"

"I can't say as I recall."

"You do so. You don't own me, Simon." Titus tossed himself into an armchair and propped his feet on the ottoman. "Did you know that the last time I cried was the day my mom went to prison? Oh wait, there was another time. After you told me I was horrible and kicked me out. Yeah, that was a tough night."

Simon was speechless.

Titus jumped up and began pacing the room as if he was encaged. "Look, are you still in love with me?"

"Whatever gave you that idea?"

"I heard you say it. From the window. After you told me to leave."

"Oh, I see," Simon said, hanging his head. "A momentary lapse. You needn't worry."

"Then why do you keep popping up wherever I go? You're spooking me, man."

"In the future, I shall endeavor to make myself invisible," Simon said with a sneer.

"Fuck you," Titus said.

"Titus, I've seen you exactly twice since the beginning of the year. That hardly qualifies as stalking. And you're the one who's been lurking outside my building and secretly photographing me. I wonder. Was it just tonight, or have you...?

"Only once or twice," Titus aid. "I wanted to have a wide choice of shots."

"Ah," Simon said. "But those other times you didn't make your presence known. Have you come up here just to upset me?"

"Oh, you're upset? Poor baby. Ask me if I give a shit."

"Do you? Do you give a shit?" Simon said, defiantly.

"No."

"Then what are you doing here?"

"How do I know? You're the shrink. You figure it out."

Simon had figured it out. If he'd been a disinterested third party, he would have arrived at his diagnosis sooner. But as a participant, his objectivity was compromised. The encounter on the beach had confirmed that they were both suffering from the same disease. Yet, Simon had made no effort to contact Titus. It would have been useless. It had to be Titus' decision or nothing would come of it.

"You know what, man? Forget you!" Titus said and bolted for the door. Simon blocked his exit. An impulsive move. As Titus reached past him for the doorknob, Simon burst out laughing.

"Sorry. I don't mean to laugh. But this is oddly reminiscent of an old romantic melodrama I watched the other day with Bette Davis; or was it Olivia de Havilland?"

"So what's wrong with that?" Titus said, resting his head against Simon. "Are you so uptight that you can't put up with a little drama?"

Simon had the good sense not to irk Titus further. Instead, he enfolded him in his arms and held him tightly. Titus whimpered and, slowly, the tension left his body and he gave himself over to the embrace.

This time, the lovemaking was different, intense and visceral but leavened with a heaping of genuine affection, words, gestures, penetrating stares. When it was over, they fell into a deep, restful sleep still entwined, in the wake of what, if they'd been lovers and not just fuck buddies, would be referred to as make-up sex.

The Emperor and the Regent

by Daniel Fisher
Indiana

"Grand Regent; the shuttle has arrived and docked, you may now proceed."

A dry electronic voice crackled through the cruiser's waiting lounge. Its tone, cold and formal. This was how the regent was informed procedures had to be. Ushered on by guards the regent once called loyal servants, through the narrow pathway to the drop ships inner cabin. No words were spoken, in fact, the regent had been kept in the dark from the moment the emperor made his wishes known. The guards piled in a cramped row leaving the regent tucked off to the opposite side, the ceremonial outfit the regent was forced to wear, taking up the bulk of the space.

The regent leaned head forward, staring down at the binding formal boots. They were locked and sealed, certainly not made for combat. The entire outfit was designed and applied to make the wearer vulnerable and frail, ensuring the regent's official capacity was as a decorative ornament for the emperor.

Being held hostage on the homeworld or stuck in reconstruction meetings would be more pleasant thought the regent, than being crammed into a federation jump carrier. The guards weren't fairing much better. The smallest of them was scrunched with his shoulder hitting the overhead carry bin. This jump ship having been designed for a completely different species, it made some sense they'd be cramped. However, that raised questions. Such as, why couldn't they have taken a ship designed for their species, or at the very least multiple ones? Probably budgetary reasons. Many of the known world's problems these days seemed to come from somebody trying to cut corners along the way. Or so the regent believed, as that was the excuse whenever problems arose on the homeworld.

The slight jolt of debarkation and they were off. Soon gravity would take hold and they would enter the orbit of whatever backwater rock the emperor exiled his mate to. The regent had to admit, this was at least a better fate than the last regent had been offered. The one prior, the last person to wear this official outfit now bunching around the waist, was ritually executed in front of their children. Simply because the previous emperor was done with them. The current regent, and youngest of the children who watched the former one's execution, had been mildly impressed how remarkably well restored the ceremonial outfit was. Age and dereliction of the body should have rendered it unusable, but whoever cleaned and patched it up even managed to get set in bloodstains out of the fussy white brocade fabric.

This was a bleak outlook for Ty, but not seeing your mate, your husband, for over an entire standard rotation of federation time, or close to fourteen months in Earth time is pushing it. Emperor or not, that man would have some explaining to do.

"Grand Regent, we apologize for the secrecy." A squished guard on the left end squeaked out his words. The poor thing so scantily clad and smushed up against the front compartment doorframe.

"Mika, I appreciate the sentiment, however, it doesn't help. Are you able to share any news, anything?" Staring off-kilter as the regent's crowned head was bumping against the ceiling.

"We're almost there." The one at the opposite end spoke. He didn't mind the close quarters resting his hand on the leg of the guardsman next to him.

"Well thank the Great Spirit herself! Seriously where is my husband?"

"Regent we can't say, we must uphold our sacred…" The smirking one, with his hand moving up the leg of his neighbor, was abruptly cut off.

"I know Maru, but at least you haven't been kept hostage all these cycles." The regent was getting pissy, making a deathly stare at the man copping a feel on his friend.

"Really Ty, is that how you're going to be? We've been loyal to you both since the war."

Ty had to breathe. The one next to Mika was right. These four men and the other three with the emperor had been true companions for nearly eight years Earth time. Even now, clearly uncomfortable in their black hide armor, hands all over each other, heads smashed into armpits and nipples they were trying to be empathetic. Their exposed chests and midriffs could have been sexy, except these guys were a bunch of fools who were more fun to spend time with, rather than use as playthings. By the regent anyway. They had each other, and their stupid genetic oaths. As well as the Federation president from time to time. Lucky her, at least someone got some, the regent mused.

"Shala, my utmost and solemn regret for such an…" *Such a stupid way to talk to fellow citizens.* "Is this cabin monitored?"

"The emperor made sure it's not, we won't speak of his plans, however."

"That's fine Nico... By the Hui itself!" Shouting across the cabin. "If I do see the emperor, I'm going to have some words. All this formality, I haven't been comfortable in months! And now, the suit of supplication... I'm going to my death for sure." Stretching cramped arms out, the regent needed some wiggle room in the white suit. "Between my mother, and not seeing my husband, I'm climbing the walls. They should just slaughter me now."

"Ty we understand. It will be worth it one day." A small smile from Nico, always the optimist. "Maybe not today, but someday." He made a slight smirk.

"I hope so."

"So what's new?" Crackling over the intercom. An odd voice, almost familiar, but cloaked by the simulated overlay.

"By the Mother of Heaven, who's there?" Alarmed, Ty instinctively reached for the dagger normally kept in the boots. It wasn't there, no weapon was, the regent was helpless in the bodysuit. The grand regent's safety was left to the imperial guard, and they weren't making a move to help.

"Come upfront to find out."

Looking at the men, nothing? They knew something. "This is one of the cousins come to kill me, isn't it?"

"No." A blushing Nico spoke, the hand in his thigh had landed its target.

Speaking to the voice. "Are you an agent of my mother?"

"That monstrous tyrant... Ha! She'd send your daughter to assonate you as a loyalty test. I'm not even that twisted." The voice cut off.

"You know, if this *is* a trap, we all die!" Wagging a finger at the group of guards.

"Regent we don't work for your mother. We're only loyal to your grand imperial mate. The imperial light of exalted heaven."

"This close..." Making a small gesture. Finger and thumb almost joined. "You could just say husband, or even Kyle, he wouldn't mind!"

"That is too informal regent, we would never."

"I'm still going to try Nico." Unlatching from the lock and standing, the regent was going to go upfront even if it was depressurized. "I will find a way to break your conditioning."

Floating to the front, the regent hit the sensor pad with a gloved hand, opening the hatchway to the front compartment. Cheap federation ships like these never had any decent tech, the seats didn't adjust, limited biometric controls, all very prewar. But they did get their home world nearly obliterated, so at least they were trying.

"Hurry and sit your fat ass down, we're about to hit the exosphere."

Ty rushed to grab the seat next to the pilot, its face covered in a helmet, probably for dramatic effect, because the regent could breath fine. An old helmet, an Earth combat helmet from the war. So this pilot was either very dated or just really unstable. Once the regent was strapped into the electromagnetic harness, the covered pilot put the ship into automatic and removed the black composite covering.

"By the Great One! Annu Mier..." Taken completely off guard, the regent was at a loss for words. Ty just sat mouth open.

"Hey, shithead. You didn't honestly think you could get away from us that easily."

"But how? Does Kyle know you're here?" Phishing.

"I can't tell you that, but I'm here as an official ambassador for the Tikal Assemblage, the Bureaucracy, and a representative for the United Federation of the Known Worlds to escort you to a very important rendezvous."

"Please tell me its war crimes tribunal against my mother?" The look in Mier's slate eyes and that harden tan skin made the regent feel alive again.

Laughing, one gloved hand over the ovoid face. "We all wish that, but no. Hopefully, this will be as good."

"To bad, so where are the kids, and that grumpy old husband of yours?"

"Who cares, I have seven Earth days away. You're just trying to get a scoop on why you're here." Smirking.

"Yes, I am. That's almost five clicks, whatever will you do?"

"Haul your imperial ass around." Both chuckling like old friends.

"Annu... Mier, I haven't been allowed to leave the Grand House in five standard cycles. It's so boring. I have no idea where Kyle is, I can't speak to Daria, and I'm being crushed by the lingering repression my mother's regime instilled. I have no real power to fix anything, and the emperor hasn't been seen in ages!" Venting at an

old friend.
"You always were a drama queen. Kyle's been seen, he's been around star system to star system... Just not by you."
"Thanks, bitch. When I see him, I'm going to kill him." Eyes narrowing in jealous hate.
"Will you?" Steely eyes meeting the gaze, like old times.
"I will. I'll fuck him first, then I'll kill him."
"Um hmm. How do you think your boys back there will take that threat?"
"They'll kill me." Thinking on it for a second. "They'll let me fuck him first, but then they'll kill me."
A broad smile across Mier's face. "And you thought, you'd been freed of that messed up empire. Now look at you, the faces have more freedom... Oh, wait. You started that revolution. Oops." Mier unzipped the flight suit, they had some time, so she figured why not get comfortable.
Removing the nano fabric pilot uniform, the first view of a sheer burgundy satin fabric top was beauteous. Form fitted and highly decorated, however, the neck and arms were fully covered. Ty balked at the modesty. Married life changed this one for sure. The regent could hardly make out the female's breasts. Ty was going to give her a pass on beaded braids dangling from the top of that boney head, but now maybe not.
"You didn't convert did you?" Worried.
"What? No, look, I love that stupid human, but I'll never understand John's beliefs. Why would you think that? I didn't lose my mind... Really?" Flummoxed, while unpinning the stuffy collar.
"You're so modest looking... No knives, no guns, you're tits are subdued. It's a little unsettling?" Moving white-gloved hands around this things torso.
"Glass houses. Isn't that what they used to say...?" Annu hummed quietly.
Ty wished the formal outfit plastered on, would allow skin to show next to her modesty. However the regent's outfit had been programmed and choreographed like everything else, and that wasn't acceptable. The crown itself covered most of the head and part of the face, ready to entrap the regent if needed. Forcing movement, ensuring servitude.
"Honestly you *have* missed a lot. Shevik made this. I've entered the third phase, and now that I'm no longer ovulating, I don't need

the mammary glands. John was freaked out at first, but our sex life hasn't been this exciting in years." Mier made a wide smile.

A slight tug on the hull, as the ship moved closer into orbit. "That's a relief. At least there's some normalcy in the universe." A hand over the chest taking a breath.

"When have we ever had normalcy? You were shipped off to my homeworld when Hui was invaded, and now all these rotations later, we're the ones cleaning up the mess."

"You are. I'm the princess in the palace. The damsel in distress, waiting for my prince to get off his ass and come home. I haven't been outside, in two cycles."

"That's bad..."

"I know, it's dreadful. I'm shuttled around everywhere because it's unseemly for the Grand Regent to be unsupervised or able to defend oneself." Lamenting. "I am less than a market prostitute these days."

"No, you twit. You really have to stop watching all those awful prewar films." She was aghast, that poor creature, stuck watching such dregs.

"I was left with the Smithsonian archives to pass the time. Sadly, I can relate to those dreadfully biased films. I pass most days with the house chaperone, watching old animated vids. Those small waisted women with their long hair and delicate features. It's so warped..." Chuckling oddly.

"Well, you did come from one of the two most gender-biased empires in known world's history." Her smile ominous.

"Funny. Only because the enemy was the other one, and they're extinct now. Thanks to us. Do you know, I haven't seen a male sex organ since Kyle left. They won't let me watch porn, the guards won't strip, and all my attendants are my mother's guard." What Ty wouldn't give for an orgasm.

"Ouch... Now I feel sorry for you. Especially, because I get all I want, John is so wonderful sexually, and now my body is primed for pleasure."

"I hate you... Please tell me you have pictures? He may be old and shriveled, but at least he has a penis. Just a picture will do." Begging, with deep dark eyes and full pouty lips.

"No, he deleted them. Now all I have are family friendly." Tapping a tiny speck on her temple just below the bone line, Mier activated a series of videos sprawling across their faces in the open cabin.

"Good thing we aren't distracted by piloting." Home movies, not helpful in finding out where they're going.

Another small jolt, the craft had entered the upper atmosphere. The regent believed that with the increased gravity, yet no intense pull, the planet they were traveling to, probably wasn't that big. However with dampener technology and re-entry paneling continuously progressing, they could honestly be landing anywhere.

"It's all preprogrammed, if we run into trouble there's an entire fleet behind us, you know to help." Mier flared her nostrils in jest. "Or, kill us if you try to make a break for it." Smirking.

"Really? I wouldn't know thanks to the closed blast shields."

"We can't spoil the surprise."

"And you're not going to tell me what it is, wonderful. Can you go ahead and vent the atmosphere now?" The grand regent was only half kidding.

"Not with me in the cabin." Completely serious. "Look, this one has John almost shirtless, you can see his nipples."

"He's handsome for an old man. Is the sex really that good?" At least Ty could imagine sex... Sort of?

"Oh yeah, we get yelled at all the time by the kids. Apparently, we're too loud."

"Does he like butt play?" The guy may be a pale old white guy, but it was the only man to imagine at the moment.

"No, I thought it was a myth, apparently not all human males like ass play."

"All the ones I know do." Ty made an eye roll.

"You're hysterical. Had I known that I may not have had so many children with him. He lets me smack it sometimes, but whines it hurts."

"He's so feeble, Kyle loves, or did love being spanked, and, you only birthed five children. That's not many for your people." Scolding her.

"And you're the last one of nine, so we both lucked out."

"Charming." The regent's thoughts shifted away from thinking about sex with Mier's husband or beating on the emperor, now that she was getting serious. "It's cruel I know, but I'm glad my sisters didn't survive the war. The Imperial Mother would still be on the throne, making them into baby factories."

"Or splicing herself into them. How the empire can allow that monster to live is beyond me." Horrified slightly, by the idea of her being alive.

"Your family wasn't much better." Scoffing, at her guffawing.

"Thankfully, they're all dead. You'd have liked my mother though."

"Melinea Five had a shrine made at the Face Palace for your mother. They call her an inspiration."

"That is so sweet." Big fake smile.

"Yeah, I wouldn't know, I'm only allowed into reconciliation sessions."

"You started that one too... Simply to get under your mother's skin. Well, and bring justice back to your people I suppose." Giving the regent side-eye.

"You're hysterical. I only want to get her skin out of other people."

"I honestly don't know how you can stomach the faces. Being around all those clones of your mother, I'd have killed them all. And here you are, trying to get them equal treatment under your empire's screwed up system of justice." She made a face like she was dry heaving.

"They didn't choose to be created, and much like me, they're only props for my mother." The regent shrugged. "So anyway, why was John deleting any of your pictures?" The regent didn't want the mood to be too heavy. Such anticipation and possible doom lay just outside. Best to savor the moments they had.

"You see, it's all your fault. Well, Dee and Kyle's too. Total transparency remember. I stopped by the DaGariner Homeworld on the way to get you. The Bureaucracy won't let me have anything in chambers that's considered insulting to their customs." Her lips sneered curling at the edges. That was a lifetime ago, however, Annu Mier was well known to hold a grudge.

"Are you being facetious, or is it only the Bureaucracy now?" Who could tell, her face, body, and tone, were all riddled with annoyance.

"You have been out of the loop... That discussion finally made it out of subcommittee to the main body for debate. Plus the DaGariner nations ratified a world government to renegotiate contracts with the Bureaucracy."

"Really, wow. I'm not surprised I didn't hear any of his."

"No one is surprised by that. Well, after about half a rotation, Dee thought they needed to make a choice. She threatened sanctions, and with the help of the Chital Hui-Ukk Fleet, and Tikal

Assemblage, plus our lovely Federation, we got them to make decisions on a lot of things."

"Let me guess, she threatened to destroy the DaGariner Homeworld and the entire habitat ring around it?"

"Oh yeah. Dee stated clearly, there were thousands of worlds that still need ecological resurrection, so they decide, or we add one more to the list." Smiling brightly.

"I love her, I miss her so much."

"I know, hey check out this vid. Harris Annu, going off to the academy. I was so proud."

"Aw. That is so nice, you getting to spend time with your children." The regent sounded only a little sarcastic. "Is Shevik wearing heels?" Were heels a thing?

"Yeah, stilettos are making a comeback on Earth."

"Those are so tall, thigh-high... They look deadly. I want a pair. Not that I could wear them out, but they'd be nice."

"Sorry princess, your fat feet are too big, and you're much too clumsy." Smirking.

"Funny... Still such a hateful creature. At least some things don't change." Curling a full lip at Mier.

"Shevik made them, I'll see if they have enough material and time. They're studying shindu, and John insists Shevik takes jujutsu if they take that." Sneering again.

"Poor child, Earth martial arts are so ineffectual in microgravity." Mier knew this, Ty just wanted to rub it in. "Has Shevik developed at all?"

"Not yet, there's a growing identity, but physically Shevik hasn't changed. I'm hoping for at least two genders... John says he'll be fine with one, but he's mostly concerned about Shevik's health." Such a concerned mother. *How quaint,* jealousy rearing its ugly head in the regent.

"The old bigot has come a long way. At least the other children's DNA blended smoothly."

"We knew there was a risk. I honestly thought we'd only have trouble with Kyte. How was I supposed to know John's sperm could degrade as he got older?"

"I don't think it's called degrading. Men of Earth don't have the same reproductive properties as the Tikal. Earth did have massive overpopulation before the invasion."

"Yes dumbass, I was right there with you. But I never thought I'd indulge in a human male, especially someone like him. At least your kid has perfectly blended genes which stabilized her. I worry Shevik may not be able to have a satisfying sex life."

"Don't think that. If you're fortunate Shevik will at least have three genders. And there's still a possibility Shevik could become a catalyst, you did come from royalty... It would give me an opportunity to throw a party." Smirking.

"A Shan? I'd love to have Shevik become a Shan, John would faint."

"You haven't mentioned that bit about Tikal genders, have you?"

"He only believes we have three. And that's taken him some years to get used to."

"Well, I expect great things for Shevik, even if John's a fool. If I survive, I might just tell him how fluid the Tikal actually are, because the high born don't reveal their secrets."

"You wouldn't?"

"Why not create some friction in that perfect marriage of yours?"

"You are so mean. I was being real, and you had to go and act all Chital." Smacking the regent on the shoulder. "Now you're never getting boots from any of my children."

"No, please. It just some harmless fun, like the old days. Before I was a hostage, and my mother stole our DNA to genetically engineer a royal heir. One who will probably commit regicide when she's done training as an assassin." The pull on the ship was getting harder, they almost there.

"Boo-hoo. I was at the betrayal she called a coronation, remember?"

"Yes, the perfect storybook wedding! Ty... Kyle. Here's the heir to the empire, now agree to join or I kill you both. Done, good... Now to ship off this genetic abomination to the cousin's so she can train to become an assassin to do my bidding... Mazel Tov." Macabre giggling from the two.

"The food was good though. You know, once the bleeding stopped."

"It was, and Dee brought those liquor's, and weed for Kyle."

"Those were fun days..." A beep went off on the control panel. With one quick flashing light, Mier knew they were there. The images disappeared.

"Were about to set down. I can tell you this, we'll be outside soon."

The look on Ty's face was one of wonder. "Actually outside? Can you open the blast shields?" Mier shook her head no.

"I wasn't going to say this, but since everything's about to change again, I will."

"Annu... Mier. That sounds ominous. You know... I expected it. I'm wearing the suit, I'll be slaughtered. The uniform will be cleaned and made ready for the next regent to wear... I can do this. I'm ready." Lying, the shaking in the regent's voice gave sway that Ty believed this was the last moments of life.

"What? No, what's that outfit got to do with anything? That's not what I was going to say, you're so damn dramatic!" Concern and annoyance, much like old times.

"My mother didn't make me wear this at the merging because the enemy destroyed the old palace... Sadly this survived. It's the Grand Regents supplication dress."

"Why would your mother insist on you wearing that?" This was getting interesting for Mier.

"The spouse of the Imperial throne is forced to join with it. It fuses with the nervous system, so I'm helpless to act on my own. In the past, when the empire was certain the line of succession is strong, the regent becomes a hindrance and was put to death. In this. Once the rituals were done, the suit was retrieved and made ready for the next regent. Marriage to death then reused, a gift to House Chital, forty-five thousand rotations ago, and you know how my mother likes tradition." A thin line across the lips, a sign of lament.

"Seriously? I knew she was sick, but that's twisted!" Annu scrunched her mouth up in mild disgust.

"The bodies are left to rot in the regent's palace. My mother was in a hurry with the whole execution or wedding thing, and couldn't get it in time." A sneer of seething hate.

"That's fucked up... Now I feel like a schmuck."

"Sorry, at least I'm with a friend, so death will be a joyous time."

"Okay, that makes this worse, shut up for a minute." She took a deep breath. "Ty, I just want you to know, all the sacrifices you've made, are making. Have saved so many lives, the Hui-Ukk would be extinct now if it wasn't for you." Taking the regent's hand in hers, squeezing.

"Annu Mier, you're exaggerating... But thank you."

"No, I'm not. If you weren't around your mother would have flung the empire recklessly into battle without allies. For a long time, I almost couldn't believe you had such selflessness in you. Sometimes I still can't." A modest smile flashed on her boney face.

"Almost? Shocking, it *almost,* sounds like you cared." Snideness, to lighten the mood.

"You were a great smuggler, just really arrogant. But that's to be expected, the last heir to the mighty House Chital!"

"Not anymore, thanks to an insane grandmother, determined to take over the known worlds using my genetically engineered child as a weapon! I'm so proud of my family." Snorting in sick laughter.

"Did you ever think she'd choose you to become the emperor?" They still had a few minutes, so why not snoop.

"Not for a second. Being the last born, I'm just a fail-safe for producing a genetically adequate heir. I was a bit surprised she choose Kyle though."

"How so? You two were already together and planning on getting married anyway."

"Because my mother is a traditionalist. She only cares about the line of succession, and how she can manipulate it. When Daria is finished with her training she'll come to kill me if the emperor hasn't already. And if she has half the programming the faces do, she'll kill the emperor and assume the throne. Kyle's a stand-in until she does." A look of sad regret on the regent's face. Regret for something the grand regent believed couldn't be changed.

"That's dark. Your people love Kyle, he's the hero of Hui. You two saved your home world and all the systems in the empire." More side-eye from Annu.

"With an entire armada backing us up. He's loved, but we both know how much genetic coding is left in the people. Obedience is ensured. The big glitch in my mother's plans is that Kyle is a citizen of earth."

"Why would that matter?"

"It buys him time. Earth would retaliate if he was killed, so his death will happen only when the imperial mother moves to take over known space." The seriousness on the face of the regent.

"The empire barely survived the last war, I know your mother is crazy, but to start another war so soon would destroy everything we've all built. Even I can't believe she'd do that." Annu Mier had a sort of confounded stare going on.

"I've heard rumors that the assassin training center is recruiting an army. In reconciliation meetings, there's talk that some old die-hard supporters of my mother have gone missing. If I don't see the emperor before I'm executed, pass it along. He has maybe six rotations before she attacks the known worlds." A flash of despair was reflected in the regent's eyes. Annu felt the seriousness of the situation. Although she had a secret that may sway the regent's view of impending doom.

"If that woman is crazy enough to take on known space, we'll be ready to blast Hui and any other world she's hiding on, into a million little pieces." Defiance in her gaze.

"So it'll be like Tikal all over again... Yippy." The regent knew she was trying to cheer up the space. No use for sadness, the regent should end life on a high note.

"That is so hateful! You monster." She stuck her long thin tongue out at the regent.

"Save that for your husband, you know I only have eyes for one person." Smirking.

"You know, I hope it's your daughter that kills you. Sneaks up behind you and strangles you with your own belt." Her narrow eyes would have been threatening, if Annu's smile wasn't so cheery.

"Strangle? Pish... She'd gut me open and spill my entrails all over this suit. Why do you think it's white... To showcase the blood. Another family tradition." The regent made a mock expression of pride.

Chuckling at the depths of perversion of it all, Mier had to wrap this up, destiny awaited. "I could sit and talk all day, but we have to go."

"So it's daytime?"

"Maybe, I'm sure it is somewhere." Her lips were sealed.

Feeling the drop-ship bump the surface, Mier stood, allowing Ty to do the same. The regent was thankful to have some small moment to reminisce about more interesting times and to make light of the harder ones to come. Annu Mier slipped off the rest of the jumpsuit, making ready for disembarking. Ty straightened the deshret looking headdress.

The uncanny similarity of ancient Egyptian headgear and the crowns of the Chital Hui-Ukk nobles was astounding. Except the earth headdresses didn't have programming involved. Ty's crown would self adjust, with wings flowing up the head and some ridiculous spine growing down the back. Joining the white brocade suit to become some overly resplendent representation of an avian, for ritual pomp and circumstance.

Leaving the cockpit, Mier escorted Ty to the main hatch, the Imperial guard had already left the ship, they were done with the regent, so they would leave. It wasn't personal, Ty knew they had no choice in their movements.

"Close your eyes." Mier put her hand over the regent's face while Ty huffed, thinking how stupid. *No world still used a firing squad, that was a waste of resources* so it couldn't be death by that.

The hatch opened, allowing them to walk down the ramp to paved stone. The regent's movements were robotic, the suit had taken control. Now, all Ty could do was be a hostage in the over the top formal attire. Walking for some ways, the regent wouldn't look, the crown wouldn't allow it, so why bother. They came to a stop after some distance.

"You can open your eyes now."

Mier was stepping back leaving the regent in the center of a wide marble circle, with four directional walkways attached. The circle was small compared to the cratered lake they stood over. Surrounding the regent, were four long pillars, this was an official war memorial, for something. So many scarred worlds, and so many monuments, it was hard to keep track.

The suit allowed Ty to move around, not to flee, that would be instant death, but the regent could view the surroundings. To the right, were the Emperor's guard, the males from the shuttle. On the left, the guard was all female, tall and wide, bigger than the men across from them. The Imperial Mother's guard. Immediately Ty believed this to be a death sentence... *But why was Annu here, if that was the case,* Ty's thoughts raced about scratching for any clue. Seeing those worried eyes searching about, Mier wanted to laugh. Instead, she joyously shouted "Look up!" pointing to the sky.

The regent scanned the heavens, all across the sky, a mass of ships were coming in closer. Federation cruisers and command carriers, the Tikal armada, large numbers of federated world ships, and even commercial vessels. The most shocking sight however, a large number of the Chital Hui-Ukk fleet were present with the emperor's command ship in the atmosphere, shining a bright light on this monument.

"Kyle's here?" Shouting to Mier, now standing ten feet in front of him.

"You shall not address the Imperial Light of Heaven with such disrespect!" The lead female guard had her hand on her blade, ready to strike the regent down for such insolence.

"Mala, I have always liked you, but piss off! He's my husband, and I'll speak about him as I see fit!" Tightness in the throat, the suit was programmed to keep the regent subordinate, and such talk wasn't allowed.

"I decree, everyone chill out!" Out from the pillar on the left, the emperor appeared. Presumably, he was hiding, laughing at his mate.

"Kyle, if this is some joke, I'm going to kill you!" Lunging forward, but only for a second.

The white formal wrapping bound the regent so tightly, sending pain receptors into overload from the stabbing nanofabric. The crown struck synapses, repeatedly inflicting more and more pain as it did. Punishment for unwarranted movement. On the right and the left, the guards had weapons ready, about to hack the regent down for threats on the emperor's life. They liked Ty, even respected the regent, but they had an oath that was genetically encoded and must kill on protocol.

"I said, I decree; chill! Everyone, calm down!" The guards relaxed, but Ty's eyes, begged for help. The regent would be dead soon if not released. "Right the suit... Sorry, sweetie." Making a dash to his mate.

Emperor Kyle, bopped over to his spouse, dressed so informally, black fabric pants, a black hoodie, and undershirt. Basic replica sneakers, all prewar. His black wavy hair and sparkling dark eyes made the pain almost worth it, as he reached the regent pressing a small hand on Ty's chest, releasing the garment, now falling to the ground.

Able to breathe again, in plain tunic and leggings, Ty snatched Kyle up into a bear hug. "I don't care if they kill me, I need you in my arms."

Kissing the regent over and over, Kyle wrapped his legs around his spouse's frame. "My big sexy alien! I've missed you so much!" Grabbing his partner's face in his hands, nothing but love in his eyes.

"You're one to talk, little human bug. You left me in the palace to deal with that monster's legacy and you're gallivanting around the western spiral arm doing who knows what." Butting Kyle in the forehead with the regent's brow ridge, all while kissing him and

biting those soft lips.
"Grand Regent!" One of the larger female guards barked.
"Kaillia shush Ty's right. I did go gallivanting around the galaxy." Smirking, then addressing his mate solely. "I'm sorry about leaving you, but we had some things to do, put me down and I'll tell you." His big oval eyes begging.
"Fine." Letting the human stand. "This better be good!"
"It is... Do you know where we are? Or what day it is?" Taking his lover's larger hand in his. Ty was smaller than the female guards, however, the regent towered over Kyle.
"A monument over a crater. So no."
"It's Earth, this spot is the Unification Memorial." Smiling.
"Okay?"
From behind the pillars, three other individuals appeared taking their place, next to Mier. Ty's eyes went wide. "MyLanthia, Twenty One, Deeana! I'm overjoyed, what...Why are you here?" The shock was so clear, it made them smile.
"Dumbass... This is where first contact was made! Where you're standing." The tall thin black woman, with skin the color of deep suede, spoke as confidently and brashly as she always had.
"First contact, us?"
"No moron, the stupid rabbit I hit with my car! Honestly Ty, first contact for Earth was a really big deal!" Her hand on the hip of a tight navy bodysuit, she was trying to entice on of the emperor's guard, winking at Mika.
Making a face at the woman, the regent had some questions, thinking her sass mouth better answer. "Dee I know it was, but why here? We met you outside of Lancaster, this is just some crater."
"Ty, the landscape has changed much. You hadn't seen the extent of damage after the war, as you were elsewhere." An ethereal lithe voice coming off the creature to Mier's left. Her pressurized suit held the contents in humanoid form, without it her gas pouches would fill, and she'd float away.
"MyLanthia it is so good to see you, I believed you'd be in spore?" Wanting to let the tears roll down, but the regent felt free for the first time in ages, so Ty mustered the strength to look strong and powerful.
"Part of me, yes, MyLanthia will be with hatchings in several cycles, until then, I leave my other selves to tend." A vibrant spectrum of flashing light cascading across its body. Her people's means of

communicating was being translated by her point of reference device into audible speech.

A beep from Kyle's wristwatch, time get this party started. "Ty, tonight marks the fiftieth anniversary of first contact! And twenty years from when we met, on this exact spot..." Cut off by scoffing.

"You're wrong, it hasn't been that long. I have known you only sixteen rotations, give or take twelve units." Looking down on the emperor to the dismay of the guard. In fairness, they *were* holding back from killing the regent.

"No, it's right! I don't pretend to understand all the dilation, and the whole Earth verses everywhere else time thing, but it's right. Twenty-one and the navigators did the calculations." Waving his hands about, as if that would prove he was correct.

"No, you're wrong, the math is wrong. Taking into consideration dilation and conversion to the federated standard of time, we've known each other less than twenty years, that anniversary will be next cycle." Smirking to piss Kyle off, and loving the death sneers from the guards. "That is still, eighteen units away."

"It's close enough! Shut up for a second so I can ask you something..." Exhaling.

"Of course, my emperor." Bowing to the smaller human.

"Bitch!" Shaking his head with a big smile, Emperor Kyle, got down on one knee taking Ty's hand in his.

"My Lord, please stand!" The male guard rushed to his side, they wouldn't lay a finger on him, but would beg like there was no tomorrow.

"What: You think this is the first time Kyle's been on his knees." Ty made such a wide grin, the female guard were ready to strike at a word.

"Princess! People are watching so keep it family friendly!" Mier bellowed while Dee, the other human present, balled over in laughter. None of them ever had much reverence for these solemn events.

"Anyway!" The emperor attempting to maintain control. "We need rings!" Holding in a laugh.

On queue, from behind the grand regent, a small figure appeared standing next to the man on his knees. Her black hair in wild ringlets down past her shoulders. With a distinctive bone ridge across her brow, a deep oval face with high cheekbones and larger than human ears, she wore matching pants and hoodie combo as the emperor, smiling brightly.

"Hi, daddy!" Smiling up at the stunned regent.

"Daria my love! Will you cut me down if I snatch my daughter into my arms?" Doing his all to keep from hugging the stuffing's out of his child.

She ran at him in a grand embrace, Ty lifted her up in his arm, squeezing tighter on his mate's hand, his family reunited. "My child, you are almost as large as your father!"

"She'll be as tall as you, I'm sure." Kyle wrestling his hand free from the painful grip.

"No, Daria will be as large as my mother, taller even than Mala. My genes were encoded to ensure it." Nuzzling bone ridge to bone ridge.

"Daddy, I removed grandmother's spliced genes, all by myself."

"You make your father's proud."

"Then hold on, Ty..." Taking a custom ring from the young girl on her father's shoulder, Kyle took back his mate's hand. "Ty Kitall of House Chital, I'm not going into that processional litany of crap..." The regent chuckled. "Will you do me the honor of being my spouse, my equal partner in all things, and in all ways? To join me in marriage, thus creating a new line of succession for the Hui-Ukk."

"I'm listening." A big smile, for his wily mate. "Go on."

"Smartass! Marry me so we can join forces and take over the empire. Complete equality between genders, and all sentient people in the Hui-Ukk."

"And faiths, the people have an affinity to the Great Mother Spirit, that I will not abandon!"

"I know, equal say for all people, as we join to become Wen-Kitall Hui-Ukk." The shorter human smirking with an evil grin.

"And topple that wretched dictator?" Ty's alien features glowed with delight. His dark eyes and hair almost shimmering from the light of the Emperor's ship.

"Yes! Your mother has to go."

"Then all we need are two things. First, from you, why should I?" a look of skepticism on Ty's face.

"Because I love you. I think maybe I was in love with you from the first moment I met you. That night, right here, all those years ago when I choked on my words." Emperor Kyle looked cocky this time around.

"You had me at smartass." Smirking, a tear in the corner of his eye.

"And the second thing, my big cheeky moppet?" Kyle's eyes welled up with joy.

"Is simply the heir's approval. And then according to Hui-Ukk law, you and I are husbands on Earth, as well as the empire. The way we intended."

"Hold on." The couple's old friends walked to the center. "Not just Earth or your dumb empire. As a representative of the Tikal Assemblage..." Annu Mier twirled her arm, in a gesture of faux grandeur.

"And the president of the Earth Alliance..." Dee announced proudly.

"Former president." Mier sneered.

"I'm American, we keep the title for life." Dee sneered back. "Former, President of Earth, the Leader of the United Federation of Known Worlds... Current."

"MyLanthia and our collective self..."

"Navigator Uniformity, probability will succeed within acceptable margin. We maintain unanimity." In stilted words, the fourth creature spoke, partly with translated speech, partly in binary code on the section of its head that was artificial. "Navigator eight- four-two-one, concurs with assessment and offers service." The point of reference device synthesizing into audible language.

Cybernetic in form, with long mechanical tendrils slinking down its backside from the top of the cranium, moving around independently from the arms and legs of this bipedal creature. The plated metallic pseudo humanoid head encased in a full-body flak suit was not accustomed to speaking aloud.

"Twenty One, that was the sweetest thing I've ever heard you say!" Getting its plated shoulder rubbed by the former president.

"The four of us, acting as representatives of our governments and the federation of the known worlds have officially signed on our support for the Wen-Kitall Hui-Ukk Empire, and its co-equal emperors." Taking a deep breath. "Shit, you two have to shorten this crap down, this is almost as wordy as it was before." Making a panged expression.

"What Mier is saying is, you guys, have the full support of the known worlds and are honorary citizens to all our member worlds. So you now command the largest fleet in history. Just in case your mother wants to put up a fight." Dee smirked at her friend.

"And finally me. As Grand Heir to a line of equals, I Daria, Kitall-Wen, of the Hui-Ukk and Earth, join my dads in marriage."

"Then yes I do!" Snatching Kyle into his arm, kissing his husband deeply. Around them, the guards dropped to their knees in supplication. Daria in one arm, Kyle in the other, Ty may have been a small compared to the females of his species, but he felt as big as the sky itself. Having to release the two for a brief moment, Kyle had one last gift.

"This is being broad streamed across the known worlds, so everyone in the empire will know." Waving up to the fleet of ships n the sky. "And you're supposed to agree before she pronounces us married, not after."

"No, now that I have a choice, I get to decide when I agree."

"Okay, anything else?"

"If I choose to burn the suit of supplication on the steps of the grand palace, I won't be killed instantly... Is that alright?" Ty wondered if some traditions might still be sacred.

"Oh honey, of course, it is. We can burn all the regalia you want." Kyle kissed and pecked his husband's hand. "You now officially have as much power as me."

A broad smile crept across Ty's face. Looking at the guard's clustered in. "Then you lot! Stand up... No more of that." They stood bewildered, not used to such freedom.

"Our sweet Daria even agreed to purge the Training center of your cousin's as a wedding present. No more assassins." Kyle's face grew so big and bright.

"What a wonderful gift. Can you stay for a few days at least?" Begging to get some time with his child and husband.

"Yes, for a few. Would you like me to slay grandmother for you?" Smiling as only a happy child does.

"Honey, she won't see the signal for a full cycle, so we can wait on that." Kyle kissed his daughter on the cheek.

"Having you offer that, makes me the proudest parent in the known worlds." Tears now freely falling down Ty's cheeks.

"How would you like a proper honeymoon?" Looking up as he was pressed into his husband's frame.

"You are full of surprises... Where did you have in mind?"

"New Kauai." Smiling a big toothy grin.

"Not the Venus ring. I'm getting fresh air for the first time in cycles, I don't want to go back inside." Ty whined, but it was understandable, considering.

"Open-air, on Earth. The ecological restoration of Hawaii is finished."

"Then yes, my Emperor. Yes!" Holding him tighter, Ty never wanted to let go.

The Last Matador

by Steve Carr
Virginia

The hotel was small and stood between two large apartment buildings as if it had been squeezed in as an afterthought. Its facade was painted a bright yellow that drew attention to it but the absence of a sign lured very few to enter through the glass door on the street level to inquire what the building was. The hotel had three floors. One of the rooms on every floor had a sliding glass door that faced the street. There was a small balcony outside each of those doors that was enclosed by an intricately designed black wrought iron railing. The hotel had set up a small cafe table, a chair with a yellow cushion, and a potted cactus on each balcony. The balconies still gave no clue that the building was a hotel, but not many looked up at them anyway, as the street was busy and crowded mostly with tourists going to and from their more elaborate hotels who had little time for seeing what was above their heads.

On the third floor balcony, Adelaide Hurque sat at the table and turned the page of a novel that she had purchased at a used book store just before leaving her hometown of San Francisco. The pages of the novel were yellow from age and many were dogeared, and a few were torn, but she considered she was meant to read it, having kept her eyes closed when she reached into the overflowing bargain bin located on the sidewalk in front of the bookstore and pulled it out. The hotel didn't have room service, but she had made an arrangement with Jorge, the day desk clerk, for him to bring her a coffee and a lemon flavored pan dulce each morning at nine in exchange for her spending fifteen minutes every day helping him improve his English. As she turned the pages of the novel she held the cup of coffee to her lips, inhaled the aroma of cinnamon that had been added to the coffee, and took small sips. She savored in equal measures the flavor of the coffee, the words in the book, and the lemony sweetness of the pan dulce that she bit into at the end of every five pages.

It was on her third day after arriving at the hotel, which had been recommended to her by a friend with similar tastes in travel and accommodations, that she finished her cup of coffee, ate the final crumbs of the pan dulce, and had read forty pages of the novel, when she arose from the chair, carried the book, cup and plate into her room and picked up the phone. “Hello, Jorge,” she said into it, "what do you recommend I do today?"

#

Adelaide generally preferred traveling to countries where the climate was more moderate. Her fair skin burned easily and she feared adding more freckles to those that already speckled her face, a condition she likened to an affliction from an early age. Her sole reason for traveling to Cancun was that it was at the opposite end of the Yucatan peninsula across from the more historically interesting Merida, where she spent the first week of her vacation while also visiting Chichen Itza. Cancun was near to Tulum, which her friend had advised her to see, but didn't really interest her.

With a light blue parasol lined with white fringe raised above her head to shield her exposed skin from the glaring sunlight she garnered amused looks and a few snickers as she sat on a bench at the Gran Puerto Cancun ferry dock. The breeze blowing inland from the warm, torquoise water of the Bahio de Mujeres played with her floral patterned cotton skirt that extended down to her calves. She kept her knees pressed tightly together and the skirt tucked between them to keep the skirt from filling with air and ballooning out. As the ferry returning from Isla Mujeres pulled into its berth alongside the pier, a man with a green ball cap with the word Matador stitched on its bill sat down next to her.

"*Discúlpeme, señora,*" he said to her. "*¿Habla usted español?*"

She was uncertain she was being spoken to because strangers seldom spoke to her without her speaking to them first. Even though he was looking directly at her, she hesitated before replying. "*Sí señor,*" she replied in perfectly enunciated Spanish. Before the trip she took to Spain a few years before she had learned to speak fluent Spanish. Since that trip, in San Francisco she attended a weekly Bible study group where only Spanish was spoken, which kept her abreast of the modern moral applications of the scriptures as well as being able to practice speaking the language. The man appeared to be near her age of forty, with black hair and dark brown eyes. His naturally dark complexion showed the signs of a lifetime of exposure to the sun, with lines that formed deep crevices in his cheeks.

"Are you and your husband traveling to Isla Mujeres for the

first time?" he asked her.

"Yes, this will be my first time visiting the island," she replied, wary of telling him that she wasn't married and that she was traveling alone.

"I was born and grew up there," he said. "Be sure to see the entire island and not just the markets. Isla Mujeres is magical but the magic isn't found in the shops that sell trinkets. "

When the last of the passengers coming from Isla Mujeres stepped off of the ferry, it sounded a horn. The small crowd that had been waiting on the pier, began to board it. She stood up and smoothed the wrinkles from her skirt while also holding it down as the breeze whipped the folds of the material.

"Thank you for your courteous advice," she said to him as she walked toward the boarding plank.

"But where is your husband?" he asked.

"I'm not married," she answered.

Following close behind her, he said, "Neither am I. I'm going to have lunch with my parents who still live on the island. Perhaps you will allow me to show you the place of my birth?"

She stepped onto the ferry. "Perhaps," she answered.

"My name is Juan-Miguel Estrada," he said, stepping behind her onto the ferry.

#

Juan-Miguel's elderly parents were polite, but mostly quietly, looking from him to Adelaide as he asked Adelaide questions one after the other about her travels and San Francisco. The four of them had a lunch, that while normal in size for typical Mexicans, proved to be too much for Adelaide. By the time the main entree of roasted chicken was served, she was already satiated by the large bowl of lime soup that she had been given. She poked at the chicken, beans and rice on her plate with her fork while answering his questions and gazed about the dining room at the numerous pictures of the Madonna that hung on the walls. Adelaide approved of how Catholics revered the mother of Jesus, but felt it should be done in moderation. The young woman who was the cook and served the meal lifted Adelaide's mostly uneaten plate of food from the table just as Juan-Miguel asked Adelaide about the bullfights she had seen during her travels in Spain.

"I never went to a bullfight," she said, happy to have the food taken away and out of sight.

A noticeable silence settled over the table as if a blanket had been thrown onto the proceedings.

"You didn't go to the Las Ventas in Madrid, or the Plaza de Toros de Ronda, or La Maestranza in Seville?" he asked with incredulity.

She took a sip of her iced tea. "No. I believe killing animals for fun is wrong."

He removed his ball cap and held it up, displaying the word Matador. "I do not kill bulls for fun," he said. "Bullfighting is a tradition, an honor, a profession that has been passed down many generations in my family. My father was a Matador and I am a Matador."

Up to that moment Adelaide had been so charmed by the attention Juan-Miguel had paid to her, and by the sparkle in his eyes when he smiled, and the whiteness of his teeth, that she had forgotten to ask what he did, or even who he was beyond being a very desireable man. She thought the word Matador on his cap had the same significance as a fast food worker wearing a Yale t-shirt.

"I had no idea," she stuttered, in English.

#

That evening while sitting on the balcony outside her bedroom window, Adelaide flipped through the brochure for the Plaza de Toros Cancun that Juan-Miguel had given to her as he walked her to the front door of the hotel. They had left his parents home after lunch and walked and took taxis from one end of the island to the other, which given that the Isla Mujeres was only about five miles long and not very wide, didn't take that long. At the south end of the island where a statue of Xchel, the Mexican fertility goddess, stood alongside a paved trail, he took her hand in his and gently kissed the back of it.

"Do me the honor of coming to the bullring to see me fight a bull tomorrow," he said.

With the shaft of her parasol resting on her shoulder, she twirled it, just like she had always imagined she would do when being flirted with by a man like Juan-Miguel. "Is it important to you?" she asked, certain from the look of yearning on his face what his answer would be.

"Yes, tomorrow is my last bullfight," he said. "I'm the last Matador of my family and my parents are too frail to come see me in my last fight. I will be fighting El Rey, a very mighty bull. It would bring me great pleasure to see you sitting in the stadium."

#

At nine the following morning Jorge delivered a cup of coffee and a pan dulce to Adelaide.

"Have you heard of Juan-Miguel Estrada?" she asked him as he placed the things on the table. She felt haggard and worn after having an awful night's sleep with thoughts of Juan-Miguel being gored by a bull named The King.

His face lit up. "Oh yes, he is a very famous Matador."

She sat in the chair and put a sugar cube in the coffee. "I'll be seeing him in his last bullfight this afternoon," she said.

"I haven't been to a bullfight since I was a young boy," he said. "It terrified me and I've never wanted to see another one although that makes me feel like I'm not a true Mexican." He turned and left.

Adelaide bit into the pan dulce and grimmaced. It was coconut flavored. She didn't like coconut in any form, especially in a breakfast pastry, and definitley not on the morning she awoke after little sleep fully convinced she had fallen in love with a man she had just met. She had another fifteen years of employment as a dentist to look forward to before retiring, after which she planned to do nothing but take ocean cruises, but that morning she had the one repeated thought recycle through her brain. *What does a Matador do after he retires?*

#

A gust of hot wind hurled dirt into Adelaide's face as she stepped out of the taxi and onto the pavement in front of the entrance to the Plaza de Toros Cancun. Spitting grit from her mouth she looked up at the lackluster stadium as the taxi pulled away, carrying away her parasol laying in its back seat with it. Following the crowd, she purchased a ticket, was handed a flier, its message printed on white paper, and found a seat in the first row that overlooked the bullring. With the glare of the bright sunlight penetrating her expensive sun glasses – the ones she bought before her trip to see the glaciers in Alaska – she stared at the print on the flier. There would be a show honoring Juan-Miguel's retirement before he engaged in the fight with El Rey, the final bullfight of the day. Not wanting to risk diminishing the thrill of seeing her newfound love in the only bullfight she had ever seen, and feeling the sun burning into her skin, she dreaded the thought of adding another freckle to her face and rose from her seat and went into the concessions area of the stadium where it was darker and somewhat cooler. The action happening in the arena could be heard broadcast through the speakers mounted on the walls. She bought a bottled water and while standing in a corner for the next hour and a half she listened to the details of the bullfights, the cheers of the crowd, took sips of water, and anxiously waited to hear the announcement of Juan-Miguel's entrance into the bullring.

At last hearing his name, she re-entered the seating area in time to see Juan-Miguel enter the arena carrying a small red cape and a long sword. With his head held high, he entered walking with a strut, displaying the graceful masculinity of his physique in his silver and black costume. She quickly scanned the arena and saw El Rey standing to one side. She had heard over the speakers that the banderilleros had weakened it with their darts, but the sight of the blood dripping down El Rey's sides horrified her – for a moment. And then as Juan-Miguel taunted El Rey with the cape, waving it in dance-like fashion in front of the bull, she felt her cheeks grow hot and felt breathless exhilliration. When the bull charged and Juan-Miguel evaded El Rey's horns she jumped to her feet with the rest of the crowd and shouted Juan-Miguel's name. She waved her handkerchief and blew him kisses. This happened several times and finally when Juan-Miguel thrust his sword into El Rey's neck and the bull fell to the ground, dead, Adelaide fainted from orgasmic fervor.

#

On the flight back to San Francisco, Adelaide sat next to a pretty young woman with unblemished skin that glowed with a healthy new tan. She said she had gotten it by spending all of her time on the beach in the Hotel Zoneria. "What did you do in Cancun?" the girl asked.

Adelaide hesitated before answering. “I fell in love and saw a bullfight.”

The girl gasped. “How could you watch an animal be killed in such an inhumane way?” she asked, her voice full of righteous indignation.

Adelaide raised the wilted rose to her nose that Juan-Miguel had given her and inhaled what remained of its fragrance. “Yes, that part of it was horrific, but to tell you the truth, I mostly had my eyes on the Matador.”

The End

The Dating Portal

by Christopher T. Dabrowski
Poland

- With this one, you'll be on good terms after the breakup. She will treat you like a friend. No sex.

- And this one?

- I advise against. She's neurotic.

- Next.

- You'll have a lot of sex after the breakup. She'll love the sex with you.

- I take it!

- I wouldn't. She will cheat on you. This one is a monogamist. However, I also advise against.

- Why?

- Bitch.

- With her, you'll get back together many times.

- Contact us - I said to the adviser on the Love-ex portal.

Love is not eternal, so today everyone cares about what will happen after the breakup.

Where I Heard my Favorite Joke

by Michelle Lisan
Florida

I met him at the park. He'd ridden his bike a long way on a hot day so we could meet. I think he wanted to make sure I wouldn't mistake it for a date – I had a reputation after all, and he was not interested in what I had to offer. I don't think I wanted that either; my love for him was not the love that us brand new adults would think of as love.

He told me stories of his senior year abroad in Germany and we walked to my favorite places. I love sharing my favorite places. They are the places I go to think and feel and dream when my world seems lacking in possibilities and space. I show people this part of my heart, but have never found anyone there when I went back.

The high rocky point looked down over the creek. Patience, strength, balance, and effort would take you to the water, but you didn't go down. You felt the empty space beneath your legs as you sat at the edge of a rock that could feel like the edge of the world. Your legs would tingle with the danger of high places.

We next went to the gardens behind the manor house. The land for this park was donated by the colonial landholder to preserve the untouched wilderness. I wonder if it occurred to him to give it back to the tribes who lived there before his invader fellows claimed it. I wonder at the goodness of humanity that doesn't recognize humanity.

The gardens are everything the forest isn't. Straight lines, even ground, orderly and managed so it will never remain itself without careful management. Fountains and sculptures. Topiaries.

The bike ride and the walking and the hot day inspired us to irresponsible and understandable behavior. We sat in a fountain. We sat there and drunk on the idiotic refreshment we talked and laughed. He told me his favorite joke.

That joke is still my favorite. I've used it as an icebreaker many times since. I am still grateful to him for that joke. I've never heard anyone else tell it. Would I have heard it from another source without him? Would it have meant anything to me if it wasn't his favorite joke?

He and I would sit on the bus together on the way to and

from small ensemble concerts. I did not get along with anyone else in our high school's small choir ensemble. He got along with everyone. I wonder if it was a gift to me or to the others that he sat with me. I often encouraged him to curse when he was bothered. He may have appreciated the opportunity. Others may have expected him to be how he always was. I told him to let go sometimes. To rant and feel. We ranted a great deal. I always had something to rant about. I was, I think, rather unpleasant.

He was so good. He was kind. He was thoughtful and smart and made me feel like it was possible for actual goodness to exist. I constantly doubted and poked at his edges to see if he really was what he seemed. I wanted to find his hidden darkness and the worst things he'd done.

I told him the worst things I had done. He was my friend.

I saw him another time at the grocery store. He was stocking shelves and shared details about his upcoming trip. I was excited for him and told him I wanted to hear all about it when I got back.

Alison called me crying to tell me that the van blew a tire, flipping and killing my friend and another boy. Three traumatized boys would return from a trip that killed their two friends.

I'd dropped out of college. I didn't know what I was going to do next. I needed the good person who knew the worst things I'd done and was still my friend.

The choir from his college traveled in for the funeral. I talked to them about the boy I'd loved. I tried to figure out if I could say I loved him and have them understand, but we were all 19 and love is only one thing.

One time he told me about when we'd met. I did not remember it when he told me. I hadn't known that it was him. When we were in 5th grade, all the elementary schools in the district sent choir students to audition. I was a sullen and angry girl. I was absentmindedly kicking the chair in front of me. The poor student occupying the chair really wanted me to stop, and worked really hard at finding a way to speak to me about it in a way that matched his penchant for empathy and kindness. I harassed this poor boy for the remainder of district choir.

That he remembered that and still befriended me when we met again in high school means a great deal to me.

What would his life be like now? He was so loved. I wish I could see the man he was going to be. I wish I could see the world that would have been with him in it.

I'm a 36-year-old divorcee with two kids. I want to talk to my friend about my life. I want to know what he'd say. I want to poke at his edges and see if he's everything I think he is. I want to believe in his kindness and goodness and see it in action.

I miss my friend.

The Dragon Dances

by Alicia Graybill
Nebraska

The wailing music, at first, set Ethan's teeth on edge. It wasn't like the fiddle scratches and wheezing concertina that the street performers played. But after he stood and listened to it for a few minutes, the pounding of the drum and ringing tambourine's rhythm began to make a type of sense of the wailing flute and strings. An older woman approached Ethan with a wide smile. She wore robes that revealed only her face.

"Come, come. Pretty dancers, come!" She waved at Ethan to come further into the room and take a place on a purple silk cushion.

"I was told to meet someone here," Ethan tried to explain but she shook her head and shooed him toward the pillow. "But I--."

She simply smiled at him and walked away. With a sigh, Ethan dropped onto the indicated seat after taking his sword off. He felt terribly naked without his Glock but Veles refused to risk his freedom on a firearm. The sultanate of Shawkat had access to 21st century technology if you were wealthy or had bribed the proper officials. Located on a small island in the Persian Gulf, access could only be gained by boat, which made Ethan more than a little nervous. Everyone else carried swords, staffs or knives and rode horses or camels. He told Vel he would leave him if he had to ride a camel.

The man next to him, a corpulent Arab in a green turban, grinned at Ethan and offered him the pipe he was smoking. Ethan smiled and shook his head politely. He had to keep his wits about him. Since Vel had gone missing nearly a month ago, he'd been worried sick, despite his repeated attempts to push the concerns away. Vel was an adult, a corporate pirate, no less, and perfectly capable of caring for himself. He didn't need someone to take care of him. *But, of course, he does,* Ethan argued with himself. *And you know you're the only one who can do that, don't you?* Veles Zemay was also an infamous art thief who was known as the Dragon. Ethan was trying to convince himself to get up and leave when the music stopped abruptly. There was a smattering of applause and then a curtain near the back of the room moved to the side. At that instant, the men around him burst into wild applause and sharp whistles. Ethan tightened his grip on the scabbard across his knees while he prepared himself for what was about to come.

What emerged from the doorway as the music started, slow and soft, was a hand. It moved like a snake, swaying hypnotically until it was followed by an arm covered in coral-colored silk. Something about the way the arm moved was familiar. Following the arm was a foot then a leg, also clothed in silk but of a dark green. When the music ceased for a few beats, the dancer stepped fully into the room, standing motionless. Around Ethan, the crowd began to snap their fingers enthusiastically. He didn't though he couldn't help but smile slightly. Though the dancer wore a mask, there was no mistaking it. He'd just found Vel.

The music started up again and as the dancer moved into the room, Ethan noticed something fluttering behind him. The veil of gold silk was held in Vel's hands and as he moved this way and that, it reminded him very much of a bird's wings. The mask helped that illusion, being as it had a beak-like nose and was covered with glossy brown feathers. During a pause in the music, the amber eyes behind the mask met Ethan's and Vel winked at him. Ethan suppressed the smile but couldn't stop his face from flushing. The music began to pick up speed at that point.

As the tempo increased, so did the movement of Vel's hips beneath the belt of coins. The dark green fabric did precious little to hide the outline of Vel's rear and Ethan found himself staring at it whenever Vel's back was to him. It had been the same that day they'd met in Vel's office; Ethan found himself agreeing to meet Vel for a "date" because of the feelings that backside stirred in him. He realized that he was enjoying the show rather too much and rearranged himself on the cushion to better hide the growing bulge in his khakis.

Why are you doing this to me, Vel? Ethan longed to ask.

Another change in tempo and now the hips were swaying like a pendulum. Ethan's mouth dropped open incredulously when he saw Vel's spine ripple upwards like a snake. He glanced over at the fat Arab to see if he was the only one who was watching. The fat man grinned back at him then calmly put a forefinger under Ethan's chin to close his mouth. With a conspiratorial wink, he nodded his head back toward Vel.

The mid-tempo music allowed Vel the time to begin to work

his way around the room. Each man present (and Ethan noticed there were only men present, as even the hostess was no longer in the room) received a visit from the dancer. Vel knelt in front of one man, the edge of the golden scarf in his mouth, the other outstretched in his hand. When the man took the scarf and pulled on it, Vel slithered like an asp into his lap then drew away with a teasing grin. As Vel spun from man to man, often ending up in some suggestive pose before them, Ethan's jealousy grew like a forge-fire under the bellows. Worse, Ethan kept waiting for Vel to come to him, to offer him the same pleasant torment, but Zemay seemed determined to avoid him. He practically sat in the fat man's lap and even took a quick puff from the pipe but it seemed as though Vel wanted nothing to do with him.

Until, however, there was another gap in the music. At that point, Vel approached Ethan and held his hand out to him. Puzzled, Ethan just stared at him. That was when the fat man spoke. "He wishes to borrow your sword."

"Oh!" Ethan could see in Vel's eyes the patronizing amusement and he gritted his teeth. "Here."

He handed the sword pommel-first to the dancer and it was drawn from the scabbard with a ringing hiss. The music started up again and Ethan watched, fascinated, as Vel balanced the sword atop his head, beginning to spin in place with the speed of a water-spout. When Vel stopped abruptly, the sword continued to spin, even as Vel lowered himself to his knees, legs widespread, facing away from Grand. Ethan had a perfect view of the pert bottom through the green fabric and how the coin belt fell to just above the split between his cheeks. Ethan had to pinch himself on the thigh to keep his mind from wandering off on its own. It was at that second that Vel took the sword from his head with a flourish and rested it on the small of his back, pushing his bottom out farther in Ethan's direction to form a tiny plateau. Ethan groaned quietly as Vel began to make the sword roll in time to the music.

"Amazing," The fat man said beside him and leaned closer to speak into Ethan's ear. "No wonder he has become the Sultan's favorite, hmm?"

Ethan nodded and it was as if someone had pitched a bottle of rum on the fire. Jealousy flared inside him and it was all he could do not to snatch the sword away from Vel and march out the door. At that point, Vel removed the sword from his rear and lowered himself gracefully onto his back so that his head rested practically in Ethan's lap. He placed the sword strategically across his hip-bones and began to roll it towards Ethan, his stomach muscles working like ocean waves.

"What do you think you're doing, Vel?" Ethan said, ignoring the glittering eyes and sweat-slicked cheeks under the mask in favor of the lips that seemed kiss-swollen.

"Buy me," Vel grunted as he moved the sword a bit closer to Ethan.

Ethan shook his head. "Buy you? With what?"

Vel's hands disappeared behind him and he raised himself up enough to grace Ethan's mouth with a kiss. At the same moment, Grand felt one of the hands slide a nicely-fattened purse into his hand. Then Vel was up and holding the sword out to Ethan by the power of his stomach muscles alone. Carefully, Ethan took the blade and slid it back into the scabbard. Vel threw the scarf into the air and removed his mask just as the music came to a sudden crashing halt. Ethan couldn't help himself and joined in the applause with more enthusiasm than he imagined himself capable of. This was all some scheme of Vel's, he knew that, but he never imagined Vel could move in those ways. The notion made him positively dizzy.

When the applause died down, a very tall, gaunt man entered the room. He spoke in English, which Ethan was grateful for. "You have seen Durra perform his dance in public. It is now time to determine for whom he will dance in private. Toss your purses forward."

As Ethan glanced down at the purse Vel had placed in his hand, he noted it had EG embroidered on it. This was all part of Vel's plan, apparently. Weighing the little bag of coins in his hand, he watched as nearly every man in the room tossed something forward. The fat man to Ethan's left gave him a look of surprise then cast his own leather pouch into the circle. Ethan looked up at Vel with a calculating expression on his face. He could see that Vel was nearly beside himself that Grand hadn't already put his money in. Enjoying the look of disbelief on Vel's face, Ethan finally shook his head and reached into his own pocket to pull out two copper coins which he added to the purse then dropped, unhurriedly, among the others. At that, Vel glowered at him, obviously wondering what he was thinking. The auctioneer began to pick up each purse in turn, returning the obviously inadequate and holding only the heaviest or fullest. There were three which he took to the table at the head of the room to count. One was the fat man's, the second was Ethan's, and the third was the purse of a man wearing all black. The fat man leaned over to Ethan again and nodded his head in the direction of the man in black. "I see the Sultan's representative made it in time to bid. Durra has many worshippers here."

Ethan nodded. "This is the first time I've seen him perform. Does he always--dance privately?"

The fat man chuckled. "Not always. We are most fortunate to be here tonight. He is quite lovely, is he not?"

"I-," Ethan started to answer but realized he couldn't. He wasn't sure when he'd stopped appreciating Vel solely for his physical charms but he was sure that 'lovely' was inadequate as far as describing Vel in his opinion. He settled for another nod while the silence grew.

The tall man returned finally, handing the purse back to the fat man, who looked rather disappointed. He glanced from the Sultan's man to Ethan and back, his hands lightly jiggling the two pouches. Finally, as if he regretted his decision, he approached the Sultan's representative and handed him back the red satin purse. He visibly pocketed the bag with the EG on it then handed Vel over to Ethan as he whispered something into Zemay's ear. Vel grinned heartily and held his hand out to Grand, who took it and was pulled to his feet. They disappeared through the door where Vel had emerged into a dark corridor. It wasn't long, though, and Vel led him into a room full of cushions and rugs. A small table with a pitcher of some liquid and a pair of cups sat to the side of the room.

"What's going on?" Ethan demanded, barely able to keep his eyes off Vel's narrow waist and the silk below it.

"Well, love, it goes like this," Vel poured them each a cup of wine, it turned out, and handed one to Ethan before settling himself into the pile of fabric. "Seems there's this legendary jewel that Sultan Raheed keeps in his quarters, a blue diamond, I believe. He tends to give this gem to his favorites just before he takes off their heads. I intend to be the last recipient of the bauble."

Ethan took a drink of the wine and wrinkled his nose at how sweet it was. "Does that mean you want to be buried with it?"

"No, dear Ethan, not at all. I intend for him to bestow the

prize upon me then for my dashing rescuer to save me from his axe-man and whisk me away to the ship and a clean getaway, savvy?" Vel's smile exuded confidence. "Come have a seat, my love. We have all night."

"So, how many other private dances have you given, Vel?" Ethan tried his best to keep his voice neutral but the sudden sly grin on Vel's face told him he had failed miserably.

"Are you jealous, Ethan?" Vel poured himself another cup of wine and topped Ethan's off. "Since we're simply friends with benefits, I see no need for you to be jealous, darling."

Ethan put the sword down by the little table and settled himself on a cushion near Zemay. "Perhaps we need to re-evaluate that situation, Vel."

"Durra, love, call me Durra. Means 'love-bird,'" Vel took another long drink of wine while Ethan studied him in the lantern light.

His hair clung to his neck in places and he still seemed to glow where the sweat had slicked over his body. His face was still flushed from the exertion though he was now breathing rather normally. Beneath the thin silk that he wore over his chest, Ethan could see his nipples had contracted to the size of peas as his body cooled. As Vel shifted, Ethan was stunned to see a small but bloody slice across his stomach. Grand reached his hand out and touched the injury lightly.

"How did this happen?"

Beneath his hand, Vel's stomach muscles jittered in surprise. The CEO's eyes widened and he glanced down at his flesh. "I'm not sure, love. Maybe when I offered the sword to you. It seems you keep yours considerably sharper than the prop ones Ben keeps to use."

"Ah," Ethan responded. Without a word to Vel, he poured a bit of the wine from his cup onto the injury then dove down to lap the liquid up before it could stain Zemay's clothing. Vel's hand seized his hair and tried to pull him away.

"*What are you doing? Ethan, have you gone mad?*" Vel's voice shook obviously but Ethan had no intention of stopping any time soon. It was a mark of Zemay's shock that he spoke Macedonian, not English. Ethan's tongue ran over the injury cautiously, tasting the copper of Vel's blood mingled with the wine.

He pressed his tongue into Vel's belly-button where the wine had pooled, sucking softly. He heard Vel whimper and grinned against the golden skin that tasted of wine and salt-water.

He set the wine aside and used his free hand to unfasten the button that held the shirt closed. His mouth found Vel's nipple and he scraped at it with his teeth, making him shudder. He moved his lips to the other side and pulled his own shirt from his pants. He hadn't worn a vest as the air seemed warmer here than in Abu Dhabi so it only took one hand to yank his shirt off over his head. The sudden sensation of his own skin against Vel's brought his cock roaring back to life.

* * * *

"Eth, please don't. Stop," Vel moaned as Ethan's lips and tongue attacked his neck, the security consultant's rough hands sliding up and down his back in turn. "Don't stop."

Ethan's voice in his ear made Vel writhe under him. "Which is it, V-Durra? Don't stop? Or don't and stop?"

"Neither and both," Vel said and applied a bit of pressure to Ethan's nape so their mouths could meet. He dropped his empty wine-cup and let his hands roam across Ethan's body. There was a strength and a vigor in the other man's flesh that Vel found irresistible. He had hoped that Ethan would be amenable to this portion of his plan but had also understood on some level that Ethan's own stubborn scruples might interfere. Apparently, his scruples weren't as rigid as his cock.

When Ethan's hands fumbled at the coin belt, pulling at it as if to remove it, Vel caught his wrists. "Wait, lover, there's a trick to it."

He used his own hands to guide Ethan's to the small of his back where the hooks and eyes were located. Once Ethan felt him undo one, he had the other two undone in an instant. When the belt was freed and tossed, jingling, to land by the sword, Ethan's fingers located the draw-string of his silk drawers and opened them easily. In his haste, Vel heard something rip.

"Easy, Mr. Grand, take it easy! Silk's expensive, you know," Vel complained.

"So are you," Ethan paused in his rush and raised up a bit to study Vel's face. "How much was in that bag?"

"About 700 dinars. Plus what you put in," Vel smiled up at him. "So how much was the final bid?"

"Seven hundred dinars and two cents," Ethan answered. "It was all I had."

"Cheap at twice the price," Vel remarked drily. "Now, Ethan, aren't you a bit overdressed for the occasion?"

Ethan rolled off him suddenly. "I thought you were to dance for me? Does that require your audience to be naked?"

Vel hesitated then grinned wickedly. "Can't hurt, love."

Ethan shook his head. "Not until I get my money's worth."

Vel laughed. "Well, then, the sooner I get started, the sooner I get finished."

"Wait," Ethan said as Vel stood and raised his hands, striking a pose. He leaned over and snagged the coin belt, tossing it to Zemay. "Put this on."

Vel bowed his head and obliged, the belt covering most of his privates except for just the tip of his cock. He gave an experimental hip-thrust and wiggled his eyebrows lewdly when his member gave an extra bit of movement to the fringe of gold-pieces. He liked the way the movement caused the lust in Ethan's eyes to flare up. Faintly, they could hear the music from the main room. It was a slow piece that Vel recognized from one of the other dancers. He pulled a solemn face and began moving his hips in figure-eights in time to the music. He turned to face away from Ethan but glanced back over his shoulder to see the techie's reaction. To his delight, Ethan was rubbing his palm along the front of his breeches nearly in time to the music.

He faced Grand then, kneeling, legs widespread, so their knees were almost touching. He leaned as close as he dared to Ethan without touching him, so close he could feel the heat from Ethan's groin. He licked his lips. In response, Ethan leaned forward so that he could brush a kiss across his mouth. Vel was no longer moving in time to the music but just hovering before Grand, his eyes searching the oh-so-serious face. When he saw something shift in Ethan's expression, he brought a hand forward to undo the breeches Ethan wore. He lowered his mouth to Ethan's breastbone, kissing and licking him gently there.

He sighed when the fabric over Ethan's hips came undone; Grand's cock shoved into his hand almost with a resolve of its own. It was, to Vel's eyes, a beautiful cock with a rosy flush, a solid two hands width when fully erect, and a pair of blue veins running up either side of it. He resumed moving in time to the music, though he wasn't sure it was still playing and not just in his head. He began to kiss his way down to the meat before him. He heard Ethan groan loudly and arch his hips up just as his lips spread to take the head of Ethan's organ inside.

"God, Vel, yes!" Ethan cried when Zemay's mouth closed around him.

Vel had to smile at the notion of himself as a deity but his mouth was too occupied to remark upon it at the time. Ethan's girth wasn't impossible to take in but his length would be a challenge. Still, he had a nice clean smell and taste which Vel appreciated. He had most of Ethan's span within and was wiggling his tongue along the underside when Ethan's fingers threaded into his hair, the guardian's strength tempered by his concern for Vel. He couldn't fight the smile back though it interfered somewhat with his action. He heard Ethan mutter something–obviously pleased at what was occurring--and decided it was time. He relaxed his throat and pushed forward, taking as much of the length down his throat as possible. At the same instant, he gently lifted Ethan's sack and applied tender pressure. Ethan cried out at that and Vel drew back just a bit in order to take in every bit of the ejaculate. It was thick, creamy and salty, which Vel found delicious. He kept the cock in his mouth until it was starting to recover. He had plans for that cock later.

Suddenly, Ethan's strong hands pulled Vel up so their mouths could meet. Vel sighed and slid a leg over Ethan's hip, letting the taller man press him back into the pillows. "When I was in India a few years back, there was this book that I found. As good as I am with languages, I couldn't read it as it was in Sanskrit but the pictures were quite remarkable. Being an art connoisseur, I had to study them thoroughly. I believe it was called the Kama Sutra."

Ethan sighed and placed a forefinger across Vel's lips. "Do you want to talk or do you want to do something more pleasurable?"

Vel grinned, "I thought you'd never ask, love. But I was just ab --."

Ethan kissed him, hard, and shifted his weight so that he was more atop Zemay. Vel lifted his hips, issuing an earnest invitation, when Ethan pulled away quickly. "Good God, what was that!"

Vel glanced down to see Ethan rubbing his penis with concern. When Grand glanced up at him, Vel made a serious effort not to smile but couldn't avoid batting his eyelashes innocently. "But, Ethan, my sweet, you had me put it on."

"You didn't tell me those things were sharp!" Ethan growled, not precisely in the mood anymore.

"Ethan Grand, you are familiar with metal objects of all kinds. I would think you might remember that metal can be pointy, seeing as how you carry a sword," Vel grumped. "Turn about's only fair play, love. Might I point out that I provided you some relief? Therefore, that would necessitate--."

"Shut up, Zemay," Ethan rumbled, the fire back in his hazel eyes. "I paid for you."

Ethan kissed him again but much more gently than the last time. Grand's rough fingers found their way to the small of Vel's back again, unhooking the coin-belt and sliding it off before it could do any more damage. While the security consultant was preoccupied, Vel buried his face into Ethan's hair, inhaling the scent of smoke and incense on him. Vel let his hands roam up Ethan's nicely-muscled arms to the sinewy shoulders then to the dark hair that brushed Ethan's nape. He was contemplating how the light caught the silver glints in Ethan's hair when Grand seized his leg and raised it above his waist. Vel gasped and voluntarily lifted his other leg. Thank the Good Lord for stamina! He sighed gratefully when he felt Ethan's blade cross his own.

"Take me, love, hard and fast, eh?" Vel muttered, unable to keep from smiling. He'd wanted this for a long time, ever since he met the man.

* * * *

Ethan hesitated. He had to proceed carefully with Zemay. If they could have something more than friendship, he was willing to reach for it. Something about the heat of Vel's body wiggling beneath his actually made his manhood seem harder than he could ever have imagined. He dropped his mouth to Vel's neck and planted a row of kisses from his ear down to his collarbone. Vel moaned breathily and whispered something that Ethan didn't catch. *He never shuts up,* Ethan mused but a smile still tugged at the corners of his mouth. *Then again, I always know where he's at if he's talking.*

"What's wrong, *ljubovta*?" Vel's voice was soft and the concern in it surprised him.

"Nothing," Ethan answered after a few seconds.

Vel pushed him up a little so he could look into his eyes. The golden eyes narrowed as they studied him. "Ethan, love, I know you can lie better than that. What is wrong?"

Ethan met his gaze steadily then sighed. "I don't know and it doesn't matter. I'm here with you and it's high time we get on with this, savvy?"

At Ethan's sudden grin, Vel's eyes widened and he smiled back. "Excellent. 'Lay on, Macduff, / And damn'd be him that first cries, "Hold, enough!"'"

"What?" The words were familiar, but Ethan couldn't place them.

Vel shook his head. "Never mind, darling. Carry on."

Ethan's response was to kiss Vel again as he pressed his cock into the velvet tunnel. At first, Ethan was a bit concerned he might hurt Zemay. Instead, as he forged up inside his lover, Vel groaned deeply and pressed himself back onto Ethan's member. Ethan took it as a sign. Holding Vel tightly in his arms, he set a rhythm to his thrusting. It must have been the right thing because Vel was soon digging his fingers into Ethan's biceps while he repeatedly cried out. "Harder, Ethan! Faster!!"

Ethan obeyed Vel's commands without a thought. It felt so good to be so connected to someone, and especially someone he loved. Zemay tensed beneath him and gasped, throwing his head back. When Ethan saw the pleasure wash across his lover's face, he couldn't hold out any longer. His second orgasm was even more powerful than the first and he collapsed atop Vel like a sail cut from the mast. He tried to stay awake long enough to ask Vel about the Sultan's jewel but the contentment was harder to resist than a whirlpool. He fell asleep with Vel's long fingers caressing his hair.

* * * *

The next morning dawned earlier than Vel anticipated. At some point in the night, he and Ethan had switched places so that he lay with his head on Grand's chest. Zemay rose and went to the kitchen to ask for a bath to be drawn for Ethan and himself. Ben cocked an eyebrow at him.

"Was it worth it?" Ben meant, of course, the very large blue diamond that Vel had traded him in exchange for a bag of dinars and one night's lodging—not to mention the dance lessons that Ben's performers had provided him.

Vel sipped at the cup of tea Ben's wife had handed him when he first entered. Wrapped in a red robe for the sake of Nedra's modesty, Vel nibbled on a breakfast cake. After a moment of consideration, he answered. "Cheap at twice the price."

At A Changing Of The Gods

by Gene J. Parola

Hawaii

It had been half a moon's passage since Lehua had spoken harshly to the *ali'i moi* [governing chief] of Kaua'i and no word had come of what her punishment would be.

She awakened at the touch of her *kumu* [teacher] and was immediately afraid. The seriousness of the situation was made clear when the *kumu* then gathered Lehua's few possessions.

However, she did not put one thing in the net bag. It was the feather *lei po'o* [head garland] that indicated Lehua's nobility. She put it on the frightened girl's brow. Then carrying the bag, she led her pupil, out of the sleeping *hale* [house], down-slope toward the thatched common area.

Unlike the pitch black meeting with the chief, Lehua had no trouble seeing who her visitors were. The sun had greeted the sky below the horizon, and two warriors were clearly visible.

Kumu Mohala turned and handed Lehua her bag, bent, breathed on her cheek, then whispered, "Don't be afraid. They will not dare harm you." Then she turned, and went back up the trail toward the *kauhale* [living quarters].

Lehua greatly admired this master teacher of *hula* [sacred dance] that she had come to Kaua'i to learn from three moons before. Politics were interfering with that pursuit again.

The men's nervousness was apparent. At the last minute, both warriors prostrated themselves in *moe* before her.

"The *kapu* [sacred taboo] has been lifted. Stand up and tell me why you disturb the peace of goddess Laka's sacred place." Her fear made her command sharper than the threat appeared. But she was taking no chances.

The two leapt to their feet. One stepped forward holding out his hand at arm's length, palm down. Bowing his head slightly, he said softly, "The king has sent us to bring you to him in Wailua."

"King Liholiho is in Wailua?"

The man looked up in sudden confusion. "Oh, no. King Kaumuali'i is in Wailua.

"And what does the 'king' of Kaua'i want of a hula *wahine* [woman]?" she asked. She was stalling for time. She needed to think.

Was this what she had feared ever since the meeting that

dark night? What might the ruling chief of Kaua'i do to her?

In an effort to speed up the proceedings, the youth spoke again: "There is news that King Liholiho is to visit soon. Our king wishes to have all the *ali'i* together in Wailua when they arrive."

Lehua considered the answer. It could be true. This summons could be an innocent attempt on Kaumuali'i's part to greet the new monarch in regal style. She had just decided that this was the case when she heard the sharp chirp of the *ania niau* bird. Turning, she saw Kiel and Maka, wrapped in a *kapa* shawl, part way up the trail.

Lehua tossed her bag to the nearest warrior and turning, said, "I must say goodbye to my *kokua* [servant]." With that she climbed to where the whimpering girl stood. "What are you doing here? You were home in Wainiha."

But Maka stopped her, and turning so the soldiers could not see her face, she hissed: "They are lying. They are not from the king. They are from the '*ohana* [family] of Keawe, the chief who ruled Kaua'i before Kaumuali'i."

Lehua started to speak, but Maka was too quick. "I don't know what they want to use you for, but it can't be any good." Again Lehua started, but was again too slow. "I'll go down and tell them that you must say good-bye to the *kahuna* [priest]. Go to the ledge."

With that she turned and bounded down toward the waiting soldiers..

After a short climb up-trail, Lehua ducked into the fern-hidden side path and was soon poised for the last step up onto the secret ledge. She was worried—what did the fussy old chiefs want with her? She was thinking back, going over everything since her excited arrival at the school with her Aunt Puahau three moons ago. A sudden movement above caused her to look up. The *maikai* [handsome] *Pake* [Chinese] was reaching down to help her up. Without thinking she gave him her hand and in a moment they stood facing one another.

Finally.

"Are you all right?" he asked in almost perfect Hawaiian.

"Yes," she nodded. Then realizing she had stood too long staring, she quickly strode past him—all memory of her arrival replaced by the one when he had stepped out of the *uniki* [graduation] crowd and kissed her.

The kiss...that strange thing that the *malahini* [newcomers] had added to her customs of intimacy...

Turning quickly, she asked, "What are you doing here?" She had meant it to be more commanding, but it came out as a simple question. "They came to Maka's *hale* in Wainiha last night asking if you were still at the *halau*. They said they had come for you. She didn't know what to do. She didn't know who to trust. Finally she decided that I would not be a part of any political group on the island and I would help you simply because...."

Lehua wanted him to finish the sentence, but a breathless Kiele interrupted at that moment with a caution to be quiet. Kiele was the smartest servant Lehua had ever had. As she climbed the last step up, they heard Maka below. She was leading the soldiers to the beach trail that led back toward Wainiha.

"Come," Kiele whispered, and beckoned them to the opposite side.

* * *

Lehua had never seen a horse close up. Once at a gathering of the chiefs in Kona, she had seen several of the animals on the mountainside. Now, she looked up fearfully as the black beast was led toward her. Her first impulse was to run. But she was not about to show her fear. Not in front of him. She dealt with it in her usual way. She took command of the situation.

"What is your name?" she demanded, stopping the advance of both.

"My name is Tong Tim, but I am called Ah Tim. My mother is a Kanaka [native] from an old *ohana* [family] on the Big Island and my father is a merchant. His mother was also Kanaka."

Lehua was calculating just how much Kanaka blood flowed through this Chinese...the part that was making him so *maikai* [handsome], when he suddenly bent, put both hands just above her hips and began to lift her towards the horse's back. But she struggled free and stepped away. He smiled. She hated him for that. But only for a moment. Then she was in control again.

"You first," she said.

He swung into the saddle. Then bending over and extending his long arm, he beckoned her toward the beast. She stepped into the crook of his elbow, and in a sweeping arc he lifted her onto the saddle in front of him.

There was not much room between him and the saddle horn and at first she pulled away from him, but the horn was uncomfortable. She wondered who would make such an obstacle as a part of a seat. However, a moment later as the beast began to move she found it a more than convenient handle.

She didn't think she would fall off because his arms surrounded her as he held the narrow straps connected to the beast's mouth. Then everything changed. The horse began to trot. She bounced on the hard saddle, up and down--each time hard enough to gently bruise her tender bottom. The stiffer she made her body, the more she seemed to bounce. Why was he not bouncing? She felt herself moving against his body. She was tense because of him. She was scared of the horse. She was afraid she might fall. All these things made her stiff and unbending. She relaxed and rested against his body; she allowed her legs to dangle next to his. She released her grip on the saddle horn with one hand and allowed herself to sway back and forth with the motion of the animal.

The foot trail had to follow terrain that could be walked over easily—sometimes when carrying heavy loads. That meant that there were gradual rises, many switchbacks and long looping curves. But the horse could leave that trail and amble through the thorny brush and lava chunks, and pick up the trail again later, up or down slope, cutting off many steps and a lot of time. Soon they were far ahead of anyone who would attempt to follow on foot

The trail went around the foot of a ridge but the horse had climbed it instead. And at the moment that the trio breasted the top of the ridge, the sun cleared the horizon. The glowing sunrise spread before them and a fresh breeze welcomed the new day.

A few minutes later, at the bottom of a ravine, Ah Tim lifted her down next to a stream. The horse drank; she stretched her legs and rubbed her bruised backside. He was doing something to the stirrups.

This time he swung up and sat behind the saddle on the horse's bare rump. Scooping her up, he plopped her into the saddle, instructed her to put her bare feet on top of his booted ones in the shortened stirrups. Then he nudged the animal forward and handed her the reins.

"He will follow the trail, but when we want him to turn off, he will go in the direction of your pull."

Lehua was spellbound. Was she actually in control of this huge beast? They were coming around the foot of a ridge. The trail would double back above them on the other side soon. With a slight tug on the rein, the great beast left the trail and picked his way to the top of the ridge, then gently plodded down to the path on the other side.

"The trail is straight for a long way. Make him go faster," she urged. At a soft command, the great animal stretched into a trot. Lehua quickly found that if she stood up on the stirrup tops and bent her knees she could keep her bruised *okole* [bottom] from bouncing up and down in the saddle. The absence of the protective arms on each side was a concern for a moment, but only for a moment. Astride on two feet, her bent knees acting as springs, she could lean forward and keep her balance perfectly as the animal swayed from side to side.

For a *hula wahine* it was no trick at all.

She began to savor the experience. The beast had a particular smell–not a bad one, just a different one. The hair along the ridge of its neck had been braided in long plaits. Its ears twitched this way and that, sampling sounds that came from here and there along the wayside.

Then something terrifying happened. With a touch of his boot heel and a quiet command, the strange wonderful man caused the beast to break into a gallop. In an instant, Lehua automatically bent low over the animal's neck and began taking the impact of the hooves with the spring in her bent knees.

The wind blew through her hair and blood pounded in her temples.

She had never experienced anything like it in her entire life.

Lehua wondered later which she had fallen in love with first, the man or the horse.

* * *

Lehua remembered the lanai of the Pake's house from the night the troupe had danced there. Now in the bright sun of mid-morning, she discovered a large garden that spread away from the rear of the house.

Tong Ah Hin, Ah Tim's grandfather, had not been able to

lease a large space in the small village of Wainiha. So he had to go quite far up the Wainiha River, beyond the many flooded *loi,* to lease land. He needed a much larger plot for his home.

Ah Tim had decided against entering Wainiha from the land trail. There was the possibility that a larger group of the Keawe ‘ohana lay in wait there for her arrival. So the great black horse had been coaxed up the last ridge before the trail descended into the village.

Ah Tim walked the horse along the ridge-line away from the village until they were up-stream of the Chinese merchant's compound. From this height Lehua was able to see the large house surrounded by a tall fence of bamboo. It was set back from the riverbank on a rise of ground. Next to it in another bamboo fence stood an additional building, larger and taller than the house. Lush green grass surrounded both enclosures and upstream at a bend in the river, an irrigation ditch guided water into a rice paddy and a flooded taro *loi.*

Lehua had seen *haole* [Caucasian] houses made of flat pieces of wood in Lahaina once, but these Chinese buildings looked nothing like them. Lehua had a very good idea of the skills required to make a Kanaka hale. But, much different skills were needed here, and different than that for those houses in Lahaina--to cut the wood into curves and make it...all fit together.

Ah Tim spoke to the horse and it plunged down the side of the ridge. Soon another nudge and the beast gently entered the river. Ah Tim slipped off its broad rump and held to a stirrup as the horse swam across, the rushing water gurgling under its belly and Lehua's feet.

Approaching the house as they did, they met no one who might reveal the ali'i [noble] arrival to spies in the village.

Immediately after Ah Tim closed the gate to the compound the two other men who had been at the hula performance greeted them. Ah Tim introduced the elder of the two as the merchant, Tong Ah Hin, his grandfather. The other, he simply called Ah Bah, which he later explained meant ‘father’ in his strange language.

Soon both men in easily understood, but strange sounding Kanaka language, welcomed her and told her that she would be safe in their home until she chose to leave.

She was quickly ushered into the house and into a small room where she was offered water to wash away the heat and dust of the trip. Ah Tim indicated that a cloth hanging nearby was to dry with. It was a strange custom. Kanaka allowed the gentle breeze to dry them. After she had splashed the scented water over her face and upper body, she touched the cloth and it was so soft and pliable in her hands that she pressed it against her cheek in a sort of caress. The water had a sweet smell, like a flower, she thought, and the cloth had a fragrance of its own. Ali'i *kapa* was scented also, but never with such an intense fragrance.

When she emerged from the room, Ah Tim was holding a length of *kapa* from her bag. He indicated that she should put it on *kihei* style with the knot on the shoulder.

It was only then that she realized that she had gone the whole morning wearing the short, sleeping pa'u that covered her only from the waist to the knees.

It was not something she understood, but she had seen it before. When the troupe danced for *haole,* the men paid little attention to the *kane* dancers and never to the hips or hands of the *wahine.* They always stared at the breasts of the women. She suspected that in their country it was *kapu* to see them.

She was led out onto the lanai and offered a strange wooden frame with a soft cushion to sit on. Lehua had seen chairs unloaded from the *haole* ships and taken to the high chiefs' *hale.*

When Lehua was settled, Ah Tim's father poured a hot brown liquid into a cup made of a very thin white shiny stuff. At first it was too hot to drink–or hold, but later when it cooled she drank it and it had a soothing effect on her stomach. Suddenly she realized that she was terribly hungry. This had been anticipated and soon there were other hot things to eat. While she figured out how to do it and decided if she liked them or not, Ah Tim was changing into dry clothes and he soon departed to learn what he could about the situation in the village.

Ah Tim had not ridden the great black horse to Wainiha; he had taken an outrigger canoe down river instead. Lehua wasn't sure where the horse was kept, but on one of her inspection trips to try and understand why the branches and leaves of a bush had been trimmed and shaped in such a strange way, she heard a noise on the other side of the high fence.

As she crept closer to the tall lengths of bamboo lashed together, she could smell the great animal on the other side. Peeking through a crack she saw the other building some distance away. In between the two buildings, the horse grazed on the plentiful grass that extended from the riverbank toward the beginnings of the Lumahai valley a long way away.

Lehua returned to the lanai with a new thought causing some concern. Why did the Chinese live behind tall fences? Were they hiding? Did they do things that they did not want others to see?

Was she a prisoner?

This last unsettling thought was still rattling around in her head when Ah Tim's father appeared with a tray of small squares and a new pot of tea.

She studied that face for as long as he remained, pouring tea and asking if she was comfortable. He was not quite as tall as his son and some gray had crept into his temples. The *Pake* in Honolulu was a lot paler than this man. Ah Bah was as brown as many Kanaka.

He expected Ah Tim to return soon, he said, when she asked. His strange, but accented language brought new questions. She had an ever-lengthening list of them, but she was keeping them for Ah Tim to answer when he came back. And she had to wait a while for that. A long while. The shadows of the tall trees that bordered the garden had lengthened and he still had not returned.

The horse knew he was back before any of the others. A soft whinny of welcome announced that its master had returned. The night ride to Ke'e, the return this morning and the round trip to Wainiha might have tired a lesser man, but Lehua saw no fatigue beneath the sweaty brow.

She said nothing as he settled himself in the opposite chair. His father appeared with a tray, and he poured himself a cup of tea. The older man left immediately and for a moment Lehua felt the weight of the lengthening silence.

"Only one Keawe soldier came back," Ah Tim finally offered. "The other stayed to search for you. The one did not arrive until the height of the sun." Lehua nodded her understanding and he went on. "But the group who wish to betray King Kaumuali'i is larger than the 'ohana of Keawe. Several of the old chiefs who escaped to Kaua'i when the great king conquered 'Oahu are afraid that Kaumuali'i will surrender them to keep the new king from attacking Kaua'i."

"What has this to do with me?" Lehua asked, with some exasperation.

"Does anyone know what else they may want from him besides

protection from Liholiho? With the power of hostages they are likely to have some, more selfish, demands."

"Yes. They have learned that Liholiho has given the ali'i moi of Hawaii Island the right to collect and sell sandalwood instead of sending it to him. Powerful chiefs on Maui and Oahu have demanded that the governor of those islands allow them to deal also."

"Yes," Lehua added. "So, now the chiefs here want to be able to sell the wood from their valleys instead of giving it to Kaumuali'i." She paused again, thinking for a moment and then asked, "How do you know all this?"

"Some information comes from the father of your *kokua* [servant], Maka. Some comes from the low Keawe chiefs who waited for your arrival. When the warriors were late they knew something had gone wrong and they began to talk of the entire scheme and what would happen if it collapsed."

"What did they say when the soldier arrived without me?"

"They were very upset. But he told them that he was sure that you did not escape. He said that they had quickly searched the *halau* and even that of the angry *kahuna,* but they were in a hurry to catch you if you had fled toward Wainiha."

"So, one stayed and one ran all the way back, thinking that I could not outrun him, right? So they will go back there and search some more?"

"Yes. They are sure that a silly girl like you cannot hide in the fern forest for very long. They will hunt and wait. Finally they will find you when you are hungry or thirsty." When he finished, his face was very serious, then they both burst out laughing.

Ah Tim's father came out to see if everything was all right.

* * *

In all of the eighteen *makahiki* of her life, Lehua had never lain in such a strange bed. There were several lauhala mats in a stack but not nearly as many as she was accustomed to. But on top of them there was a huge sack made from *haole* cloth. Inside it was stuffed with the fluff from the young fern leaves. On top of this pad, was another cover. In fact, upon a closer look, she found that it was two layers of a shiny smooth cloth with several layers in between.

In the center of the top layer a terrible green beast with red eyes, a long tail and short legs had glared at her when she first entered the room. Afraid at first to touch it, she soon learned that it appeared out of the cloth by way of hundreds of individual stitches of different colored threads.

She had no intention of sleeping on such a creature. So to solve the problem, she turned it over and lay on the pure white silkiness of the other side. A gentle aroma of dried flower petals wafted up around her as she sank into the soft depths.

For the first time she understood how the chiefs had been taken by the things the outside world had to offer. Had there been anything like this carried into the *hale* of a chief?

Lehua saw her world, the world of the Kanaka, under attack from all sides—the most pathetic of which was from within its own *ali'i.*

The social structure that had served the *Kanaka Maoli* for more years than she had been taught to count, was in disarray. The wisdom of the accumulated years—religious and common--was called into question.

And it was into her world of confusion that Tong Ah Tim had thrust himself. He would prove to be a difference so great that she could not imagine its size.

She lay thinking of the day's events.

"We must find a way to get you safely to Kaumuali'i," Ah Tim had said as they sat on the lanai after eating a strange evening meal. It was dark and the single large lantern hanging from the ceiling made a pool of light just large enough for the two as they sat facing one another.

"Why did you say 'we'?" Lehua asked. "None of this is your *kuleana.* If the rebels find out that you are involved, they may make a great deal of *pilikia* [trouble] for you and your *'ohana."*

"If Kaumuali'i finds out that I could have helped you and I didn't, he will make a lot more trouble for me and my ohana than those sad old chiefs can," Ah Tim said flatly.

Lehua studied the man a moment then with a hint of a smile said, "So you have no interest in me. It's just a service you do for the king of Kaua'i."

It was Ah Tim's turn to study the face of this impudent girl. Then, with his hint of a smile, he started to speak. But the loud jangle of the gate bell interrupted and he quickly rose and went to answer it.

He was back soon with a panting Maka in tow.

"What are you doing here?" Lehua yelled. "Don't you know how dangerous it is for Ah Tim and his ohana?"

"I"m bringing good news," she squealed. "The plot has been foiled. The rebels are scurrying like rats." She stopped for breath. "But part of it was true. Kaumuali'i wants all *ali'i* to meet with him in Waimea as soon as you can get there."

Now, as she lay in the sweet smell of the soft silky quilt, Lehua wondered what Ah Tim's answer would have been had Maka not chosen that moment to ring the bell.

Was all his effort just because his grandfather's business might be threatened if he had not helped her escape? Had he no other interest in her?

The kiss at uniki made her think otherwise.

* * *

Even before Lehua's 'ohana arrived, Hanalei Bay was filled with boats. The king dallied
there, so Chief Naile, had no trouble in getting leave to deal with family business.

Lehua had gone to Hanalei to greet her mother when the great *kaulua* [double canoe] arrived and they tarried there only long enough for her father to arrive before sailing on to Wainiha. Almost everyone had gone to the festivities in Hanalei. Those few who had not, had been hired to cook for the Tong's guests. Pyramids of *kalo* [taro]waited for space in the smoking *emus.*[earth ovens]

Ah Bah had been able to make every outrigger in the village available to their visitors. There were many paddlers among the relatives and after several trips up and down river, all seventy of them were at ease on the great meadow between the bamboo stockades. Some lounged under trees or under the several thatched lanai that had been hastily built to shade them..

For most of the day, the three Tong men made their offer of marriage, then left Lehua's *kupuna* [elders]to discuss her fate. Outside, she joined them immediately, but they simply shook their heads at the questions in her eyes, and brought her to an outrigger that would take her to face another quizzing where the great canoe lay in waiting.

* * *

The next day dawned cool. Already there was much activity around the great double canoe that seemed to dam the mouth of the Wainiha River.

The craft had been beached on the village side of the river. Fifty paddlers milled about, checking the lashing, pre-stepping the mast and readying the craft for the sea.

It had not been a comfortable night for Lehua. The entire *'ohana* had congregated in the thatched lanai to hear her explanation of why she felt it was *pono* [correct] to marry the Pake. And more troublesome: to obey the Queen's edict.

They were less interested in this *wahine's* decision to so quickly embrace the new law as they were in the possibility of losing precious land—from which all wealth flowed.

One old chief was particularly angry at the freedoms granted *wahine* by the lifting of the *kapu.* "We must not only bear your presence while we eat, you flaunt the eating of those forbidden foods."

"No longer *kapu,* my grey bearded uncle. We have long watched you eat the *pua'a* [pig] and *niu* [cocoanut] and wondered what the gods would do to us if we ate them." The night air was still. It was a sensitive subject. "The answer is nothing."

A rumble of angry grunts rose up from the men and she spoke up again louder to be heard: "Was this one more *kapu* by the *kahuna* and the *kane* to make men feel special? Many moons have passed and the gods have not struck us down."

Lehua might have won the whole argument had she not pushed her luck. "Or is the *maia* [banana] the problem? Has the *kahuna* so frightened you that your *ule* [penis] will not rise? Do not blame a hungry *wahine* for a lazy...." She was shouting now.

The crowd was on its feet too and only the calming words of Makamae prevented some terrible condemnation. When it was quiet she spoke slowly: "The time of the old gods and the wooden spear has been replaced by the new God and the fire sticks. The queen has spoken. What chief will stand against her?"

There was no response. The failed battle at Kuamoo was still fresh in their minds.

But, the decision, made late into the night, left no doubt that Lehua had to be taken back to the circle of wise chiefs who would continue her education about things noble. And tomorrow morning was not too soon to start.

Now, in that morning's early light, the passengers had begun to collect on the platform that bridged the huge canoe's two hulls. Most of the paddlers sat at their stations, with only a few still on shore waiting for Lehua to board so that they could push off.

When she boarded, the craft would be pushed into the river, and the first splash of paddles would wash away the most dramatic events of Lehua's young life.

She had just given her net bag to the remaining paddler to toss aboard when she heard it the first time. When she turned toward the sound, she heard it again.

It came from a short way upriver and on the opposite side. A man in a wide brimmed leather hat sat on a huge black horse that had recognized an old friend. It said goodbye.

When Ele'ele saw Lehua turn toward his whinny, he sounded again.

There was no bridge across the river, so as Lehua ran upstream on her side, the great black beast strode into the rushing river and when she got near enough to wade into the water, Ah Tim scooped her onto the saddle in front of him, and he turned the great black head toward home.

It had all happened so quickly that only the one paddler who was ashore finally gathered his wits and began a pursuit. But Makamae called him back. And soon the clear chant of Auntie:

The god dwells in the woodlands
Hidden away in the mist, in the low hanging rainbow.
Oh, Being, sheltered by the heavens,
Clear our path of all hindrance.
Inspire us. Oh, Laka, and dwell on
your altar. Free us.

The Stone

by Christopher T. Dabrowski
Poland

It was love at first sight. They felt that they are destined for each other. Passion, affection and the impression that days are too short to lose it apart. When she missed him a heart-shaped stone always comforted her. It was the symbol of their love.

One day the stone disappeared. She called him. He did not answer.

She had written on Facebook. He did not reply and didn't return home.

She worried sick.

He was dying in hospital after an accident.

The doctors were not allowed to contact her because they weren't married.

Their hearts were made of stone.

A Surfeit Of Love

by Timothy Naslund
Florida

The unrelenting sun brought me two things, both unruly in nature: a strong desire for a drink and memory of you. Perhaps it was the heat I'm burdened by now, the sweat accumulating on my brow and racing down the sides of my face, only to drip into my roof's aluminum gutter I'm currently bent over, repairing. These beads of sweat exploding upon impact on the scorching metal, absorbing the sun's relentlessness all morning, as this particular chore was taking longer than expected, seemed akin to the invocation of your memory – its sudden and abrupt gestation.

Last night's storm had ripped the aluminum off its poorly fastened braces and the metal had crumbled to the mercy of the ferocious winds as nature took out its fury on the helpless gutter, twisting it back and forth until it hung pitifully off the side of my newly bought home. Having the following day off from the storm that persisted throughout the hours of yesterday paired with a spark of ingenuity, I found myself removing the damaged portion of gutter and replacing it with a gleaming, eight-foot piece I had purchased from the hardware store. The perks of being a homeowner, the burden of responsibility falling upon my lap, but I digress.

I typically found physical labor, arduous in the dead of summer, always a great catalyst for my mind to plot out and program a task for my body to complete, while it was left free to wander. And amid its wander, it comes as no surprise that my mind would traverse to the depths of its memory bank where the files and chapters containing every heartbeat-timed moment shared in your presence were held. We fall on a day around the same time of the season two years ago, during one of the last moments where we saw each other and spoke in person rather than on the phone where our conversations were spoken without the fervent honesty that our eyes always convoked.

As circumstances played out, we happened to both separately pick the same reclusive beach town to spend our holiday. You were with your mother for the weekend and I my brother, although, for the sake of this memory and my brother's perpetual lateness to even moments of leisure, I was alone as he was set to meet me halfway through this intended, idyllic vacation.

I had rented a hotel, The South Beach Inn, titled after a

much more famous and crowded beach miles south from its actual setting. The pastel pink, green, and orange stucco walls of the hotel, along with the beachfront location I saw on the booking website enticed me to book the room and was delighted to hear I was able to procure one of the limited rooms overlooking the ocean. When I arrived, I was pleased in the hospitality of the concierge, the view outside of my hotel room overlooking the crashing waves onto the glistening coast, and how once I stepped out from my room and walked down the squared staircase, my feet landed promptly in the sunburnt, white sand welcoming me to the beach and a nice reprieve from the cold concrete I was so accustomed being surrounded by at that time.

After spending my morning entrenched in a wonderful novel underneath a parasol speared into the sand next to me and an inclined beach chair I rented for the entire weekend, I decided to ask the concierge where I should go if I wanted a drink at a bar not trying to lure in every tourist that walked by its neon open sign. She was kind enough to give me the address and directions to a pub located a few blocks in from the beach. Evidently, it was in where the locals lived and where they spent their time and money buying drinks reasonably priced, and when they weren't making more watered-down ones where all the non-natives went to frolic. I thanked her and asked her how long of a walk it would be and was happy to hear it wouldn't take more than twenty minutes if I took up a brisk pace.

From the concierge's directions I managed to find myself in front of the bar, even after taking several detours into small shops whose names caught my attention and warranted a chime from their front door bell. Names like, "The Rusty Hook," "Wilson's Wares," "Jacob's," all intrigued me in their own, quaint merit, and while I didn't walk out of their establishments with anything, I was impressed with the peculiar yet ornate décor each one was meticulously dressed in.

But all of this was me simply wasting time. That's what vacation is for after all – the deliberate wasting of time that would be otherwise spent worrying about how to allocate the remaining few hours left in the day. I had nothing to do in this beach town aside from loose plans and roughed-out ideas of excursions I thought would be entertaining to indulge in during no particular part of my vacation. Most of the plans I had made before my trip were for once my brother would arrive, so for now I was left alone to waste my time how I seemed fit. And I seemed fit to blissfully watch each hour gradually grow in size until its apex on top of the twelve-digit clock, when I presumed I'd be either too drunk to worry about its transformation back to one, or asleep.

Little did I know I was simply wasting time until I were to see you again. I arrived at the pub, sat at the bar, and ordered a beer from the heavy bartender stationed behind the myriad of bottles all varying in the amount of liquor remaining in each. His high cheekbones were further accentuated by the hearty black beard he wore, outgrowing the cropped length he kept the rest of his receding hair. He was rather amiable and when I asked him for a recommendation for a beer to compliment such a lovely summer's day, he poured into an ounce-sized glass an American grapefruit pale ale and reveled in my earnest approval of a reaction, proceeded by me commending his choice. He filled a larger, frosted glass of the hoppy ale and offered his services if I needed another recommendation for my next one.

It was as if you knew I was there, watching me all the way since "The Rusty Hook" where you saw me pick up and then put back the miniature sailboat comprised entirely of toothpicks and a ripped, white tablecloth. You might as well have been a dream, and better yet if you were, for if it wasn't for the wide base of the glass I drank my pale ale out of it would have surely shattered as it slipped from my hands, slamming back down to my table, reverberating a shock that reflected the thought of seeing you.

I was stationed at the corner end of the bar. My line of vision covered the entrance to the front door. As it happened many times before this scene, when you first walked in, I didn't believe it to be you. I thought I was merely projecting your reflection onto the face of a fair-haired woman my age who I didn't see coming up from the window, but who walked in alone, allowing your eyes to dance around what seemed to be the entirety of the pub before landing upon my own confounded glance. Unlike the countless amount of times it happened before, your image this time didn't fade from the woman's visage and I was left staring into your eyes – eyes that separated me from the rest of the world, the pub defying the laws of physics and departing from the foundation it was built upon, hurtling out past deep space until there was nothing, where there wasn't anything outside this close proximity we shared. Here in this four walled establishment, in front of your mesmerizing smile, I found the full contents of my universe. You always did inspire in me such maudlin behavior.

We didn't bother to speak of the coincidence of seeing each other in a town neither of us had been prior, nor knew of the other's plans to visit such a place. What would have been the use? We found it just as inconsequential as questioning why the ocean never seemed to pardon the land and instead punished it relentlessly for departing from underneath its loving embrace.

You ignored the bartender's beer recommendation with a flushed smile and asked for a drink I never heard you order before. You wanted to move to a table, so it would be easier for us to talk, and so we did.

We spoke of things from the past. We spoke of things concerning us both and what had filled the gaps between our last time apart. We had a knack of interjecting ourselves into each other's stories, apparitions appearing in memories, the subconscious thought of the other materializing, becoming more prominent in the memory, reminding the other we were always there. This came with no ounce of apprehension for such vulnerability. We were long past the trifles of the cuts and bruises of worrying how one's love would be reciprocated. The scars that we indirectly carved into each other over the years built up enough tolerance to rely on nothing but pure honesty and equal amounts of providing and accepting the benefit of the doubt that I felt the same as you and you the same as me.

Once we had enough to drink, you insisted on leaving the dreary lighting of the bar and to go for a walk while the sun was still out. We walked parallel to the beach, to avoid getting any closer to the coast and the cluster of half-naked bodies that were otherwise distractions to our sudden reunion. Besides, you pointed out, neither of us were particularly dressed for the beach. Instead, we walked through a neighborhood of tightly built-together townhomes, a prismatic collection of painted stucco, defying any sort of pattern and making it impossible to decipher what color the next house would be. These polychromatic townhomes were only on the side of the road we walked on, facing away from the ocean. On the other side of the road were little dead-end alleys, leading toward little clusters of stores or clusters of multi-colored homes not as intimately positioned than the ones standing in tight file along the road.

You told me you came with your mother. It was her idea to come and you, reluctant at first as you always were to any structured thought, told me you were glad you didn't let your mom come alone.

In front of the fences outlining the perimeter of the townhouse lots, sat a bench. It sat anchored into the sidewalk between two houses, one a faded red, the other a tortilla yellow, both donning a roof comprised of blue shingles, dirty from the rain that bombarded the town earlier in the season. You wanted to sit down on the bench and explore why they had placed it there.

Years ago, you had told me you always thought a bench, or any public seating must be accompanied with a beautiful view. There was a reason, whether intentional of the engineered design of the bench or not, of it being there. Yet, if I tried to remind you of this passing declaration you made, you probably would have denied ever saying it (and maybe you were right, but alas, then how compelling is the thought of the necessity I find in conjuring up such thoughts I believed you gifted me). We sat down and looked toward a cul-de-sac comprised of just four homes. Having green and brown patches of grass between them, each house had more space than the two-walled houses, each butted up to one another that were now to our backs. None of the houses in the cul-de-sac, however, had any fences and it was difficult to see where one person's plot of land ended and the next person's begun.

In the middle of one of the home's driveway were two kids playing with a soccer ball, a boy and a girl. Neither were old enough to have the motor skills to kick the ball with any coordination; well, maybe the girl who looked to be the older sister if they were indeed related. The two were content with letting the ball roll back and forth between them, propelling the ball in any manner they sought necessary to keep the game going. At one point, after an emphatic kick from the boy missed the ball completely, the boy fell and looked as though he were going to cry, but after glancing toward the girl, who stood at the end of the driveway, looking at the little boy lying where the grass met the concrete, got up without a word. He dusted away the white asphalt embedded in his knees and held the ball with two hands, like Atlas holding up the world, until throwing it back toward her, the burden of such a weight vanquished along with any visible repercussions in his face of the fall. It soared over her head and rolled to the neighbor's driveway. The girl ran after it while the boy capitalized on her being turned away and rubbed the lingering pain away from his knees.

When I brought up the two children playing you commented on how they were left out there alone and forbade any other transgressional thought from forming in your head by changing the subject.

You asked me if I still loved you. You looked at me, directly into my eyes and I looked forward toward the children. I regretted bringing attention to the children, an insensitive gesture by me, I know. You stopped picking away polygonal chips of paint from the bench's armrest once I told you I still did, but something hung over us from words I was unable to articulate or capture yet knew the silence you left for me after I responded was reserved for something more.

We left the bench and kept a slow course along the neighborhood until our senses were dulled by the different color houses and yearned for the more muted colors of the sand.

You asked me if I wanted to see your mom and I told you I did. We were throwing around the idea of having dinner at a restaurant along the water advertising their fresh catch of the day among their daily specials written in yellow and blue chalk on a sandwich board next to the entrance. You thought for a minute about running to go get your mother, so she could also join in on the bliss we allowed ourselves to be enveloped in when in each other's presence. Your body jerked toward the direction of your accommodation, but you stopped suddenly.

It was a peculiar feature time adopted whenever I was with you. For some reason – perhaps it had something to do with some electromagnetic field I possessed interfering with your own causing some disruption on a molecular level – the corrosive qualities of time seemed to strengthen immensely. What was once unfathomable elation was now compromised, first fissured in front of those children, and oxidized holes of rust formed in places that were broken once before, that had slowly healed over after time apart, now breaking the picturesque lenses that first covered my eyes seeing you walk through the bar.

When I asked what was wrong, you said it was fine and that we should just spend the time alone. You suggested seeing her tomorrow just before the hostess asked how many in our party – two, just two – and once we sat down, I asked you if you were going to order the calamari or the mahi-mahi tacos, the two items you read aloud from the special menu outside. You ordered both for the two of us.

After dinner, we walked some more along the beach. You took off your shoes and I held them in one hand, your hand in my other, and I watched the sand stick to your feet as you dragged them along the cooled sand, now yearning for the warmth of the beating sun. As it turned out, our aimless walking left us only a block away from my hotel. I invited you to come by, to see the homey studio suite with the gaudy patterned and uncomfortably rough fabric couch with mismatching drapes I was spending my nights in. Perhaps it was in the way I said it, but you were hesitant in your response. The underlying promiscuity and overtly presumptuous nature of the question while not my intention, was inevitably felt and surfaced the carnal tension that was rising in us both. No doubt, our past oversights have spurned us before from allowing such vehement and sweeping sensation to disintegrate the physical boundaries separating us, our souls taking part in the ritual of heralding life, sacrificing sweat and the pouring out of love for something we harmoniously fused, impassionedly, desperately between one another.

You asked what I was doing tomorrow, and I told you my brother was coming in. You seemed pleased, warmed by the sound of his name as if his name was part of your family as well.

You asked how he was, and I said he was fine.

You told me we should all get together, and I agreed.

We sat down on a clear patch of sand and faced the dark ocean. The lights coming from the town overran the luminescence of the moon and so it shrank in the starless sky, feeling unneeded and unwanted. In between the cries of the crashing waves, we spoke of anything that would come to mind, prolonging the farewell that was inevitably coming. We both saw it in view but knew neither of us wanted the night to end, each of us wanting more time with one another, even though we knew it was well over.

And one can ask themselves the question I often asked myself when I was brave enough to reflect on such feelings: Why are you and I not together? There was no doubt, what we shared was love. A love (and maybe this is a little presumptuous for me to declare) that seemed not only impossible to replicate but also impossible to be overpowered by an attraction toward another living soul but your own. And although I wavered sometimes with precarious doubts about your outlook toward me, I nevertheless was invested in the idea that you spoke with mutual earnest whenever you told me those beloved three words, words I only ever wanted to hear from you. Yet, bestowed by the cruel hands of god knows what drives us all, and the uncontrollable, adversarial forces we all fall victim to from this world, we were not compatible for any type of long-term engagement with the other. Both against our will and desire, we would grow cloy when presented with the seemingly infinite time of until death do us part. At no fault to us, we always seemed to lose our balance. Over-encumbered with such angelic happiness we forget what it is like to suffer and feel the need to thus bring it upon ourselves, and a race to the end commences.

Our goodbye was equal parts warm and numbing. We broke from our embrace, a hurricane of despair left in the wake of the paradoxical winds that encompassed us. You said goodbye and we reminded each other of our love.

I love you.

Those words when spoken by you, if there was a merciful god, should rupture my heart upon hearing the last syllable uttered. And I would hope that the feeling that coursed through my body whenever I heard and saw the words leave your precious lips, directed toward me in my now ruptured-heart state, would stay with me forever. The feeling, departing my body alongside my conscious, I pray would guide me toward heaven where I could wait for your soul to reunite with mine, where the trifles of our humanly shortcomings couldn't interfere with us any longer.

I watched you walk away and told myself this would be our outcome. In the meantime, I would fill up my time with stories I'll relay to you until our next reunion, making up for the time spent apart and reveling in the timeless future we will eventually be allowed to occupy.

The Culprit Was Winter

by Timothy Naslund

Florida

Late December chills persuaded our ears further into our coat collars. Our extremities screamed inward with frozen numbness cries to our legs to pedal us into a direction of some place warm and well equipped to inebriate the senses to comfortably ignore such bodily warnings. We succeeded in finding a refuge from winter's beckoning, a second-floor bar overlooking the unknown named street.

A bar of this degree: one where flocks of bundled up adolescent souls, wrapped in middle aged bodies fighting the cold with their chesterfields and parkas, buttoned up to their wool knitted scarves, battle the wind whistling between the maze of buildings enticing their indecisive minds to decide on a haven to pass the time in social interaction while passing their crumbled bills and worn credit cards across an epoxy resin, wooden counter top, decorated with festive, seasonal green and red coasters and half emptied, watered down cocktails (their ice melted away and forgotten). Despite the bar's atmosphere akin to its tepid temperature, it seemed a better alternative than winding through roads with illegible signs, written in Korean, hoping to find a more energized bar - if we were fortunate enough to stumble on another bar at all before freezing.

The necessity for a vacation was upon us both - a retreat from the mundane normality of our patterned days, gridded neatly in a page of the calendar not yet flipped to. A red, circled date where we ritualistically prayed to until our words were heard and eventually announced it was upon us with its ephemeral moments of relaxation and adulterated liberation, only to end carelessly, swift with the despair of having to fight through the weeks and months once again in order to reach the next chance to indulge in more fleeting days of reprieve. We found ourselves vacationing in a city that I was sure to butcher the name if I tried to repeat it, in my rushed and mumbled tone, saving my tongue the embarrassment of its phonetic shortcomings and overall lack of confidence of the Korean language. We hung our coats on the back rests of our bar stools (a comfortable luxury I cherished whenever I was ever at a bar where eventually, half way through the night I always found it a battle to keep from slouching as I'm turned, listening to whomever has captured my attention or who held the best conversation during the night – usually, I admit, my wife) and once seated, proceeded to give the bartender who greeted us our drink orders as we staked our claim at his bar.

Amelia, she always ordered a gin and tonic, a drink I wasn't sure how she could stomach, much less enjoy, and I, being more of a bore in my preference of man's liquid burden ordered a familiar, German beer the bar had on draft.

The bar was dimly lit, but even still without the aid of any shining, fluorescent light overhead, Amelia was radiant, as she always was, smiling through sips of her lime accompanied drink, strands of her sun-kissed streaked hair sneaking over her shoulders as she leaned forward, her nails grasping the glass painted a midnight crimson, contrasting her soft, marble white hands, delicately sculpted with enough subtle imperfections to invoke intrinsic beauty in even the most objective eyes. Her nose permanently turned upward, influenced by her elevated cheekbones, gave off the initial impression that she was perpetually in a state of constant delight, yet the apathetic posture of her rested, half-pursed lips played the role of her facial antithesis, balancing her countenance to a more content and neutral pose. She was, and always is, a delight to behold.

Amelia. Even the slight utterance of her name enamored everything within me: the first syllable, one of astonishment, ah! My tongue suspended in awe to chase a hungered touch of the lips – me – then part, ready to sing a lolling syllable of the tongue touching teeth, only to end in equal astonishment, as I am whenever I'm anxiously awaiting a response after calling her name, left in the wake of her will and eventual anticipated retort. Her eyes were her only giveaway to how she felt, and I, in the four years of knowing her, from time to time still was uncertain what those malachite jewels foretold. My face, however, contrast to her complexion, constantly reflected my current state of affairs in transparent fashion, and in this moment, a gracious smile encumbered my visage as I stole a glance from my left, taking a sip from my white foamed, amber ale.

Although few tables were unoccupied and almost every stool at the bar had someone hovering over a drink, the bar didn't seem too crowded. Music was drowning out a lot of the conversations around us, yet it was not too overbearing where it interfered with our own shared intimacy. Amelia and I talked for some time with one another, mostly about what are plans were for the following day and any peculiar sight we saw earlier today that caught our interest and prompted such reflection. We were having a pleasant time as the bar grew warmer, our bones thawing out the night air's chill, now on our second drink, our bodies being heated up internally by the sensation of alcohol mixing with our blood, giving the tongue an absurd amount of confidence and slowly overcoming the extremities with careless movement, unabashed by any possible transgressions, when our conversation was abruptly derailed by an older gentleman sitting to my right.

"You want to know how I can tell you're American?" he said to me, his top lip covered by a bristly, salt and peppered moustache.

"Excuse me?" I responded.

"You're American," he said in smug fashion, "I can tell." He looked to be in his late fifties, perhaps even his sixties - double our age. He was a burly man. His protruding gut pressed against the bar as he leaned forward, facing toward me and Amelia. I wasn't sure how drunk the man was, if he was drunk at all. His face seemed to keep a naturally red hue around his cheeks and forehead, and his speech didn't seem altered in the least bit - his booming voice not once slurring or hesitant on what his mind wanted to say.

"How can you tell?" Amelia asked, leaning her way toward me and the inquisitive man.

"You're damn loud, that's how. Only Americans talk that loud, especially in another country, like you need to let the whole damn world know you're here. I know because I'm also American and loud." He chuckled; lifting his glass of scotch up, toasting the seemingly obnoxious similarity we shared. "But you-" he said, pointing his glass toward Amelia, "you are not American, though you certainly play the part well."

He was right; Amelia was not American in the traditional sense, although she lived there currently and for the later part of her childhood. She was born in Dresden, where her parents raised her until she was nine, and then, due to an employment opportunity for her father, she was unearthed from her native soil and had to replant her roots into the foreign dirt of the cavalier state of Virginia. Her father and mother spoke enough English to not harbor fear for such a diasporic decision, but they neglected to teach Amelia much English, mainly in part of this choice of emigration being spontaneous and absent of much planning. Coupled with her basic knowledge of English grafted from her parents and primary schooling in Dresden, daily English lessons with a language tutor re-forged her tongue, hammering away at any German accent and tendencies that lingered through the process, turning her into a proper English-speaking immigrant in a few years time.

"Well if I'm not American, what am I?" She asked, looking up at the man as she sipped her gin.

"European." Was all the man said.

"But where in Europe?" She continued to ask. "You can't just guess Europe."

"The hell I can. Doesn't matter, all the same as far as I'm concerned." He sipped his scotch once more. "Bunch of recreants, the lot."

The man slapped the table and let out a loud laugh, as if it were intended not only for our ears, but any other pairs that could have been eavesdropping on our conversation.

"I'm only kidding. Besides, I'm no mind reader, dear. I can just spot an American when I see, or in this case, hear one." He chuckled again, this time at a more intimate tone, and tipped the rest of the brown liquid in his glass into his mouth, exhaling loudly as he firmly placed the glass down onto the bar. "More drinks," He said, "shall we? The night is still young, and it's been a while since I've gotten to chat with a couple of folks who speak half-decent English."

Before we had a chance to interject, he motioned for the bartender and ordered our drinks, knowing what we had either by sight or by overhearing what we ordered before. Nevertheless, seeing how both of our glasses were almost empty, we didn't decline the man's offer. We too were lustful for interaction with a common tongue, fatigued from choppy speech, slowed down and spoken at a pace and pitch we felt made language seem somehow more palpable. It was exhausting hearing a language not your own all day, your mind processing unfamiliar sounds that stick to nothing as the walls in your mind crave for some adhesive comprehension to form.

He sat in silence waiting for the drinks, watching the bartender prepare each one until our respective glasses appeared in front of us, ready to be absorbed. His stare wasn't an intimidating, or an intruding one toward the bar, but more as simply a spectator, in regal stoicism, watching any craftsmen execute his work to a tee.

He didn't seem to marvel at the practice, yet showed his admiration for the bartender's labor in his idle attentiveness. Once we received our finished products, the man nodded to the bartender in approval and Amelia and I were instructed to lift our glasses and to toast.

"To what are we toasting?" I asked.

"The only thing worth toasting for -" He collided with our glasses and took a long sip from his iced scotch and I didn't know if he was referring to the drinks or something more. We followed suit, Amelia giving me a playful look as she brought the drink to her mouth, indicating she was up for our guest and wasn't the least put off by what I perceived as a mutually charming yet intrusive manner. Like most couples who have allowed enough time to pass while in the another's endearing presence, we grew accustomed to reading into such subtle motions, depicting a hidden, malleable language we spoke in moments like the one we found ourselves in now, letting the other know if we were tuned to the same frequency of the current state of affair occurring.

"How rude of me," the man continued as he placed his drink back on the bar, wiping his palms down the front of his collared shirt "My name is Nathaniel, pleasure to meet the two of you."

He reached out his hand in my direction.

"Nathaniel." Amelia repeated. "Such a traditional name."

Nathaniel scoffed at Amelia's remark, "It's a shit name." He said with such deliberation, I didn't feel a need to argue him off the point and instead simply laughed.

"My name is John, and this is my wife, Amelia." I said, gesturing toward my heart's proprietor.

"What are the two of you doing over in Korea? Don't tell me it's your honeymoon; what an appalling destination if it indeed is."

"Why would here be so appalling for a honeymoon?" Amelia inquired. "I find it quite a charming country."

"You don't come to Korea for a honeymoon, especially during winter. Two young souls, enamored in the way you two are, you both should be in a place that matches your inhibited and sweaty fervor. Like Paris or Dubai, or some other ostentatious city. Believe me, I was young like you once and a much smarter and a better-looking lad too, so I should know a thing or two about these things."

We sat there as the night grew in its pale darkness, each one of us listening with supposed earnest to whoever was speaking. We told him we were on vacation and chose to come to Korea out of spontaneity and on a whim from a recommendation from one of Amelia's colleagues, whom had taught English there, which persuaded us to book the trip during our window of vacation.

Nathaniel told us that he was in Korea until a little after the end of the year – as his plane for Thailand left on the seventeenth of January. He was, as he so eloquently put it, trying to see how many countries he could get piss drunk in before it was his turn to die and he had already covered much of Europe and South America. Nathaniel came across as a remarkable man. Brash in most instances, but genuine enough to perceive this trait as endearing rather than unappealing. We found ourselves laughing at his crude jokes we would have otherwise never uttered ourselves, but found each one wickedly amusing, like some harmless transgression, done in muted shadow that felt more satisfactory the more its prohibited. He was a military man, spending over a decade with the Marines, fighting in the tail end of the Vietnam War and spent some time in Grenada.

"Awful time there, humid as all hell under that military garb." He proclaimed. Amelia had a look on her face that supposed she wanted to ask Nathaniel a question, but she opted instead for silence, turning her attention rather to the drink in her hand. Nathaniel, noticing her silent caprice, looked her way and said, "What, you want to know if I've ever killed a man, isn't it? Well, go on then, ask away."

"Have you?" She asked. She was a little embarrassed he knew.

"Yes," He said, "but what of it. Men shot at me and I shot at other men." He opened his mouth to say more but stopped and stared down at his glass, looking as if he was contemplating taking another sip while mulling over the paused thought stuck in his throat. The scotch was announced the victor as he downed the remaining liquor in his glass. He spoke, this time without any hesitation. "War simply happened."

Never participating in any wartime myself, I remained silent, as did Amelia. When speaking to anyone, like Nathaniel, someone who had witnessed war firsthand, my own opinion always felt inconsequential to the intricacies of such a brutish, yet seemingly inescapable experience.

Breaking the short spell of silence, Amelia excused herself as she made her way toward the bathroom, leaving me alone with Nathaniel.

I offered to buy the next round, to which Nathaniel happily obliged.

Nathaniel watched (again in the same concentrated fashion) the bartender prepare the drink order. It seemed something in his eyes elicited pain for a moment: the moist glisten that occurs around one's pupil, the veins in the eye glowing red with blood, anticipating the moment when the locked door holding in the emotional outburst is rammed open with the first shed of tears. This fleeting glimpse of pain, however, dissipated with a blink of his eyes and even further as he cleared his throat, the despair perhaps drowning in the copious amount of alcohol that was accumulating in his stomach, as it was in mine as well. I wanted to follow Amelia and get up and go to the bathroom too but felt rude leaving our newly acquired acquaintance alone with three drinks, so I briefly ignored my bladder's plea and remained in my seat.

Nathaniel thanked the bartender as he placed each drink in front of its corresponding stool. "I have to know," He began, "how did such a lovely woman get stuck with the likes of you?"

I thought for a moment.

"Two things," I finally said, holding up two fingers, "fortune and persistence."

"Bah." Nathaniel scoffed. "Pure dumb luck is more like it."

I began telling Nathaniel how Amelia and I met. How we both were invited, through a mutual friend of ours, to a Halloween party during Amelia's first and my third year in University. I told him how while I was getting ready, a friend of mine begged me to switch my costume of a methamphetamine dealer from a popular television show at the time with his police officer uniform that was too tight on him, but he insisted would fit perfectly on me (it was a little tight on me too, but by the time we got into each other's costumes, our ride was honking his car horn at the end of the driveway, so I was stuck with a police costume that left little to the imagination). After I reluctantly said I would swap with him, wouldn't you know, once we got to the party and started mingling about, I saw Amelia. She was leaning against the island in the kitchen over a bowl of chips, dressed in convict's clothes and her face made up grotesquely to look like a zombie. I told him how she was the first to say anything between us cursing at me from across the room, middle finger waving their first hello, saying I had left her in the back of my patrol car and that's why she was now dead. I told him how we talked the entire night, migrating from the kitchen, to the outside patio, and then eventually the living room couch, our eyes never too eager to leave the each other's unattended until the host politely kicked everyone out and we were left to say goodbye and drive home, anxiously anticipating when we could speak and see each other again.

"She said I looked ridiculous in that police uniform, too. I even told her it wasn't my costume and when I introduced her to my friend, she told me she had no clue what he was dressed up as. I called her the next day asking her to meet me for lunch which she agreed to, and now, four years later, here we are."

Chuckling as he took a sip. He tipped the glass gently up to his lips so the ice wouldn't move as he closed his eyes to enjoy the first sip of his freshly poured scotch. "You're alright, kid. Here's to you and your wife." Nathaniel lifted his drink, indicating for yet another toast.

I responded by knocking into his drink and tipping my head back, showing my appreciation for his gracious gesture, as the beer began to taste smoother as the night waned on. Holding out his glass, he said, "This is what it's all about, remember that." And I was a little unsure of what he was referring to. Just then, Amelia returned from the bathroom and asked what we were toasting to now.

"Good fortune." Nathaniel said, not missing a beat, before I had a chance to respond.

Amelia took her seat and the conversation moved on to more trivial things as the shorter hand of the clock passed both its apex in height and numerals and started its drowsy descent down into the fainter hours of the night.

After a couple more successions of drink orders, Amelia tapped out and substituted her gin and tonic for plain soda. There were now some empty seats at the bar, but the tables remained crowded with empty glasses and talkative Koreans, now more boisterous then when we first came, but not overbearing loud. The bar was filled with warm energy from the energized souls that surrounded us. The three of us were commenting on how it was remarkable how some of the young couples in Korea seemed to match outfits when they were out in public and not afraid to publicly display their affections in ways I considered a bit excessive, but admittedly admirable.

"Well, I think it's cute." Amelia concluded.

"All I know is when I was young and dating, if my fellows back home ever caught me matching like that bloke with my wife, I wouldn't hear the end of it." Nathaniel said, looking over at the couple, shaking his head with a smile.

"So, you had a wife?" I asked, "Or are you speaking in general?"

The smile evaporated from Nathaniel's face as he met my eyes with his. "No, no generalities here."

"You had a wife?" Amelia repeated, her attentiveness being projected in her now perked posture in her bar seat, leaning toward both me and Nathaniel.

"Yes, I had a wife." He said taking a sip. Before bringing the rim of his glass to his lips once more.

"She's gone now." He added.

The air grew stale between the three of us. Our conversation - taking a turn into unchartered waters, where neither we nor presumably Nathaniel wanted to venture - had lost its sense of direction, and we didn't know where to turn our course now, unable to find the preserving winds of banter. Instead we sat undulating in place as we averted meeting eyes: Nathaniel busy with his drink, Amelia looking over her shoulder, back toward the matching couple, and I, ripping away at the damp coaster that housed my previous beers, rolling up the wet paper between my thumb and index - an excruciating couple of seconds it was. I noticed my beer and Nathaniel's glass needed refilled; a saving grace, I thought.

"I'll get the next round." I said, managing to catch the bartender's attention.

"I'll be damned, have you no manners?" Nathaniel asked, and for a moment - similar to his very first words to me - I was unsure of what he was referring to.

Reading the confusion on my face, Nathaniel clarified by saying, "Has the beer filled you up so much that the overflow is spilling into your skull? I'm no floozy you met at the bar; it's my turn to get the drinks, you had the last round." His belly vibrated the residual water that melted from the ice in his last glass of scotch as he sat chuckling, contagious in not only eliciting laughter from the two of us, but fortunately also clearing away the fogged air of tactlessness that was surmised by Amelia's and my own lack of sensibility in prodding at matters we shouldn't meddle in. Nathaniel, however, steering the conversation's course back to those obscured waters once the bartender arrived with a new beer and scotch, said, "She was a lovely woman, my wife. You two remind me of her and me: young and itinerant. I mean, look at you two, fully enchanted with one another. How I wish to be there again, to have this weight of age off my porous bones, to be flooded with the spirit of youth with my love next to me talking to some old bastard about nothing all goddamn night. Although we tend to never remember the bad days as much, I assure you there weren't too many for us."

We thanked him for the compliment, but I was unsure what to say next. Luckily, Amelia came to the rescue, always being the more tactful one in situations where such a quality was imperative.

"What was her name?"

"Sheila." His eyes glistened at the utterance of her name, the same glisten that appeared during each preceding drink order – the alcohol slowly impairing my perception of the passing time, which I only could conclude as soaring steadfast toward daylight, as we would eventually look behind us out the window and see the once shadowy streets ablaze in the orange glow of sunrise, wondering how we managed to converse and drink ourselves through the night (alas I recalled the bar's closing sign saying it closed at a rational four in the morning, leaving no chance for us to be on these upright barstools witnessing such a serene scene).

"Sheila, Sheila, Sheila! Ah, how could I forget the day we met." he started, an act of clairvoyance, knowing (or perhaps just fresh on his mind from our earlier conversation) the next question he guessed Amelia would ask, "I could forget all the countries I've ever stepped foot in a thousand times over, but that night – and any moment where I was honed in to the faintest of her breath – is forever engrained into my memory." His tone shifted from its natural deep pitch to a weaker, more mawkish level, breaking through the integument of his enigmatic character he seemed encased in all night, simply revealing a drunk, heartbroken man finding solace in good scotch and company willing to lean into the night with him.

He told us how she was a waitress at her family's restaurant by day, a bartender at night. He told us how he would come to her bar every night, watching her pour drinks for him and others. How he would beg for her time outside of work, "Just one date, that's all it'll take, I promise." Nathaniel would say to her near the end of the night when most of the other customers staggered off to their homes. How he would eat lunch every week at her family's restaurant, eventually befriending her father in his jovial nature and always showing the upmost respect to her mother whenever he thanked her for such angelic cooking, as he put it, eventually speaking to her and her to him as if he was already inundated into the family. After some time, Shelia finally conceded and went out on a date with Nathaniel. He was right, and shortly afterward they were planning a wedding.

"She was playing hard to get, I knew that." Nathaniel explained, "She adored seeing me grovel, come back time after time after each gut wrenching rejection, her eyes inviting me back to the same bar stool the following night, or the following afternoon to the table closest to the kitchen, always the table closest to the kitchen. We got to know each other very well in that time, her and I, and even though during the whole song and dance I was driven mad by her consistent rejections, I admit, the chase was damn fun and well worth it."

He went on and on, and we listened diligently, Amelia's fingers grabbing at my thumb, pressing against my knuckle in moments when Nathaniel's recollection invoked empathy and a quick smile from me to her whenever I caught her stare out the corner of my peripheral. How remarkable one's own mawkish memories can be selfishly absorbed by its audience.

He told us how she died from a case of walking pneumonia going untreated, during a hiking excursion they were having through Switzerland in early January, around this time, he added.

"She never liked to show frailty, she was a strong girl. She thought it was only a bug, something she would get over soon enough and not something that would affect the three night hike we had ahead of us that week. By the time we finished, her cough had gotten worse and she was deathly sick, but still, she wouldn't let me lay a finger on her as we were coming down that mountain, never once complaining about the cold." Nathaniel drank the remainder of his scotch in one, long sip. "Hard-headed girl. Too damn stubborn. Too damn stubborn."

We ordered two more drinks and another soda for Amelia.

"If my memory would so happen to betray me," Nathaniel started, swirling around the contents of his newly poured scotch, the booming echo in his voice diminished to an intimate murmur, "leaving me a blank slate whenever I thought of my Shelly, then that would surely be the end of me, friends." He cleared his throat, managing to get his intonation back to its voluptuous tone, "But, until that day–"

"To Shelia."

We rose our glasses and the still image of the wet smile on Amelia's face, the reddened cheeks of Nathaniel, and whatever facet of my emotional state my face was outwardly portraying is the last memory I have of that night. Although I know something had to follow, the final scenes of that act seemed too frivolous to hold onto: them being perhaps a few more exchanges between us, the inevitable departure and journey back to our hotel which Amelia made certain, and the obvious curtain-call undressing and collapse into the white sheets of the unfamiliar, hotel bed, was all lost know. These moments were sacrificed to the keepers of time, leaving me with the proper ending of the story of how I needed to remember that night, as inimitable as it was. And I would wake up next to Amelia the following day, our heat mixed underneath covers, the light of day peeking in on us, and know for some, and hopefully us, that is all that's ever needed.

The House Sitter

by Keltie Zubko

British Columbia - Canada

Years after she'd left, he wondered where his wife had found the house sitter.

He didn't though, not yet, each day on their Holiday to Save Their Marriage (as he called it), lying in the sun on a beach on some mid-Pacific island Marg chose, far from their home on Vancouver Island. His mind was still back there, showing the house sitter around their property, before they'd left it for a whole month in mid-winter. He was just that close to going AWOL with the rental car, back to the airport and grabbing a flight back.

Of course he wouldn't do that, he owed Marg, so he clung to those scenes, hid in them from the sun, sand, and constant socializing with others in the same time-share. She wanted to rub sun block on his pale body, so he let her, coconut-lime smelling lotion the only cool thing about the place. She did a thorough job, telling him to relax his legs, that they were as hard as tree trunks. She whispered in his ear how glad she was to see his naked feet, lolling in the sun instead of clammy inside boots that never dried out.

He grunted, turned over and retreated into his mind. Marg had installed a wide variety of books for him on her Kindle, with streams of grey-black characters on a flat white paper mimicking screen, but his eyes just could not focus, so he closed them.

Then, he could almost smell the undercurrent of mold beneath the biting fresh deep woods, Douglas fir and yellow cedar, moss overgrowing everything, the florescent red and acid-green fungi, leather-leaved salal dripping cool water onto the forest floor.

From there, his mind slid always to images of the house sitter Marg had found to free them for this trip. His face flushed under the sunburn, and he wondered again why he hadn't told her the important things about the house, neglecting the very point of having her.

Of course, he hadn't wanted her in the first place, a stranger in the house. All the way over, confined to his seat in the aircraft beside Margaret, breathing recirculated air, he wondered how he'd been lulled by the house sitter.

She materialized just a little before their neighbor arrived to take them to the airport. She wore a paint-stained green jacket, faded just like she was faded. He couldn't remember the colors of her eyes, her hair, her face. She was as pallid as if the west coast rains had washed all pigment from her skin. He wondered what color it had been when she was young, for she was his age or even older.

She seemed to slip like mist out of the deep forest, rather than arrive in that beat-up van, stuffed with huge canvasses, her work. She was an artist from up the island, Marg said, "and Charlie, you'll like her stuff." He doubted that, having seen too much art Marg thought he'd like. The glimpses of mere edges and impressions did intrigue him, though, the colors echoing those around their property, up the side of a hill far above the river. They were inland from the coast enough to smell salt, but removed from the vistas of ocean meeting horizon, hidden within the vast swathes of winter mist, wrapping the tall trees that had reached for hundreds of years out of the valley.

His mind balanced between the house sitter and Margaret.

Margaret talked a lot. She said too much, hurt his feelings. Once she'd said he was like some kind of fungal creature, thriving like the mushrooms do, at the base of the towering trees in damp and musk. The smell of the woods, rotting leaves, choked her, making her cough. She preferred the smells of a coffee shop, or restaurant, with warmth and comfort, manmade things, or the excited heat of a show, or a store with that plastic smell of new electronics, or the clean commercial undertones of dried paint in her gallery.

Not the smell of the woods. He would open the door and inhale it like he was trying to ingest something into his soul. So too, the smoke that hung around their valley when he started the fire, mixing with the icy morning fog. He liked the salt tang from the cold ocean that crawled inland to where they lived, with its rank undertones of dead fish and things that could live in that chill under water.

At least, he tried to joke, the putrid mill smell was gone. She didn't laugh at that. With the mill, his job had gone, too, even though he'd been lucky and able to take early retirement remaining in the small town, in his grandfather's house, the last generation of loggers.

There was never enough sun, she complained, and the deer stripped all the little seedlings she tried to grow in the alkaline soil, the peat bog soil, that only liked blueberries and rhododendrons and azaleas, not Prairie plants basking in sun from an unobscured sky. She'd gone through a phase of featuring Prairie artists in her gallery in the city, finding a market among inlander ex-pats yearning to move back.

She bought scented things to expunge the wood smoke permeating their house and clothing. Margaret still wanted to banish the woodstove, get a heat pump instead, so she could flick the thermostat on rather than build a fire, with its time-consuming ritual and dependence on factors she couldn't control, like the atmospheric pressure, the right mixture of kindling, and patience.

She never built the fire, refused to haul the chunks of fragrant wood that always had, to her, some drawback: the pine wept sticky sap all over her hands and clothing; the cedar made her itch, splinters crawling into her work gloves. Hemlock was too heavy, no matter how dry it was. He liked to start the fire from scratch but not her. It took too long to heat the house and the discipline of making and feeding it tied her down and irritated her. "We live in the 21st century. I don't want to live my great grandmother's life."

And off she'd go to the city, leaving him, wrapped in the winter darkness, like a blanket, comforting, not oppressive, as she claimed. She had a different attitude to sky and horizon and space. On the Prairies, she said, storms couldn't sneak up on you. You saw them coming for miles and could mentally prepare, unlike here, the hills around the coast of Vancouver Island, with tricky micro climates that lurked over the next rise.

Here, things stalked you, coming closer, skulking behind enormous weathered tree trunks, jaded from having seen it all, until whatever it was, popped up, pressed its face against your windows, or dropped down suddenly on the shake roof with a heavy thud. Margaret kept the curtains drawn at night even though he said there was nothing out there. The darkness, she said, was too close, was darker than a midnight sky, heavy with towering trees and swooping branches, or opaque sheets of rain.

Not for her, cooking on a woodstove, but rather the microwave and every possible short cut to meals eaten on the run while she talked on the phone, hurried out the door.

Her tools were mostly digital. Now that he was retired, his were the chainsaw, pickup truck, bungee cords, chain oil, the splitting maul. His thoughts plodded on as he cut and hauled the rounds, heaving them from the truck to a messy pile in their yard, where they shed their bark, littered the place outside the woodshed, so the grass refused to grow.

There, with the dog's complicity he made a ceremony of gathering their wood for the winter. "But Charlie, you're not getting any younger. You won't be able to do that forever." He scorned the machine she dragged him to see at the tool store, went back to his axe and hours of work, splitting and stacking. Those hours still honed his muscles, made his arms like iron and weathered his face with the combination of sweat, rain and thought.

He shivered and felt chilled even now, at the sunny beach. Some people thought the heavy rains of the Pacific Northwest drove them mad, or at least just a little bit odd, from the pummeling water on roof tops, car tops, and their skulls under the weeping, morose sky. Perhaps that's what had happened to him, stopped him from enjoying the beach and the sun and Marg's perpetual currying of contacts, networking, and outreach to new customers, new clients, new opportunities for her business, even on this holiday.

He couldn't open his eyes fully to the beating sun, squinted instead, listened for any conversation coming too close, pretended the shush, shush, shush of the waves was wind shifting the trees above the old house that squatted beneath their swaying height and expansive branches.

He hadn't shown the house sitter the basics because of time, and because that would have felt like peeling his clothes off in front of her. Hard enough to see it through Marg's eyes, much less a stranger's. And so now he worried how she'd manage, reviewing what he hadn't mentioned: the outside things, the woodshed, emergency lanterns and matches, kindling all split and ready, where the compost was, the tools (though he doubted they'd be necessary), where the garbage and recycling was picked up, way down at the road, not up by their house.

He'd led her briefly around the property, not the acres surrounding the house, nor the house itself with its deep roof incline, covered in shakes, cut from the land it stood upon. It was bigger than a cabin, with well-insulated walls against the penetrating winter damp and the summer strawberry-scented heat. She followed him and the dog followed her.

He had meant to show her the intricacies of the locks, where extra keys were kept, and tricks peculiar to the heavy doors even though he could feel the old house protest like an elderly bachelor, protecting his solitude.

Of course Margaret had made a comprehensive check list, but instead of going over that, the house sitter distracted him by pointing to the weathered cedar plank, secured to a log down at the end of their driveway. "Deep River," read the carved words.

"Why the name?" she asked, "there's no river up here, is there?

"The Sooke River is way down there, but that's not what it means."

"The song?" she asked, one colorless eyebrow, twitching.

"As a matter of fact, yes. Not because of the song, but the singer..."

"Robeson?" she asked, "but why?"

They'd stopped, stopped right in the middle of the driveway and turned to each other. He noticed a tinge of pale blue in her eyes, which he'd thought were the impenetrable grey made by sheets of rain.

"It was around the time of his concert at the border, when his passport was confiscated. He was banned from leaving the states."

She barely nodded. He continued, "The story is he crossed into Canada, here, by boat, to give a concert just for the loggers, working up in these hills."

She said nothing, listening with her eyes holding light as if winter was over and sunlight hit the drops of clear water resting on the leaves after a rain, before the wind blew them down. Deep, clear luxurious drops of crystalline water. Now, on the beach, sprawled in the grit, his mouth hungered for such cold water.

The house sitter waited. Margaret did, too, patient in her own way, talking to the neighbor by the car with their baggage inside. He continued.

"Old timers tell how he came in by boat, across from Washington into the harbor, here, and then about the concert for the workers, by the enormous old growth they were logging. He sang like in a concert hall, on this very land, way in the back." He stopped, as if hearing the sound, then finished. "My grandfather made that sign."

Margaret had called him then, so he abandoned the rest: emergency generator, who to call in case of trouble. She said nothing more to him. He didn't want to ask how she'd manage hauling in the wood for the fire, each day.

They reached the back door, and Margaret said, "Did he tell you everything you need to know?"

"Enough."

"Well, enjoy the studio. Hope it gives you what you need."

"Yeah," the house sitter answered Margaret. "Check out that gallery, if you get a chance."

"I will."

* * *

On the first day, she slipped around their house, deferring to them, as if they were lurking just past a corner, phantoms skittering into the shadows when she turned her head.

Her priority was to move her canvasses into the empty studio that Margaret had offered her first off, seeing her work in the gallery where they'd met. It was the clinching point, a vaulted ceiling with skylights and broad windows to capture what light there was in mid-winter, surrounded by towering trees that shed their debris on the yard and buildings. That, and of course, solitude.

Margaret had shaken her head about the loneliness, claiming she couldn't stand it, stuck up that steep road in winter amid the driving rain, the dark, the mold and moss entombing everything that didn't move, trapped the way the smoke from their wood fire couldn't find its way out of the valley, wrapped around the tall trees, unable to reach the sky in darkest winter. And of course, if even a large branch, much less a whole tree, fell across the road, she wouldn't make it to the city for work or even to the village for groceries or a cup of coffee in the single coffee shop, with the noise and warmth of other people. The house sitter had smiled at Margaret.

Now, she lifted her oversized canvasses out of the damp van, unwrapped them and positioned them around the studio, finding each its right space, so they could breathe and face her and the others. It got dark early so she didn't fuss too much, waited for the next day to see what illumination would light her way through the mysterious, groaning, swaying, watching forest. She didn't need much.

She shivered, though the wood stove had warmed the whole

space with its soothing dry heat in the damp that crept into bones and joints if you let it, making your nose drip and fingers ache.

That was at least one thing he'd shown her, looking skeptically at her size, she knew, as he led her past the rows of aromatic seasoned firewood. She'd have to haul it in to heat the place. She didn't care. It was a very small tradeoff for just being there, to work within the breathing, singing forest.

On the day after they left, she walked through the empty rooms, still feeling they were watching her, the man with his grey green eyes, slow and steady, like an icon brought inside from the rain, face carved of wood, lines running down it like the rings in trees, a contour map of his life. Margaret, of course, was different: quick and alert, an organized bird, ready to fly up toward the sunlight between the tree tops, fleeing. She was the same size as the house sitter, but arranged differently, wore spiky heels, and wore them bravely as if she was almost ready to leap out of them to the sky. The house sitter couldn't imagine that, clinging as she did, by the soles of her feet to the forest floor.

Funny how Margaret had to ask her that question to make her notice they were the same size. She certainly didn't feel at all equal to Margaret. "What size shoes do you wear? Your feet look the same as mine. I've got lots of rain boots and gloves and gear, outdoors gear you can wear. Help yourself. I'll leave them all out for you."

She'd walked through their house, exploring, hearing its creaks and groans, feeling a dreaming presence, just barely breathing in the warm cedar boards of the high ceilings, the scarred stone hearth upon which the wood stove sat. Even the remnants of food in the refrigerator seemed caught in another time, opened all the cupboards and pried into the freezer, finding a stash of local salmon, and precious halibut from the deeps in the strait, and frozen blackberries, the dried apples sprinkled with cinnamon.

She fingered the work clothes hanging by the back door, examined the boots and gloves, hats resting there as if just stashed. She touched the ground-in red dirt on his gloves, like it was pigment for her paintings, unearthed from the forest floor around the house. Margaret's gloves were stiff, and unmarked. The house sitter tried them on. They fit her.

* * *

Tropical sun weighed on his eyelids, made them burn and he flipped over onto his stomach, remembering the house sitter's tiny hands, hoping they were strong.

* * *

On the second day after they'd left her, she spread out her own meager belongings. She'd slept late in the guest room with its small bed and bare closet because it took the dawn so long to reach back there, where the hillside joined the house. Their bedroom had a skylight and a fireplace and flopping down on their bed, her body sank into the old, forgiving bed. Margaret was right: she should sleep in there. She closed her eyes then opened them to watch the tall trees move in their dreams, leaning over the skylight.

She spent the rest of the day laying out her tools, paints and brushes, palette and her easel with a fresh canvas amid the others already in the studio. She wanted more than one blank canvas, here, in this place, felt her hands beset with ideas.

* * *

On the first day at the beach, he mentioned to Margaret the odd thing that the house sitter had heard of Paul Robeson, and even more, seemed to know a bit about him. She looked like he'd dragged a sloppy wet rag down her shining face, leaving it scrubbed blank and eyes blinking. He tried again. "It isn't a contest, you know. You don't have to like what I like. I don't mind what kind of music you like." She shook her head, turned away. He felt like the time he'd tried to hold an unruly sapling from her as they climbed an overgrown path in the forest behind the house and instead it snapped out of his grasp,
rebounded and whipped her bare neck.

After that, they only settled deeper into their routine, Margaret scouting the stores and artists, he biding his time. They ate, slept, shopped, talked frugally, except to other people, occupied their spot on the beach and ate and slept some more. He abandoned the Kindle, bought books at the secondhand store, with crackling spines, and read them but often couldn't remember where he left off, and took to cleaning the sand out from underneath his nails with the corners of the pages, while he read. He knew she hated it, but he couldn't stop himself. Grains of sand got in between the pages, marking the days and his progress through them.

Margaret established a small group of other people, gravitating to her, at the center, the apex to which their new acquaintances clung. That always happened. She spoke for both of them, since he was too slow for their questions, perhaps didn't hear or just didn't bother. They were boomers, holidaying amid other boomers.

So when did you retire? What did you do?

He shrugged. How could he say, "I work, I will always work. I will never retire."

He lay in the sun, the heat drying up his words, recriminations and conciliations, both. She became more active, like a bird always spreading her wings, preening in the same glare that held him paralyzed. He needed the quiet running water, the cleansing rain. He waded into the ocean, but waded back out again before it could pull him deeper, before the land fell away from his searching feet, completely.

* * *

In their house, the house sitter ate their food, made her way into the village, endured her first interrogation by the local shopkeeper, and heard stories about Charlie's old man. She picked up their mail, and hurried back to the house.

On the day she lost track of how long she'd been there, she slipped into a pair of Margaret's unused rubber boots to walk down the steep hill to the road. They were dusty but didn't even have the price tag removed. She clipped it off, and by the time she climbed back up the hill, the rain had washed them clean, though little yellowed pine needles from the edges of the puddles clung to the shiny toes.

She laundered the sheets from the guest room where she'd slept the first night, and made up the room again so it was ready. Each night she climbed into their bed with the flannel sheets, where she could watch the fire, which she stoked after hauling wood up the polished wooden stairs, dipped and worn by decades of footsteps. The dog settled into a heap, whined and chased squirrels in his sleep, heaved himself up, turned around and collapsed again with a grunt.

She moved Margaret's clothes to the side of the double closet, and wedged her minuscule wardrobe into the middle. She studied her few things, beside Margaret's colourful clothes, hanging like a work of art in dramatic blues, reds, and purples, the wild prints and vivid silks, making a rich collage, replete with promise like freshly squeezed paint, in pure, rich hues. Her own dark colours and jeans shrunk back in embarrassment, closer to Charlie's clothing, just a few suits and dress shirts, some plain ties, worn and friendly work clothes.

Winter storms lashed the windows and beat on the roof, sending showers of pine cones, needles and small branches down with the rain. The trees bent and groaned outside, but the house held her, so she slept well. The power didn't go out, and anyway, she could see by the light of the embers whenever she woke, gold on golden walls. The dog slept in his spot nearby.

She painted, but began each day exploring outside before she settled down to work. All the things open to the weather seemed more personal than even the bedroom. She pushed open the door to his workshop, stepped inside, noticing the way he organized his tools, chainsaws carefully parked, the handles worn by his solid grip. She fingered the engraved "Made in West Germany" lettering on the casing. Antiquated, she thought, and imagined him, sharpening the chain, a tedious job: Shritch, skritch, with a gentle round file, a light stroke to keep the angle perfect so the chain would cut, and not burn through the wood. She could feel the respect of his touch on all the tools, placed in a way that made sense to her, like the way she organized her brushes and paint in a certain order.

Long she painted into the darkening afternoons, until she could barely tell what her brush was doing on the large canvas, not sure if she used paint or something else, some new, indescribable medium to create the picture unfolding from her mind.

She went again and again to the staging area for splitting firewood, like some empty altar. The fragrance of various native woods lingered in the air, and years of bark littered the ground making it cushioned and even springy. His axes lined up in the tool shed nearby according to their various duties: a splitting maul, a hatchet, a heavy axe with a handle she knew would leap to the warmth of his palms.

Bordering the area, log rounds gathered to memorialize the

first cut, made when he'd fallen each tree. She saw the single straight, brave incision, three-quarters of the way across and then the down-cut at a drastic slant to make it crash to earth in the right direction. She saw what it took: delicacy, intuition, skill and strength. Those pieces were never easy to split. But he'd gathered them in a circle around this area. What were they? Seats for ancient spirits? No human being could sit on them. She almost heard Margaret wondering why. If, that is, Margaret had ever been out there. Yet another picture presented itself and her fingers pulled her back to the house to set it down, at least as a sketch.

Often the dog drew her up the paths carved in the red dirt to the back of the property where generations of other dogs had gone before. And people, too. She paused and felt the stillness, amid the plunk, plunk, plunk of the heavy drops, delayed by huge branches on their way down, long after the rain stopped. She felt the loggers of the past waiting just over the hill, with their primitive equipment, springboards and two-man crosscut saws, felling saws and bucking saws. They had no gas powered engines, no helicopters, no chainsaws. They too, paused, hearing that deep, rich forbidden voice freed to the listening forest.

* * *

Margaret had a finger in it all, knew everyone, kept track of everything in the gallery scene, the old, the new, experimental, boring and bored. But she'd surprised even herself by the flashing identification and sudden decision she made about this particular artist's work, the moment she saw the first canvas.

Vast paintings, almost the size of the walls behind, the rain-misted colors of a west coast winter, depicting the "Freda Kahlo of the Pacific Northwest" since the slight, faded woman had insinuated herself into every painting, sometimes almost barely visible, but always there, like part of the primeval landscape. A wood creature, a sprite, a water fairy, and most often, these days, an aging crone surrounded by the vivid colors, untouched, unmoved, uncolored by burgeoning life around her. Like she could see it but not be it, Margaret thought, until she felt such boiling impatience she wanted to snatch up a paint-laden brush herself and give the woman's self-portrait color, vivid, living cheeks, an azure flash in her eyes, make her flesh hot and alive. She thought of the way Charlie's fires in a freezing winter deluge overheated the house, baked her right to the core of her bones. That was the image, that one particular image which gave Margaret the answer she didn't even realize she was seeking.

They each tried to talk, but nothing could ever get said, until it seemed that silence held them captive unless, that is, the crowds assembled round her. All those chattering new friends now left him alone, so he spread himself out, like her background, as it always ended up. He didn't have the words for her, or for them, so let the conversation wash over him like cold torrents of the rain at home.

He still thought about the house sitter, pictured her in the house, knew that the cupboards would open for her without sticking, the windows would let in the wintry sun for her, gathering each tiny cold ray, so she'd have the light she needed. The paths would unfurl as she stepped further into the deep woods high above the river. She would hear the echoes of that voice so low it just rumbled and hummed through the land, seeping into your guts and your brain.

"Come into town with me," Margaret said on a day when he'd left the beach to shelter under the trees around their patio. "I just want to look at a couple of galleries." He shrugged and let her haul him there, to the stretch of shops, ones like she was building in the city, back at home. They catered to the tourists from the cruise ships, and the wealthy timeshare owners. Once, he'd eagerly sought her tutelage about the artists.

He wore shorts and a linen shirt like it was a costume, revealing too much of his browned skin, tanned by this time, socks in his sandals, despite Margaret's protests. She, however, fit in, he saw, like the parrots gathered on the man's arms for tourist pictures, or like she'd flown out of a painting in the expensive galleries, a tropical bird, an exotic flower, a painted face, with vivid makeup, big eyes, and big smile. He knew her smile was genuine but that was not enough.

They strolled along the boardwalk, she leading, though they went side by side. He was too slow for her, so she went ahead into the galleries until the last one, where she caught his hand and drew him with her. "Just this one and then we'll get a drink and a bite to eat."

He stepped over the doorsill, wide open to the crowds on the boardwalk, and flinched at the overwhelming size and variety.

Another place with tiny signs advertising big prices beside the huge canvasses. They were both local and international. At least there were other people shuffling around, admiring the giant works of art, and they weren't all grotesque, these ones.

He made his way around the room. Giant dolphins. Vivid ocean. Surreal skies. Paradise, wherever it was. Margaret spoke to the owner in the corner.

He breathed as if the air itself was expensive, moved to the next one and came face to face with a forest, like home. Old growth fir and sun coming through the mist. He gulped the fresh air exuded by this one, not cloying, tropical flowers, heat, lotions, grilled street food, money, but the fresh breeze off a much colder ocean. Shards of light peered through deep forest and he felt the light of it lay a cool hand on his forehead.

His body relaxed, and finally in all the weeks they'd been there, he could even open his eyes wide. He saw that the moss on the tree trunk of the six foot tall painting enclosed a form, that of a woman, made of the tree trunk, made of the forest, revealed in the sunlight, disguised by the mist, but there, a face peering out of the disguise, half-turned away, but also half turned toward him, her moss enclosed arm like in a velvet dress, she peered at him, hand extended, come on, come on, come here, come home. It was her.

He shook his head, gulped again.

Margaret crept up beside him stood silently, watched him, and the painting.

"You like that," she said in a voice he barely knew. He nodded.

They each waited in silence.

Finally, she spoke, "I have a ticket for you, you know, anytime if you want to go home early. You decide."

He still had no words. He squinted at the name of the artist, but it made no difference. It was the house sitter. Then he looked up again at the figure in the painting, the face drained colorless by the mist and the forest, the small body enclosed in the emerald lush moss, her figure half turned away from him, half turned to him, the hand outstretched, beckoning.

* * *

She had long found Charlie's stash of vinyl and played

them over and over again, turning the sound up, so it was really not just by chance that late one night as she worked, she didn't hear a car drive up the steep road past the sign, and stop in the yard.

She heard Robeson's voice, singing, the bass so deep it was a vibration in her bones, from her spine to her fingertips holding the brush, connecting with the canvas. He drew the sound out like she drew the paint-laden bristles, luscious and full on the meshed surface, so that the friction and its traces were everything. "De-e-e-e-e-e-p ... Ri-i-i-i-ver ... Oh, don't you want to go? To that promised land ... where all is peace...." So deep, she felt the house sigh and relax around her as the door opened, and Charlie came home.

The Promise Of A Kiss

by Robin Pond

Canada

The walk home is awkward. The conversation doesn't exactly flow. It spurts more like water from a corroded faucet, punctuated with elongated bouts of uncomfortable silence, in danger of drying up completely. Harmon has already used up most of his ice-breaking questions and amusing anecdotes over dinner. Melody has appeared receptive, smiling and laughing in all the appropriate places. But he hasn't budgeted properly for the after-dinner walk.

Whenever he thinks of a question, she answers it readily, factually, and far too succinctly. Then he has to search for yet another conversation-starter. His efforts make the interchange seem more like an interrogation than a friendly chat. He prefers talk which doesn't require so much thought. After all, it's not like he really cares about the answers to any of these questions. He's merely trying to find some common ground, something upon which he can build. But the ground keeps shifting, and he knows any foundation he has managed to construct so far is shaky at best.

It is late spring, but still chilly. They are both bundled up against the cold but he is perspiring slightly. He finds it physically challenging to be this on edge while giving the appearance of strolling along casually. He is glad she doesn't live very far from the restaurant. But then, as they turn the corner and the final half-block of sidewalk stretches out in front of them, he desperately searches for a new topic. After all, she is cute. Her shy smile, dainty mushroom nose, all-encompassing eyes quick to crinkle with amusement, totally endearing.

So Harmon, in the absence of any better ideas, begins to praise her choice of neighbourhood, how nice it is, how convenient. He asks her how long she has been living here and she answers "Eight...going on nine months."

He continues to say how nice it is and she agrees noncommittally. "For this stage of my life, it's perfect."

She slows to a stop. "So...here we are." She faces him and smiles. At her back is a red door, the entrance to her building.

"This is it?" Harmon makes a show of examining the tall, narrow red-bricked building as if he has some reason to doubt this is really where she lives.

"Yes. This is it." She assures him.

"Nice." He nods approvingly, continuing to praise her living arrangements.

An awkward pause, with each second stretching into its own self-conscious eternity. He shuffles a bit closer to her.

She hesitantly offers her hand. "So…I had a really good time tonight."

"Me too." He leans towards her, studiously ignoring the proffered hand.

"That was a great little restaurant." Melody compliments him on the choice.

"Wasn't it?"

"And so out of the way. How'd you ever find it?"

"Got an e-flyer on my phone."

"Really?" She seems genuinely surprised.

"Yeah."

"I don't think I've ever found a restaurant that way."

Harmon isn't sure she is impressed by his admission. He quickly explains. "It was an impressive e-flyer. Lots of glossy pictures. Action shots—thick cuts of meat, steam rising off the vegetables, luscious salads, all the friendly, smiling waiters—and the descriptions made every special seem really very special."

"Sounds impressive."

"Yeah." Harmon concludes. "It was."

He senses the beginning of a rapport. But unfortunately, while this hope flickers through his mind, another pause descends upon them. They both stand there in slightly defensive postures, each ready to react to the next move of the other.

Finally Melody begins to edge back towards the door. "Well, then…good-night, Harmon."

"Right." Harmon pursues her. "Good-night Melody"

He moves in for a good-night kiss, but she jerks away. "Woah! What're you doing?"

He is immediately apologetic. "I…uh…I just thought…I mean…You said you liked the dinner."

"It really wasn't all that great." Melody crosses her arms.

Harmon is forced to agree. "I know. I was disappointed too."

"My vegetables were cold."

He points out the portions were small.

She sighs. "But I'm not sure I'd have wanted more."

"And that waiter was downright surly." He continues, strangely relieved by this onslaught of honesty.

She nods in agreement. "I think he was having a bad day."

Feeling the full weight of his disappointment, Harmon adds sadly, "You've got to wonder what this world's coming to, when you can't even trust what you see in an e-flyer."

"I know." She commiserates.

He smiles, realizing the ice is finally breaking. "But at least dinner gave us something to talk about."

"And laugh about." She agrees.

Emboldened by this sudden mutual understanding, he steps forward, trying to take her in his arms. "Then maybe we can get passed the disappointing dinner?"

But she pulls away again. "It's not just the dinner."

His self-confidence melts away, replaced by frustration. "What then? What's ruining the moment? Is there something stuck in my teeth. I should've known. That happens a lot. It's an orthodontal thing. I knew I should've gone and checked in the mirror, before we left the restaurant. But I was afraid to leave you."

"Afraid I'd bolt?"

"It wouldn't be the first time." He admits.

But her tone is more sympathetic than defensive. "No. It's nothing like that. Honest. Nothing personal. I really like you. And the dinner was...it was okay."

But now Harmon is confused. "What then?"

"It's just...well...I need to know, before we–you know–I need to know where this is going."

He objects. "It's just a good-night kiss."

But she earnestly explains, "A kiss is never just a kiss. It's a promise. A promise of what the future will hold."

"Yeah. Okay." Harmon, being forever hopeful, will agree to almost anything. "That's what I'm trying to find out."

She studies him for a few seconds, and then, as if convinced by some silent exchange, she takes hold of his hand. "Okay then."

Still holding his right hand in her left, she leads him to the door, fishes her keys out of her pocket, unlocks the door, and pulls it open. She hesitates on the threshold. "Do we really want to find out?"

Harmon makes an effort to not appear too eager. "Nothing ventured..."

So she takes him inside and leads him up the stairs and into her modest apartment on the third floor. By this point, his earlier confusion has given way to a cacophony of conflicting expectations. He has absolutely no idea what is going to happen next, but he is extremely eager to find out.

There is a closet just inside the front door. Melody slips off his coat and hangs it up with her own. She entwines her arm in his and escorts him into the living room. It is a small room. The downtown apartments are never very large. But it is well-furnished. Everything is neat, ordered, pristine. He recognizes several copies of famous pieces of impressionist art adorning the beige walls, but he doesn't know the names of the paintings or artists. He would ask her, but he doesn't want to do or say anything that might derail the promising mood.

She leads him directly over to the couch. They sit down together. Without a word, she reaches over to the coffee-table and picks up two strange-looking helmets with large black goggles protruding from the front. She hands one to him. He regards it quizzically, turning it over in his hands, and she explains simply, "FV view-goggles. To see what the future holds."

He understands immediately. He has heard of the Future Vision 500 system on the info blogs. They apparently allow the wearers to project a type of co-created future, a potential virtual reality made actual as a function of the desires and motivations of those wearing the helmets.

Melody smiles shyly as she adjusts the settings on the view-goggles. Then they both put them on. The graphics are amazing. Even though his eyes are now covered, he clearly sees them sitting together there on the couch. They meld together into a long, passionate kiss. He feels his heart pounding in his ears.

The beige walls of the tiny living-room dissolve into limitless space. Time flickers by at an amazing speed, unconstrained by the necessity of physical instantiation. Harmon watches them walking along the street, just like earlier this evening, but appearing much more relaxed as they stroll, arm in arm, chatting, smiling, laughing, enjoying each other's company.

Melody begins to narrate. "So we date a few months, then maybe we move in together."

"Sounds good." He eagerly follows her narrative. Scenes of their courtship flash by. Moments of passion. Moments of joy.

Occasional disagreements ameliorated by fervent reconciliation. Any misgivings he might have had dissipate quickly. Even though only simulated, this is already the greatest relationship he has ever experienced.

She continues to narrate. "We become a couple. All our friends are couples, too."

"Some of my friends are singles." He points out.

"You'll have to lose them."

He hesitates. But none of his friends can compete with the scenes flashing before his eyes. He quickly agrees.

Her narration continues. "We inevitably marry. Move to the house in the suburbs."

"We're living in the suburbs?" Harmon is more of a downtown type of guy.

But Melody appears to favour the suburbs. "Good schools. Good access to shopping and other conveniences."

"Or maybe a downtown loft." He suggests.

"No." She insists. "A downtown loft's no place to raise our kids."

Harmon straightens up as the images continue to bombard his consciousness. "We've got kids?"

"Two." She confirms. "Maybe three."

Harmon chuckles. "Why not more?"

"I'll make you get a vasectomy."

"Ouch!" He is sweating heavily by the time the images of the operation pass by.

She continues. "But we'll have several pets."

"We need pets too?"

"Kids have to have pets." She tells him. "Some fish, maybe a hamster, or a rabbit, and a cat–"

"Or a dog." He interjects. "I like dogs."

Melody compromises on this point but reminds him, "You'll have to walk the dog every night. Later on twice a night."

"Twice?"

"It develops a bladder infection." She explains.

Harmon takes a deep breath. The initial passion of the narrative has been replaced by softer but deeper feelings. The images of his adult life flow quickly past. He mutters, "A lot of responsibility."

"Constant worry. And a lot of expense." Melody responds

with equanimity. "Life doesn't come cheap."

Harmon's face scrunches up with concern as he watches them plod through their projected lives. "No it doesn't. Mortgage. Two cars. Clothing. Food. We probably won't even be able to eat out much anymore."

"No." She agrees. "Not with all the special after-school programs for the kids. Summer camps. University tuition. Doctors. Orthodontists."

Harmon begins to object. "Just because dental issues run in my family–"

But the images fly by as Melody continues to narrate. "A lifetime of apps to collect e-coupons. We'll both be working so hard to pay for it all the years'll go sailing by."

The images continue their assault. Their faces become wrinkled. Their hair begins to grey. He has a paunch forming around his waist. "All this launched by a single kiss." He mutters thoughtfully.

"An intimate commitment." She declares.

"Mapping out the next 10 to 20 years of our lives."

"And beyond." Her narration continues. "Before we know it, we're past middle-age. We're old. The kids are grown and gone. And we're left there, all alone, in that big rambling house. Just the two of us."

"Just the two of us." He echoes.

The program fades to black. Harmon shakily removes the view-goggles. He blinks as he scans the room uncertainly. The beige walls still don't seem completely solid.

After a few moments of recovery, she asks him if he would like a night-cap before heading home, but he says he's fine. She escorts him to the door in silence, but as she hands him his coat, he acknowledges, "You've certainly given me a lot to consider."

He pulls on his coat and she moves closer, straightening it and then gently running her hands down his arms. "I'm sorry if it was a bit too much...too soon...on a first date. But I've got to know, when we're left there in the greying light, there at the end–I've got to know–will there still be as strong a bond between us?"

Harmon takes her in his arms. This time she makes no attempt to pull away. He smiles. "There's only one way to find out."

"You mean–?"

"Give me a little kiss, and we'll say good-night." He leans in and kisses her gently. It feels as good as virtual.

"And you'll call me in the morning?" She prompts.

Harmon shrugs. "Maybe."

Her eyes widen. "Just maybe?"

"Yeah...Maybe." Still flushed with the intimacy of the Future Vision, he has a strong desire to be entirely honest. "I don't really like to plan that far ahead."

Lost And Found In Space And Time

by David M. Hoenig
USA

Friday night, 7:58 pm, March 10, 2017

"LET'S...GO... 'PODS!"

To Gretchen Falkirk, the roar of the crowd rose and fell with an unintended symmetry eerily reminiscent of a heartbeat. *An overly fast heartbeat, in fact, which would be reminiscent of my own at the moment.* For what felt like the millionth time, the coach of Miskatonic University's female wrestling team—the Fighting Cephalopods—looked at her number two wrestler in the 53 kg weight class. "Where the hell is Roth?"

Sharon Carmody waved her arms helplessly. "I've asked everyone! I tried her cell, and called her room... No one knows, Coach!"

"If she's not on the mat in two minutes, we'll be automatically disqualified, and Yale will win the match by default!" Falkirk tilted her head and vertebrae popped as she stretched the tension in her neck. "How's your knee, Carmody?"

"Not good enough to take on 'The Tempest', Coach. Heck, not even if it was bionic; only Stacy's got any shot at beating her!"

The enthusiastic chanting of the predominantly Miskatonic U crowd abruptly surged to something better approximating someone having a heart attack as they demanded their champion. "ROTH!...ROTH!...ROTH!"

"The Ancient Scots had their warrior-poets, why can't I have mine?" Falkirk muttered.

"What was that, coach?"

"Nothing." She drew in a deep breath and tried not to scream her frustration as she looked at the clock counting down. "Definition of irony—Stacy's missing the absolutely literal intersection of poetry and physics she's always going on about."

"Huh?"

Falkirk waved irritably and instead focused on the clock, unaware of how tightly her jaw was clenched. *Where the hell is she?!*

#

Somewhere, with continuous variables for x, y, and z,

Somewhen, within quantum foam fluctuation values of either positive or negative for time or energy

"Isn't this amazingly cool, Temi?"

Temidayo stared around her, mouth agape, and turned to take in the view. Instead of a lightly forested trail on the Miskatonic University campus, she and Stacy stood on a rocky footpath beside a lake. To the distant south, the vague impression of a city stands along the shoreline, blurred by distance and overlying smog. Twin suns overhead lie veiled behind thin, cirrus clouds parted down the center, the unlikely heavenly scene above reflected in the surface of the lake below. The faint strains of a cello can be heard just above the whip of wind across the lake.

"What...? What just happened, Stacy? *Where are we?*"

"Well, I've got a theory."

Temidayo waved her hands to take in the heavens above. "*That* is just not possible."

"It is. Let's walk, and I'll explain. Or at least try to." Stacy took Temidayo's hand in hers, and they headed along the trail in the direction of the city. "So, this happened to me twice before, always in the same place on the trail and time of day. I'm pretty sure it has to do with the music we heard playing outside the Zann Conservatory."

Temidayo stops and tilts her head. "I think I can still hear it."

"There's a special guest cellist playing with the University Orchestra this semester. He starts tuning his cello just before six every morning, and then he's off. The first time I hit that point in my run, and...*this*... happened, it freaked me out, Temi! At first, anyway. But nothing bad happened once I was here, so I just ran for a while around the lake to check it out. Eventually, I sort of followed the music back to Miskatonic."

"Well, I'm totally creeped out."

"But it's amazing, isn't it? I wanted you to see it, partly to make sure I wasn't nuts or something."

The young women made silent progress towards the distant structure, but its details remained indistinct. Temidayo broke the silence. "This all reminds me of, well, something I've read once. I'm not sure what."

"I know, right? I did some research after the first time I came here. I think the two suns are... wait, what's that?

Temidayo shielded her eyes with one hand, squinted. "Looks like a man and a woman."

"Well, that's new."

"You haven't seen them before?" Temidayo glanced behind them. "Um, should we be leaving? I mean, if we want to go back to Miskatonic?" She bit her lip. "I'd like to go back ten minutes ago, if we're being honest. This is too weird."

"We should be okay. The last time I was here I ran the trail for a while. Getting back home wasn't all that difficult."

"I'm assuming because the cellist was still playing?" Stacy chuckled. "Relax, Brainiac. He's going to play for hours. And I'm not sure, but I think time's different over here anyway.

"That's impossible."

"Like this whole trippy trip, you mean?"

Temidayo grinned suddenly. "Okay, you have a point."

Stacy pulled the other girl to a stop. "That smile just does it for me. I want you to know, I really like you, Temi."

"Well, I..." Temidayo looked down, then back at Stacy's earnest face. "You are the most amazing person I've ever met."

When the kiss broke, they turned and walked hand in hand down the trail until Stacy, looking ahead, stopped them. "Wow, okay, no."

Ahead, a woman watched them approach as she caressed the manhood of a polished, mirror bright silver statue. The metal-man was muscular and nude, with antlers protruding aggressively from his head as if to stab at the strange sky above. "Have you heard the song?" she asked the girls.

Temidayo's brow furrowed. "What song, ma'am?"

"It is that which the Hyades sing, counterpointed by the disharmonious tatters of the King."

"No, ma'am." Temidayo exchanged a glance with Stacy. "I mean... we did hear something earlier..."

The woman turned to regard the statue before continuing. "That song is not a paltry thing. Who are you?"

"This is Temi and I'm Stacy. And, uh, you are...?"

The woman smiled sardonically, trailing her hand off the manhood of the statue. "Left wanting, I'm afraid." She circled the metal-man, the curves in his structure reflected everything—lake, sky, and the three women—in bizarre caricature. "Have you never before beheld the Phantom of Truth?"

Temidayo shook her head. "No ma'am. Who is, or was he?"

"He represents the Great Truth."

"What truth is that?"

The woman looked adoringly at the statue. "Peace through superior firepower." She reached out to touch the statue's chest, and skimmed yellow- and black- painted fingernails across the shiny metal. "Marvelous; he remains as warm as if he yet had heart beating out the seconds."

Temidayo stepped backwards. "Omigod. Stacy; we need to get out of here, and right now."

"What? Why?"

The woman turned. "'What? Why?' The Phantom's day of leveling threat has long passed, and I, would bid you formal welcome to Court, at last."

Temidayo reached for Stacy's hand, held it. "What do you mean exactly, 'of leveling threat'?"

"He lived to bring peace between the two cities."

Stacy looked puzzled. "Which two cities?

"Why, Carcosa and Alar, to be sure! Uneasy peace, no true cure, and these days seems it especially fragile, as if counting down all the while. But in his day, when he was most potent? The mere threat his temper *might* erupt brought all parties to the table."

Temidayo yanked on Stacy's hand and turned them both to go back the way they came.

The woman called out. "But where do you go? I have invited you..."

Stacy had no choice but to follow as Temidayo pulled her into a run. "What's going on, Temi?"

"The metal statue! She's talking about it like it was a weapon of mass destruction—'Peace through superior firepower', right?—used as a deterrent to war. And she says it's warm to the touch..." She bit her lip as they hurried. "I think it could mean alpha particle decay."

"I have no idea what that means."

"Honey, it...that thing could be made out of *plutonium.*"

Stacy's face paled, and her reluctance disappeared. The young women followed the trail, and left the woman and statue behind as quickly as they good.

Out of sight of the strange encounter by the lakeside,

Temidayo slowed them to a walk. "We've been here too long. How do we get back?"

"We need to find the music."

"I don't understand that at all, Stacy."

"Me either, but we really need to get home. I'm really scared."

Temidayo shuddered. "If you're scared, I'm terrified! So, where do we find the music?"

"I don't hear it now."

"Then how do we get home?!?"

"We have to wait for the music. It'll be okay, Temi; I promise."

Neither girl registered more than the sudden brightening before Stacy would never be able to fulfill her promise.

#

Friday morning, 5:45 am, March 10, 2017

Stacy Roth jogged out of the trees into the clearing behind the Zann Conservatory, her broad shoulders seeming to float above the wooded trail as she ran with quick, economical steps. When she saw who awaited her, she bounded over and kissed her on the cheek. "Temi! You made it."

Temidayo Abiona stood bundled in a heavy sweater, arms folded tight for extra warmth, but smiled. "This is crazy early and crazy cold, but here I am. How long have you been out already?"

"About fourteen, give or take."

"Minutes?"

Stacy laughed and checked her watch, kicking her legs out as she walked over. "Miles, goober. I've been running for a bit over an hour."

"You're superhuman. What time did you get up?"

"My usual–four."

Temidayo shook her head while grinning. "Take it from a physics geek: four in the morning qualifies as an imaginary time. Heck; that I'm out of bed before six is nearly beyond belief."

"Thanks for coming to meet me."

Temidayo put her arms around Stacy and they hugged. She laughed nervously. "You're so warm."

"Aerobic training'll do that. Anyway, uh..."

"What's this all about, anyway? Why'd you want me out here this early?"

Stacy tucked her hands into the pockets of her sweatshirt and kicked at some leaves on the trail. "It's the best place to show you what I was talking about, what I'm doing my thesis on."

"The poetry thing?"

Stacy laughed. "Yes, geek, 'the poetry thing'. It's like when you were telling me about your work in theoretical physics, and you said that you were working on a new solution to the Einstein-Rosenberg equation..."

Temidayo laughed aloud. "It's *Einstein-Rosen bridge as a solution of the Einstein field equation.*"

"Right, all of that." She flapped her hand by way of apology, and rambled on. "Anyway, the way you were explaining it makes sense in a weird, poetic way, and this is the best place to show you why."

"You're putting me on, right?" When Stacy shook her head, Temidayo's grin faded to be replaced by a serious look. "Explain it to me."

"Okay. Check it out. Rilke wrote this elegy:

Ah, but the City of Pain: how strange its streets are:
the false silence of sound drowning sound,
and there--proud, brazen, effluence from the mold of emptiness--
the gilded hubbub, the bursting monument.
How an Angel would stamp out their market of solaces,
set up alongside their church bought to order:
clean and closed and woeful as a post office on Sunday.
Outside, though, there's always the billowing edge of the fair.
Swings of Freedom! High-divers and Jugglers of Zeal!
And the shooting gallery with its figures of idiot Happiness
which jump, quiver, and fall with a tinny ring
whenever some better marksman scores. Onward he lurches from cheers
to chance; for booths courting each curious taste
are drumming and barking. And then--for adults only--
a special show: how money breeds, its anatomy, not some charade:
money's genitals, everything, the whole act

from beginning to end--educational and guaranteed to make
you
virile . . . .
. . . . Oh, but just beyond that,
behind the last of the billboards, plastered with signs for
"Deathless,"
that bitter beer which tastes sweet to those drinking it
as long as they have fresh distractions to chew . . . ,
just beyond those boards, just on the other side: things are
real.
Children play, lovers hold each other, off in the shadows,
pensive, on the meager grass, while dogs obey nature.
The youth is drawn farther on; perhaps he's fallen in love
with a young Lament . . . . . He pursues her, enters
meadowland.
She says:
"It's a long way. We live out there . . ."
Where? And the youth follows.
Something in her bearing stirs him. Her shoulders, neck--,
perhaps she's of noble descent. Still, he leaves her, turns
around,
glances back, waves . . . What's the use? She's a Lament.

Temidayo shivered. "It's beautiful, but wow, so, so sad."

"So you see the connection, right?"

"Um. Not really." She smiled to take any sting out of the response.

"Remember Rilke's 'Letter to a young poet" I mentioned last Saturday night at the recital?'

Temidayo furrowed her brow. "The 'We Move' one?"

"Right! See, I'm pretty sure he knew. The 'City of Pain'? I think I've seen it." Stacy bit her lip at Temidayo's evident confusion. "I'm doing this badly. Okay, forget that part for now; remember the other day you told me about your thesis, how negative energy was a theoretical way to solve the equations without having to have huge gravitational mass like a black hole, which, since you can't escape it, makes wormhole travel a moot point, right?"

Temidayo blinked. "That's... actually... I mean, yes. Bring it on, science jock."

Stacy grinned, then exhaled slowly before continuing

more soberly. "You also said that weird things happen at the quantum foam level, like unexplained phenomena appearing and disappearing without any obvious source."

"Um. Yes, actually that's pretty much exactly right." Temidayo's eyebrows rose. "But..."

"I paid attention, even though it was a bit unusual for pillow talk."

Temidayo grinned sheepishly.

"Anyway, is it possible--however unlikely--that a specific point in space-time could generate negative energy--whatever it is--spontaneously?"

"Um. Theoretically, yes. At least in transient, miniscule amounts, anyway."

Stacy beamed. "Cool! Now imagine that you had a device which amplified that somehow."

Temidayo considered that and was beginning to nod when she tilted her head sideways. "Do you hear that?"

"Right on schedule!" Stacy checked her watch. "It's from the Zann Conservatory, behind you. He always starts tuning up just before 6 AM."

"'He' who? And what does that have to do with anything?"

Stacy grabbed Temidayo's hand and pulled her with her. "This!"

There was a burst of light like a flashbulb going off as the two young women disappeared into thin air. The radiance slowly faded in a jerky way, exactly in time with the strains of the cello emerging from the nearby building.

#

Wednesday night, 6:47 pm, March 8, 2017

Temidayo pushed the buzzer for apartment 5G. While she waited for a response she muttered to herself. "I can't believe this is happening, that this is real."

The intercom lit up. "Temi?"

"Yes, it's me."

"You're right on time. Come on up; I'll meet you at the elevator."

The door buzzed and Temidayo jumped at the sound, then reached for the handle and went in. She walked to the elevator and pushed the 'Up' button, then checked her overly generous figure in a lobby mirror, opened her coat and smoothed the knit black dress she wore beneath it as she muttered again. "What am I doing here? She's *perfect,* and I've got more curves than Arkham Route 20."

The elevator dinged and its doors slid open. She inhaled deeply and blew it out, then walked in and pressed the button for the 5th floor. It rose smoothly, and when the doors opened, Stacy was there, smiling. "I'm so glad you're here." She wore black jeans that looked painted on over her narrow hips, and a maroon, crew neck, cashmere sweater. "Let me take your coat."

Temidayo shrugged out of her coat and handed it to Stacy, then followed as she went down the hallway, arms folded under her breasts. "So. Um. Off campus housing?"

"Yes. Part of my athletic scholarship--I need to get to sleep for my training far earlier than I could ever manage in a noisy dorm."

"Really?"

At 5G, Stacy opened the door and held it. "I'm usually in bed before 9."

Temidayo licked suddenly dry lips, poised on the threshold. When she spoke, her voice was a little hoarse. "And tonight?"

Stacy fidgeted before looking Temidayo directly in the eyes. "I was hoping maybe a bit earlier even than that," she said in a soft voice.

#

Saturday night, 8:19 pm, March 4, 2017

Temidayo whispered to Debbie Connaught. "Thanks for convincing me to come. Who knew poetry could be this dynamic?"

The young man sitting next to Temidayo glanced at her and shushed her.

Debbie gave him a dirty look, then whispered back to Temidayo as she pointed to a name in the mimeographed program. "If you think the last one was good, wait'll you hear the next artist. She's brilliant; she really blew me away with one of her pieces last month."

At the front of the auditorium, Stacy Roth stood up from a front row seat and took her place center stage. The audience quieted down as she cleared her throat.

"Oh. My. God." Temidayo breathed. "She's so hot."

Debbie grinned. "A little butch for my tastes, what with those shoulders and the asymmetric double taper haircut, but hey, if it works for you..."

This time it was Temidayo who did the shushing.

Stacy had already begun her introduction. "...and Rainer Maria Rilke's work has had a profound impact on me. And for reasons which go beyond my thesis." She smiled widely as the audience chuckled appreciatively before continuing. "I'd like to paraphrase from one of his Letters To A Young Poet... 'Many signs indicate that the future enters us in order to be transformed in us, long before it happens. The future stands still, but we move in infinite space.'"

Temidayo stared raptly, and didn't see the little smirk as Debbie watched her regarding Stacy Roth.

"We move through space and we move through time, but ask yourselves if it's fair to say that time and space also move through us." She paused, composing herself for a few moments. "My offering tonight is titled 'Time Only Passes Where There's Movement':

The hours move like sliding sand
which shifts at gravity's command.
The days flow past like water brushed
against scoured skin before it rushed
away down river's bed. Do stand

and watch events which, rude, demand
attention. Fail, misunderstand,
all focus dimmed, importance hushed;
the hours slide like moving sand.

The overload is all unplanned,
and brain's slipped gears and can't withstand
the deluge of the moments crushed
in tidal flow of all that's flushed
away in sweep of second hand-
the hours drop through glass, like sand.

“The title--that’s *physics*! In poetry?” Temidayo squeaked before she sat back in her chair, speechless, as the audience broke into enthusiastic applause.

Debbie leaned close to whisper into her ear. “Yeah, it’s almost like you were made for each other.”

The look she got was disbelieving. “She’s *so* out of my class.”

“Maybe, maybe not. So; you want me to introduce you two afterwards?”

Temidayo’s eyes widened even further the instant before she nodded and turned back to watch Stacy return to her seat, and then kept watching.

#

Saturday morning, 8:47 am, March 4, 2017

Temiday cut up her pancakes as she wound up her explanation. “So, technically we *are* already moving through time, in the forward direction. Motion only occurs when you can measure time…”

“And time only passes in a place where there’s movement, right?” Debbie put down her coffee.

“Exactly! But since things tend towards entropy and not the reverse, time moves forward rather than backward.” Temidayo took a bite and chewed, swallowed. “No matter how many weird solutions to Einstein’s vacuum field equation are given, unless we can define anomalous states like negative energy or negative mass. Which, I might add, even quantum theory has difficulty with.”

Debbie held up her hands in a ‘wait, wait’ gesture. “Okay, okay, super physics geek. But what about consciousness and quantum theory?”

“You mean biocentrism?”

“Yes! I don’t get it.”

Temidayo blinked. “Not many people do. Seriously though? In second semester, basic physics?”

Debbie shrugged. “Maybe? Just, you know, nutshell it for me so I don’t look like a complete idiot if there’s a question on the exam.”

Temidayo drummed her fingers against the table for a few seconds, then sighed. “Um. Okay, think of it like this…consciousness allows choice, right? So, what we choose affects how events unfold over time. Quantum theory, at least, allows for both outcomes to exist at the same time as parallel events or universes, if you will. Maybe they both persist forever, or until one of the probabilities collapses…"

Debbie plonked her head down on the table. "Enough, roomie--my brain is full." She sat up abruptly. "Oh! Before I forget." She reached into the pocket of her hoodie and pulled out two tickets. "You want to go with me to this poetry recital tonight, Temi? One of the artists is someone I think you should meet."

"Um." Temidayo looked up from her breakfast and considered. "I was going to study--I've got a Physics of Sound midterm on Tuesday. Professor Whitlock's done some brilliant work on vibrations and quantum foam fluctuations…"

"This'll be more fun. Promise. Besides, you can study before and after."

After a moment more, Temidayo shrugged and smiled. "Okay; why not?"

#

Saturday morning, 8:50 am, March 4, 2017

"This'll be more fun. Promise. Besides, you can study before and after."

After a moment Temidayo shook her head. "I got to ace this exam. Next time?"

The disappointment on Debbie's face was clear. "You're passing up something really special." She considered. "Okay, here's 'next time': are you free this Friday night?"

"You mean the 10th?"

Debbie nodded.

"I can be; whatcha got in mind?"

"The Fighting Cephalopods are going up against Yale, and I got an extra ticket for that, too."

"Wrestling?" Temidayo shrugged her lack of enthusiasm. "Um. I don't know…"

"Hey now! Where is your Miskatonic U school spirit, girl?" Debbie grinned.

A long sigh. "Fine." Temidayo picked up her orange juice. "Count me in."

#

Friday night, 8:07 pm, March 10, 2017

Temidayo leapt to her feet to try to see over the group of very tall freshmen in front of her who had, themselves, jumped to their own and completely blocked her view of the match. "What happened? What'd I miss?" she yelled to Debbie over the excited roar of the crowd.

"Roth got a great drag on the Tempest!" she yelled back. "She was so fast."

Temidayo had to tap the guy in front of her twice before he turned. "Hey! I can't see through you!"

"Oh, crap! I'm sorry." He moved closer to one of his buddies to create room for her but was already looking back at the action. Stacy Roth had not been able to take advantage of the takedown by the time Temidayo could see what was happening, and she saw the referee make them both stand up to face each other again in the center of the mat. The crowd remained standing, and chants of "ROTH!...ROTH!...ROTH!" dominated, with the occasional "GO 'PODS!" rising and falling in the background.

"God. She is just. So. Perfect."

Debbie leaned over. "What was that, Temi?" she shouted, but her roommate was watching the action avidly.

The two wrestlers were circling, pushing off each other, probing for an opportunity. The Tempest went for and got a front headlock with a quick move, and the predominantly Miskatonic University crowd collectively gasped before Stacy broke the hold and got an arm around the Yale wrestler.

"WHOO!" yelled Temidayo as Stacy pushed to take advantage of it, and forced her opponent out of the ring. "Did she just win?" she asked Debbie.

"No, but she got another point. She's up now, and it's the final round. She just has to stay ahead of DeHaviland."

"Who?"

"The Tempest, Temi!"

"Oh. But..." Temidayo went silent as the two wrestlers, brought back to the center again by the referee, burst into motion. "Damn! She is so fast." She stretched her shoulders. "I had no idea wrestling was so... dynamic."

Debbie glanced away from the match, and saw Temidayo

raptly watching Stacy Roth. She smirked and nudged her in the side. "Want me to introduce you to her after the match?" Shock brought her look away from the wrestlers. "Wait: you *know* her?"

Both missed seeing Stacy make a lightning-fast move against the Tempest, but the roar of the crowd brought their gazes back to the action in time to see her employ a double leg takedown which flipped them both out of the ring, ensuring the Miskatonic win. The noise level of the gym went supersonic as Roth leapt to her feet, fists pumped into the air in victory.

Debbie watched Temidayo, gaze fixated on Stacy doing the sportsmanship thing with an obviously disappointed DeHaviland, then follow her as she moved to celebrate with her coach and teammates. Once the noise levels fell sufficiently to again make conversation possible she nudged her. "Yeah, Temi, I know her. She's a bit butch for my tastes, what with those shoulders and the asymmetric double taper haircut, but she's one hell of a poet, too."

"Really?"

"Yeah. When things quiet down a bit I'll introduce you two. You should hear her go on about the intersectionality of physics and poetry…"

Black Feline Love

by A.L. Paradiso

New York

Love is love, no matter the species, no matter if it breaks some rules. This is one of those. There's no way I can tell her whole story yet. I simply don't have enough tears in me.

It always gets worse, or at least more frequent, on Halloween. It began twenty-one years ago, just before the first anniversary of her passing on 11/3/1998. I was with her for her last breath. She used the last of her strength to make her way to me and lied down at my feet. That was the last time she put her trust in me instead of finding shelter to die, just as her mom did five years earlier. She routinely trusted me above all others and above her own natural instincts. What was different, was that she growled at me for the first time in her sixteen-year life. With her failing strength, she told me she was upset with me and my heart broke.

Throughout the year, once or twice a day, as I sit and work on stories, I often detect a fuzzy, black feline push past curtains which don't flutter. It comes just past half way into the blue-carpeted room and every time I turn to focus on it, there's nothing there. Sometimes it's the size of a legless rat, other times it's the size of a stalking puma. No flare, no explosion, no puff of smoke, just not there. The same path every time. The same path my Jaguar would follow when she'd come down from the bedroom late at night and scold me for staying up so late and keeping her waiting for me. Long black hairs, fluffy tail and head up, she followed that path chattering like a concerned mom saying, "What are you doing up so late? Come on; it's bed time. Let's go. Are you coming?" Half way into the room, she'd U-turn and walk half way back, still chattering to herself, then U-turn back to me and scold me again. Her circling said, "Follow me already!"

I'd laugh and love her more for her concern and quickly shut down the PC to follow her. That frequent routine included her waiting for me at the foot of the stairs, crouched like a sprinter at the starting blocks, ears back, face focused on the top step. She'd wait for the 'starter pistol' to go off, my foot on the first step, before racing to the top and sitting casually to
wait for her slow dad.

We had a bathroom routine where she hopped onto the sink and watched (over) me until I said "bedtime." She'd hop down, race to the bed and wait for me to get in before curling up against me for the night.

Usually, I found her in the morning still between my arm and my ribs if she was not already up and waiting patiently for our morning progression, which she knew lead to food. For a short time, she'd wake me early by poking my nose or licking me until I woke then racing to the sink for the next step. I had to put a stop to that when she began waking me an hour before the alarm clock went off. In one of the few times I scolded her, I'd point at her and loudly say, "NO. Food waits." It took a couple of days to get her to understand.

For the next few weeks, I woke to her sitting on my chest with her HUGE face nearly touching my chin. Her arms folded under, she stared down at me until I opened my eyes and startled. After a quick meow, sometimes with a nose lick, she'd race to the bathroom and wait for me. I got the message, "It's about time. I've been waiting so patiently for you and didn't wake you." What could I say? She did exactly as I asked and got her breakfast a little sooner. Trust and love both ways bonded us for life.

That bond began at her birth. She was not only a breach, but being the last of four, her mom, Phoenix, nearly died of exhaustion. I was with her for the last two births. Every time mom paused (pawsed?), Jaguar's sac retreated. I knew I had to help, so I pinned the sac down as Phoenix rested between contractions. Two more cycles and Jaguar was out. Unlike the previous kitty, Jag had trouble ripping the sac. I watched a few seconds until I feared she'd suffocate, then tore the sac for her. She wobbled to my voice and I became her life long dad. Phoenix was too exhausted to clean her or call to her so I moved Jag to her mom and she immediately nursed.

Our bond was evident in several instances when she terrified vets and other incidents where Jaguar trusted me and relaxed just because I asked her to. When my wife and I separated, she insisted on taking Jag with her. They moved in with a friend and I insisted on visitation rights though I just wanted to steal her away.

Though I demanded Jag remain an indoor only cat, she was tossed into their huge yard because she'd leave a liter trail in the house. I was furious and afraid for her, mostly because I'd made the mistake of having her declawed before I understood how that injures cats and leaves them nearly defenseless. When I heard she hadn't been seen for three days and didn't respond to anyone's calls, I raced over there.

My voice cracked as I imagined the worst and called out for her. We heard a tall fence rattle more than 100 feet away; saw a fuzzy, long-tailed blur race along the top of a narrow fence then hop into the long yard and race directly to me, tail up, she chattered all the way to me. I heard her scolding me, "Where the hell have you been?" over and over until she reached me. Then she wrapped her tail around me, purred loudly and looked at only me as she repeated, "I'm so glad you are here." My tears of fear and remorse and love flowed like two tiny dam spillways as I hugged her.

When her mom died, 1-23-93, Jaguar's behavior changed and told me she was depressed and upset. Instead of sleeping with me, she slept under my bed. Instead of running to me when I called, she stayed there. When I discovered her under the bed and signaled for her to come out, she ignored me and just stared at me. I had to drag her out to read her body language. She was listless so I curled up with her on the floor, stifled my tears and begged her to stay with me just five more years. By then I hoped she'd find a reason to live that included more than just me and stay with me another twenty years.

Just over five years later she got ill and when that horrible night came, I saw her struggling to lift her head and breathe. I whispered to her that it was OK for her to let go and wait for me with her mom at the rainbow bridge. I lied. She died a few minutes later and took a piece of me with her. I reach out to her in tears often and apologize for not doing
more then still beg her to wait for me.

Come October every year, I see that black speck enter much more often on her way to scold me. She never makes it to the first U-turn before she disappears. That speck brings it all back until her deathiversary every November third. It may come as many as twenty times in a day to remind me of her. Love is love. I hope she's saying, "I'm expecting you at the rainbow bridge. No hurry. I can wait." Perhaps she's just saying, "Don't forget me." As if I could.

Intersection

By Silvana McGuire
Indiana

On a fall morning in mid-October of 1983 I went a little bit crazy. Staring at the red traffic light at the intersection of Ford Road and Main Street, I pulled the steering wheel of my Ford Truck and made a right turn. It was almost 7:30 in the morning and I was on my way to work. Except that, to get to work, I had to wait for the red light to turn green and keep driving ahead, uphill on Main towards the highway intersection. As if watching a movie from the backseat of my truck, I observed my head turning left and right, then my arms moved and we headed towards the dip on Ford Road instead, then drove over the bridge above Snake Creek; I saw that I adjusted my legs and sank deeper into the cushion of the sofa-like seat of my white vehicle, while the road led us through widening fields of corn and the houses became more and more sparse. I watched myself reach up for the neck of my plead shirt and unfasten the top two buttons with a heavy, relieved, lung deep sigh. My knees spread wider apart and I rested my left elbow on the armrest on the door. My back molded to the back of the seat. The muscles of my neck and my jaws relaxed as I inhaled the fresh, cold air coming in from the window I had cracked open.

She was waiting for me. I knew that is where we were going. We were going to meet her yet again. It was a Tuesday morning and she had no appointments. I couldn't wait to see her again.

Me, but not me, was watching everything from the back seat, allowing whoever took control of my body to do as he pleased. The driver and I observed the thickening of the bushes on both sides of Ford Road, then a left hairpin turn deposited us under a tall colorful canopy of trees that hid the sunshine and blue sky. The tires slowed down and we could see through the windows the details of the branches and every flower and bird nestled in there. In here, deep into the park there was still some moist from the early hours of the morning; the long leaves were glistening and sparkling with droplets just now being touched by the golden rays of sunshine streaming through the foliage.

My eyes focused on the rearview mirror. In that instant I could see me in the back seat of my car. Watching me see my grey eyes and thick brows move closer together, the familiar crease I notice every morning as I prepare to shave, the twinkle of pleasure and anticipation in the eyes of the madman on the small mirror centered atop the wide windshield.

She would be waiting in her whicker chair lounging on the white porch that wraps around the home. She would be wearing a large colorful hat with flowers on it just like every time we meet at night. Her curled blonde hair would be loose on her shoulders. Her dress would be recently ironed and perfectly fit to her slim figure. I felt my mouth tingle in anticipation of the kisses we would exchange.

Her eyes were the color of love. Her eyelids heavy from our lovemaking that morning. She smiled a thousand smiles at me and repeated "I love you" countless times. I could hear her happiness from across the bedroom. Her laughter had the consistency of a dripping honeycomb. I wanted to taste her laughter again.

The pair of eyes in the rearview mirror met mine once again. I stared deep into his and could see our entire life ahead of us. Behind us. We had met in high-school and she never looked at anyone else since. I could have had any of the other girls who were interested in an athlete, a football line backer at that. But I didn't want any of them, the other girls. I wanted her.

When I proposed, she had tears in her eyes. I don't think she was surprised though. We had been going steady for so long and I had just gotten the job at the automobile factory. She knew. She just pretended to be surprised and we were both so happy. For a while.

When later we learned of her diagnosis, I confess I spent many a night awake, looking into the ceiling, listening to her pretend sleep next to me. Her pretend sleep at night, her pretend smile during daytime, her pretend satisfaction with our life together.

It was all that pretense that did us in, I am sure. We should not have pretended to know what we were thinking, wondering, expecting. We should not have kept living as if we were going to grow old together. We both knew the truth and the truth was that love is not forever.

Love is for those days when the skin is not falling off your flesh, those days when your breath does not stink of decay and disease. Love is for those days when there are no nurses and doctors and needles and medical trays around. Love is intimate. Love is not public.

Our love had become public. She had become a patient and I had become a caretaker. There is no love there, only compassion.

I am not a bad person, of course I would spend my last days taking care of her. Whoever she was. Whoever she had become.

Then she was none. Just last summer.

As I approached the intersection of my heart and reason, I looked right into my heart and saw nothing coming in. I looked left onto reason and that was full of logic and arguments. As I was watching the traffic light and expecting it to turn green so that I could keep driving ahead uphill on the road of a loveless life, I went a bit crazy.

I turned right into my heart and went down towards the dip of the bridge over the creek. There was a white light in the distance where the orchard parted into a gravel road. I saw her waiting for me on the porch in the distance. I jumped ahead into the driver's body and I said, "I love you".

And I was no longer crazy.

Observable Universe

by Marlon Martinez
New York

My friends called her *Shapes* on the count after that one summer she spent in Florida and came back with a body that shouldn't've belonged to someone her age. Most of us, by then, had grown hair on the *parts* of ourselves we thought only grew on our parents. The kids whom this happened to first were the ones who started calling her Shapes to her face. I always thought the nickname was a brutish classification. At least in the context of how they said it. They were boys who thought growing up in Queens automatically grandfathered them into being hoodlums. Teenagers who were under the impression that, because their home telephone numbers began with a *(718)*, they had garnered a degree of credit from *the streets* to which they had not earned. *Shapes* was a lackluster description too simplistic for something as complicated as her.

I adopted calling her Shapes because of the things she would tell me when she'd sneak into my room at night. After climbing the tree that led to my window. After evading her father when he'd come home belching flammable vapors, looking to project on someone the anger he felt, that had nothing to do with the *screen* he was projecting it on to. She'd hop the fence of our conjoining backyards and throw a counted amount of pebbles at my window.

It was the time in our lives when we were beginning to rethink our stances on the whole B*oys vs. Girls Conflict.* We'd been waging a war against each other all our lives but for the life of us couldn't figure out why or who started it. This was before our bodies began to make the specified odors that would eventually drive every single one of my friends, myself included, into a hormonal madness that could only be quelled by the attention of the person, who you desperately hoped, was seeking yours as well.

It was prior to full blown puberty that Shapes told me personal things that sounded like they came from a diary she would claim she didn't keep. Details about herself that no one knew but me.

No, I called her Shapes because she was a kaleidoscope when you looked inside her. If I *held* her to the light, and twisted one way, she would fragment into a million different pieces and colors. Twist the other way, a million more.

We carried on like this almost in to high school but we

never told anyone.

When you're in junior high, there are mandates that restrict certain interactions. I was the boy who had extensive knowledge of *Middle-Earth* and *The Galactic Empire.* She was the girl that wore makeup and would go shopping for bras on the weekend. It was okay that we never talked outside of my room because Shapes had told me that her father was a *regular* at the bar up the block from our neighboring houses.

When the school year was over, well into the weather turning hot, Shapes would sneak out wearing less clothes that showed more skin in an attempt to keep *cool* while she slept at night.

There were a series of freckles scattered all over her. Her body looked like the night sky in reverse. On her left calf was a *brownish* constellation in the same pattern as *Cassiopeia.* Shapes would stretch her arms, fingers interlaced over her head, and show me that above her belly button lied *Orion's Belt.* By her chest, before your eyes got to her cleavage, was the star cluster, *Pleiades.* Her birthmarks were strewn across a porcelain *sky* that perspired on summer nights, leaving sweat trails containing the chemicals that would make me her prisoner if they ever bonded with my own.

Her physical features were this universe that I increasingly needed to know.

I wanted to traverse the expanse of her *complexion,* explore each inch that separated one beauty mark from the next. Every awkward mole and blemish. The patch on the inside of her forearm that lacked the same pigmentation as the rest of her skin. All the details and nuances she thought she needed to hide, I would show her that she shouldn't.

This was her super power.

Her strength over me.

The Gate

by Christopher Clawson Rule

Florida

The early Spring sky was a beautiful blue as Marianne walked out of the sliding glass door of her beachfront home. She took note of the few clouds that spotted the horizon, then taking a moment to scan the powder, sandy beach in front of their Madeira Beach home. She smiled inside with a great sense of satisfaction that her life had brought her here to this land of paradise. Looking out through the tall dune grass at the many shades of the green and blue in the waters of the Gulf of Mexico was one of her favorite things to do. She found and drew great strength and support from the waters of the Gulf. Marianne and her husband, Henry, of 42 years, purchased this modest beach home just about two years ago. Their plan was to come down a couple times a year and then rent it out for a couple years, then move down from Michigan and occupy the home full time. That time had finally come for the couple. They had made the extra money from the rentals that they had hoped for and were now able to comfortably live full time in their beach house. They picked a date and stuck to the plan. It had been only three months since they had moved down on January 1st. Now it was April Fool's Day and they both were enjoying their decision and the move. They had already spent a lot of time remodeling the house. Walking on the beach and working on their tans lines. Not to mention the moonlight swims and love making on a blanket just off the shore. They had found a place up on top of one of the dunes; it overlooked the water as well as gave them plenty of privacy. On a clear night the moon and its reflection would be just enough light for them to enjoy. For them, there was nothing better that touching, kissing, joining with each other late at night in the open air. Feeling the sensation of each other skin and the sounds of the waves crashing were just a welcomed added bonus.

Marianne continued down the boardwalk that Henry had built to very end of their property line. There she found him building a gate to keep them secure. Or at least that is what Henry was telling her. She still didn't know from what, sand crabs maybe.

As she walked she made sure that she was careful not to spill the two tall glasses of lemonade and ice she had made for them both. Slowly she walked feeling the coolness of the stained wood boards beneath her feet. While she made her way down the wooden path she took note of Henry, the kind gentleness of his character, the trim lines of his body, the muscles that held him together and the way they all this worked in tandem to make him the man that he is.

"Hey there Good Lookin!!!" Henry said as Marianne approached, offering her a flirtatious smile. "Whatcha got cookin?"

Marianne giggled just a bit at his corniness and said, "I cooked us both up a couple of glasses of ice cold lemonade. Interested?"

Henry watched Marianne walk toward him. It had been 42 years of a very good life. They have three grown children with eight grandchildren, a nice family, a good family. The perfect size for holidays, birthdays and a family get together. Now, their children bring their own children down to visit them on the beach. Most times they would come for a week, spend some time on the beach, make a trip to Disney or Sea World and then just relax for the remainder of their trip. Both Henry and Marianne loved having the company and spending time with their family. But they were also very excited to have them leave so that they could get back to their everyday lives. Casual days, sleeping in, coffee on the deck in the mornings, walking around the house naked, wine on the beach at night while watching the sun go down. They cherished their quiet walks and picnics on the beach, something that they couldn't really enjoy in the same way with their grandchildren under foot. They had both worked hard for all of their married life. Now it was time for them to enjoy what their hard work had brought them.

"Well, thanks, Sweetheart! A cool drink sounds great right about now." Henry said taking the glass she offered.

"You're welcome," smiling down at him. "Soooooooooo tell me again why we need a gate." Marianne asked, as she looked down beyond the gate and saw an empty box as well, "and apparently now an empty box."

"It's to keep you safe." Henry started, taking a drink of his lemonade. "Wow, that's perfectly tart. Thanks Babe," smiling over at Marianne. "Besides, isn't it pretty?" He asked, using his hands to show off his work like Vanna White or one of the Price and Right girls would do. "The box is for our shoes. That way we can just leave them here so they won't get all sandy."

"Well it is pretty, and I suppose the box is a good idea." Marianne replied. "What a lovely day. We should walk later."

"We can walk now if you'd like. I'm finished here." Henry explained.

"Really?"

"Sure, let me put these tools away and we can go." Henry replied, almost gitty for the opportunity to get to spend another moment with his favorite girl.

"Nice!" Marianne smiled as did Henry. He loved how easy it was to make her happy. A simple walk, holding her hand, a gentle touch as he walked by. Even coming up behind her and holding her for a moment gave her so much joy that he thought for sure that it would make her extraordinarily happy for a week. He never really thought about it until it happened. And when it did, it also brought a smile to his heart.

Henry hurried along, put his tools away, picked up a better pair of sunglasses, some sunscreen and met his love out on the beach.

"Which way?" She asked, reaching out her hand for the sunscreen.

"You decide." Henry said as he started to follow her north up the water's edge.

"So what are you reading now?" Henry asked, as he moved himself a little deeper into the water.

Since they had arrived Marianne had read probably 25 novels. She had always read a great deal, but what she was doing now was like some speed reading training class. She was well known at the Madeira Beach Library and knew all the employees by name.

"I'm not. I just finished a dollar store book that I found. I wasn't impressed." Marianne said, handing the sunscreen back to him, looking over at him and thinking how well he had aged. He still had most of the color in his hair and he was still in good shape. Smiling inside, he still hadn't gotten that mid-life belly that men his age seemed to always get.

Henry wasn't extraordinarily handsome or sexy. He wasn't some gym rat muscle bound man. He was just your average guy with a decent body. At the age of 62 he was still slim, having just a slight belly. The grey in his hair actually made him look better. What Marianne loved most about Henry was his smile, his easiness and willingness to love her. It seemed to bring him an amazing amount of pleasure just to make and see her smile.

"So are you going to gift that one to the library?" Henry

asked smiling and taking note of the green and silver bait fish swimming around his legs as he applied the sunscreen to his face and shoulders. When he was done he drove the bottle of Coppertone into his back pocket.

"Yes, and I was thinking that I might want to try my hand at writing my own story." Marianne added, looking down at the sand, waiting for Henry's response. “Christ on the cross, if some of these other books can get published, why can’t I do it?” Thinking to herself that she was also trying to talk herself into it.

"Well, I think you should! You've always said that you could write a better story than some of the books you've been reading." Henry started. "We could set up a space for you upstairs or even out on the deck. That way you could see the Gulf and be outside while you write." He continued, letting his mind race to how he could make that work.

Laughing just a bit at his enthusiasm and the look on his face, she knew what he was up to. "I think you just want a new project or something to build. I'm not sure if you think that this is a good idea or not." Marianne said, laughing again.

Henry laughed with her. "You may be right," smiling over at her. "Honey, I think you would make a great story teller." He continued as he gave her a flirty wink.

Looking over at Marianne, Henry realized how proud he was of the woman she had become. They were very young when they first got married. She had proven to be a wonderful partner, wife, mother and grandmother. Kind, caring, always there for him, she tried to be as supportive as she possibly could. Over the years she had grown to be a very lovely, mature, woman. One that he loved more than he even thought possible. What he really loved was watching her eyes change colors. Typically her eyes were a gray blue, when she was really happy the color changes to a beautiful sky blue. It was just one more really good reason to love her and make her happy.

"Well, thanks, it won't be easy, I'm sure. But really, what is? And, how wonderful would it be to see and feel your creation, your own book in your hand. To hand it to someone and have them read what you've created. And then for them to tell you what they thought and learn from that." Marianne said, reaching out for his hand.

"When do you think you'll start? And do you have a topic in mind?" Henry asked with interest.

"Tomorrow, and nope! I think I'm just going to start writing and see where it takes me. I was going to go to the store later this afternoon to get all the supplies that I need." Marianne explained, a bit nervous about the idea now. She had been journaling for years, now all she had to do was to put her thoughts into a story.

"Sounds like a plan." Henry said urging her to turn around and head home. The sun warmed their faces and they opted to set further out into the water for the rest of their walk.

Once they got home Henry held the new gate open for her so Marianne could walk up the boardwalk. He felt amazing pleased with himself that he was able to create this walkway for her and the gate as well. He took a moment to hook the latch and take one last look out over the Gulf.

"What a beautiful day and a perfectly lovely gate." She said, reaching back for his hand. "Come inside with me Henry." She continued. Henry had been very supportive and looked so sexy doing it that all she wanted now was to take Henry up to their bedroom and make love to him.

The Gate - Chapter 2

Marianne was writing at the kitchen island when Henry came bounding home. He was smiling and seemed overly excited, almost gitty, not able to stay still. When she looked up she noticed that he was waiting for her to ask him what color the canary was that he ate.

"Blue?" She asked with a smile.

"GREEN!" He replied, offering a smile in return.

"You seem to be a bit over the moon at the moment." Marianne said putting her pen down on her story covered pad of paper.

"I am!" He replied, still smiling, not given away his surprise.

Laughing a bit. "Care to share?" she asked, pushing her pad off to the left.

"I have a surprise for you." Henry said still smiling from ear to ear.

"Okay, so I gathered. What is it?"

"Come see," he said, grabbing her hand and pulling her toward the sliding doors and lower deck.

"Henry?"

He stopped, grabbed her shoulders and kissed her, and then continued to pull her toward the door. Once they reached the sliding doors, she noticed that the drapes were pulled closed. Obviously the surprise was hidden behind the drapes out on the deck.

"I'm so proud of you. Over the last couple of weeks you've been really dedicated to writing your book and I wanted to get you something." Henry started, still very excited. "I think you'll like it and it will help you."

"You didn't have to get me anything." Marianne said, eager to see what he had brought home.

"Okay, close your eyes." Henry instructed. Marianne did as she was told. Slowly he moved the drapes and guided her out to the deck. "Okay, open your eyes."

Henry had bought her a desk. It was a beautiful deep blue color, similar to the Gulfs water and was made of steel. It looked like a metal drafting table because it sat higher than a normal desk. The chair was also metal and matched the desk. Henry had already purchase a cushion for the chair. It matched the other cushions on their outdoor furniture perfectly. He had already cleaned it up and placed a vase of peach colored tulips on the top to brighten Marianne's view.

Marianne smiled with excitement and almost cried at his thoughtfulness. She slowly walked over to the desk and lightly ran her fingers over the top of the smooth surface.

"Henry, it's perfect. Where did you find it?" Marianne asked, reaching out for his hand. "I love it!" Then reaching around his neck to hug him tightly. "And you, I love you, too." She said softly in his ear. "Thank you, Honey!" Then Marianne kissed him with so much love for him.

Henry smiled from ear to ear. One of his greatest joys was to make Marianne happy. It was obvious that the desk was a major hit.

"You seem to like it." Henry said, taking one of the tulips from the vase and handing it to her and kissing her cheek.

Smiling at his gesture, "I love it, and you!" Pausing a moment. "Let me get my pad and pen."

"Wait! There's more." Henry said "Look! It's wired so you can bring out your laptop and hook up some music and a light, if you want to writing into the night hours."

"Wow! This is like the Cadillac of all desks." She said as they both laughed.

Soon Marianne was set up out at her new desk, looking out over the powdery beach. She took note of how lovely the new gate looked against the sand and Gulf view. The natural wood totally stood out against the green blue waters in front of her.

Henry was inside watching Marianne write at her new desk. It was a beautiful sight to see her in this element. Whether she got published or not wasn't the point, it was great to see her enjoying a new project, and trying so hard to be dedicated to her work.

The pink lemonade he was drinking was hitting the spot until suddenly a cloud came over him. Slowly he walked over to the book shelf and took out his favorite book, "As The Crow Flies". Opening it up he found the letter from his doctor. The one that let him know his test results. He hadn't told Marianne yet. She didn't even know that he'd gone to the doctor. At that point he didn't want her to know. Now, knowing the results he wasn't sure that she needed to know. The doctor had said that it was going to be fast.

Henry was going to die.

The Gate - Chapter 3

"How's the story coming?" Henry asked as he walked out on the deck.

It had been three weeks since Henry had brought home the metal desk. Marianne, true to character had used it at some point of every day. She was working hard on her story and Henry gave her the time and space to do just that. He was extremely proud of her. So much so that all he could think about was trying to find ways to help her. Find her time to do what she really wanted to do. Henry found himself spending more time cooking, cleaning up and washing the dishes, just so Marianne could get back to work. Many afternoons he would bring her lunch out of the deck so that she continue to write while he just sat over in the corner reading the paper of a book.

"Good, I'm in a great place." She answered, barely looking up from her tablet.

"Do you have time for a walk? I'm headed to the water." Henry asked, coming up from behind her and putting his arm around her shoulders.

"I always have time for you. AND, a walk on the beach."

Marianne said, with a little giggle as she started to close up shop and put her pen and paper in the hide away drawer.

"Great!" Henry said, stepping back to give her some space.

Sliding down off the steel stool she said. "Let's go," then exchanging her reading glasses for a stylish pair of sunglasses.

The two started down the boardwalk toward Henry's new gate.

"Henry, I love looking out over the beach and seeing your gate against the blue water." She said as she lifted the lever to go through.

"Thanks." Henry smiled at her. "I'm glad you like it." Inside Henry was thinking that his plan was going to work.

The gate was a marker, a reminder of him and all the love he has for her. The desk was positioned perfectly so that every time Marianne sat down to write she would see the gate and remember him and how much he loved her.

Henry closed the gates door behind them, they slipped off their flip flops and then they both headed for the water's edge. Their conversation ranged from Marianne's story, to their children, Henry's next project, which was still undetermined, then eventually dinner. They decided on something light. An easy salad topped with chicken.

"I think that we should bring dinner out to the beach and watch the sunset. Maybe even bring down a bottle of white wine." Henry said, moving up to hold Marianne's hand in his.

"That would be really lovely." She said, looking over at him. "Soooooooooooo, whatcha got going on over there, Big Boy?" Marianne probed, knowing her husband well enough to know that something was going on in his head.

"Going on?" Henry replied, knowing that he'd been caught but unsure as to how to begin. Marianne would always ask him 'whatcha got going on over there,' when she saw him thinking too much.

"Yeah, you're typically very good about making sure I feel loved." She smoothed.

"Really?" Henry asked smiling at her. "I'm glad that you think so." Hoping he could talk himself out of this.

"But, lately you've gone the extra mile. You're being very attentive. Very romantic, sexy and extremely loving." Pausing a moment. "So, I'm asking you, again." Then stopping and turning toward him. "What's up?" Marianne finally asked again with a look that meant that she expected an honest answer.

"Nothings . . . up. I just love you and want you to know it." Henry said, thinking that he needed to think quicker on his feet so she wouldn't trap him into telling her.

"Henry?" Marianne asked, stepping away from him, up out of the water and into the wet sand while the waves rolled over her feet. She noticed that her feet started to sink beneath the sand and water, but she didn't care. She wanted an answer, she wanted the truth, and she wanted it now.

Henry stopped and looked at Marianne. Her look was one of concern. He stood there, unsure of what to do or say. She had every right to know exactly what was happening and what he was going through. Not to mention his outcome. The problem was, he didn't think he had the courage to tell her. And he didn't want to her hurt. No one should have to deal with this and something that he was trying to protect her from.

Blowing the stale air in his lungs, out. "Marianne," pausing a moment to gain additional strength. "About three months ago I went to see a doctor."

"Why didn't you tell me?" She asked, tilting her head. "I'm sorry," catching herself. "This isn't a lecture, I'll let you finish."

Henry smiled at her correction. "I was afraid. Afraid of what was going on. What the doctor would say. Even what you would say and how you would react." Henry explained. "Yes, I should have told you. I should have taken you with. But . . . I was trying to protect you."

"Henry . . . from what? What's wrong?" She asked with an air of real concern. He was now frightening her, and though she wanted to know what was going on, there was part of her that was happy not knowing.

"Honey," Henry started, looking down at the sand and water then back up at Marianne. "Sweetheart, I have cancer." He said softly, as if he was trying to keep from letting anyone who might be passing by from hearing and knowing.

Marianne felt a huge weight hit her causing her shoulders to fall, her heart to sink and lungs fail her. It was as if a spot light from outer space instantly shined down on them as they stood there on the sand. She wanted to say something but she mouth felt dry. She could feel her body creating weight as she stood there. Her feet sinking deeper and deeper into the sand with no strength to step away. And her eyes quickly filled with silent tears as her knees went weak. She bent at the waist and grabbed her thighs to balance herself.

Henry said nothing more, he just looked at her. The fear and shock on her face was apparent. As if she was like a deer frozen in a pickup's headlights. Quietly her stepped over towards her, lifting her upright and holding her tightly. Doing his best to reassure her that everything would be okay.

"Marianne, please say something." Henry said as he saw another tear fall from her grey blue eyes.

"Your Dad has decided to not go through any treatment. As hard as this is for me, and him, for all of us really. I can understand why he wouldn't." Marianne paused a moment. She was speaking to her three children, their spouses and her grandchildren. "The doctors have said that treatment really wouldn't help. It may prolong his life for a short time but really there is nothing that they can do. This tumor is moving and growing at a rapid pace. And he would rather live out his life at home and with his dignity." Being silent for a moment, "we're hoping that you can understand and accept this decision."

The room was silent. She saw tears run down their children's faces and knew from her own experience that they were in overload with emotions and had a rash of questions.

"So, no more tears, lots of hugs. AND, I want some BBQ," Henry said, standing up to direct his family.

"Dad?" He heard from the room.

"BBQ my friends, BBQ!" And Henry headed for the deck to turn on the grill.

Maybe it was rude, maybe it was cold. But the fact is, he didn't want the attention, he didn't want the sympathy. He didn't want more looks of sadness. If he did end up going there. If he went down that road he would have to go to that place of reality. And at the moment, he just didn't want to deal with that. It was easier, for him, to just go on with life as he wanted it to be, not as it really was.

Marianne walked out on the deck, closed the sliding glass door and looked at Henry. Between them there was nothing but silence. Henry still hadn't looked at or acknowledged the fact that Marianne was even there. He calmly went about his business getting his grill ready for BBQ chicken. It was a favorite of his and his children. Marianne had stood there, quiet, her arms and hands hanging down by her sides, just waiting for him to realize. She could tell that Henry was already upset and getting more uncomfortable with her presences.

Without warning Henry turned toward Marianne and said. "It's still my life. The weeks or months that I have left are mine to do with however I want."

"No one is disputing that. But remember, you've had months to get use to the idea of your current situation. We've had, what, five minutes? Maybe a little understanding on your part would be good here. We are, as you well know, losing our husband and father." She was calm when she said this. Almost void of emotion.

Henry stood there as Marianne spoke. He took note of her calmness and non-confrontational, yet direct demeanor. He knew that what she was saying was true. Granted they didn't understand that was he was losing was a little more valuable. But he also knew that he needed to make this easier for them, the loved ones he was leaving behind.

"Marianne, I understand. But I don't want to be, or looked at as, sick. I don't want to make everyone watch me suffer. Hell, I don't want to suffer." Henry said, putting the grill utensils down on the steel fixture. Hanging his head, not really knowing what to do. His plan all along was to just go on with life and not tell anyone. Foolish as it was, he just wanted to save them the pain and the memories of seeing him that way. He'd seen and heard from Cancer therapies could do to you and to your family. And he just didn't want that, for him or for them.

"I know Henry."

"Okay, then what's the issue?" He asked becoming a bit overwhelmed by the conversation.

"Henry." Looking at him and then walking up to hug him. In his ear she whispered. "But they don't know that. Try to understand and try to make them understand how you feel so they can feel better about all this as well. Also, do you really want them to suffer in your place?"

She released Henry, stepped back, looked at the tears welling in his eyes and smiled. At that moment, she knew that she had gotten through.

"I didn't think that this was going to be this hard." Henry said, fighting more tears away.

Marianne smiled at him. "It doesn't have to be. If you all show each other some compassion and respect, you'll be fine." Marianne continued, then waiting a moment. "One more time?"

"But the . . . " Henry started looking back at the grill.

"That'll keep." Smiling again and holding out her hand. "Come on."

Captive Maiden

by Francis Currier
New Hampshire

Eerie shadows cast by flickering candles jumped across pale walls, adding to the ominous feel of the room. Dark, unrecognizable shapes cluttered the floor along the walls. Quilts and blankets lay in a rumpled mess in the middle of the bed, and she could just make out the shape of some strange animal half hidden under them.

She studied the shape, her thoughts momentarily diverted from her situation as she attempted to figure out what the animal was. She stepped closer to the bed and then bit off a curse when her foot hit some unknown object. Her breath held. Still as a deer, she listened for any noise outside the room. Nothing. She was on edge; the desire to pace so strong her muscles ached with it. She held back, afraid to make noise and bring attention to herself. If she were quiet enough, perhaps they would forget she was there.

A small noise outside the room brought her gaze to a large, plain mirror attached to the dressing table. She tensed as she watched the handle of the door move downward and the door inch open. A large man entered the room and closed the door. His careful, silent movements at odds with his size. He met her eyes in the mirror, no expression on his face.

"Why have you brought me here?" she asked quietly.

He stayed by the door a moment more, his expression suddenly distant, listening for a sound only he could hear.

Finally, their gazes met again and she watched through the mirror as he approached. Even though she knew it was coming, she flinched when he grabbed her arm firmly and swung her around to face him.

"Do you know who I am?" he asked her roughly.

"I know who you are. You're a thief and a coward!" she replied hotly. "I demand you return me to my family!"

He laughed lightly, humorously, and reached out to touch her thin, straight hair. "You, madam, are not in a position to demand anything from me." He stepped away abruptly and paused again in the direction of the door. Listening. After a moment, he pulled a bottle off the bedside table and poured golden liquid into a light blue cup. "Drink, my lady?"

"I want nothing from you but my freedom," she said.

"Like your father gave me my freedom?" he asked her

before drinking deeply from the cup.

She watched his stubble-covered throat move as he drank. "My father showed you mercy," she said, sharply. "He gave you honest work for fair wages and a place to sleep. And this is how you repay his kindness?"

The dark-haired man barked a laugh, coughing slightly on his drink. "Kindness, you say? Mercy? Where I come from it's kinder to kill a man than slowly grind the life out of him. Your father used my family. We had nothing to survive on. A hovel to sleep in. Food that wasn't fit for a dog. Yet you wonder why I turned to thievery?"

She narrowed her eyes at him. "How dare you speak of my father that way! If it wasn't for him, and for the kindness of me and my sister-"

"Your sister is a bitch."

"How dare you! You ungrateful bastard!" She moved forward swiftly, raising her hand as she went.

Just before her hand struck his face, he caught it and squeezed. "Think carefully before you strike me, woman. You will not care for the repercussions."

She tried to pull out of his grasp, but he held her, squeezing slightly harder, and then released her.

"Your father was an old, greedy man who cared nothing for others. All he cared about was putting coin in his pockets. And about his precious daughters." He turned away from her and returned to the bedside table. He refilled the cup and drank. "I should actually thank him. I learned to be an unfeeling criminal from him and it's served me well."

"You hate him so much, hate his daughters, and yet here I am. I would think the last thing you would want is to be near me." She watched him, noting the way his shirt stretched across his shoulders and belly.

He smiled when he caught her looking. "I've always been near you. I tracked you down years ago, and I've been watching you ever since. Every move you make. Every breath you take." He quickly took another drink, but not fast enough to hide the twitch of his mouth.

She narrowed her eyes and asked, "Why now? If you've been watching me all these years, why wait so long take me?"

He studied her, taking in her full breasts and hips, and

slightly rounded belly. "Before your father is gone, I want him to know that I have you. It will kill him to know that I have his favorite daughter. To know that I will be the one to take her for the first time. To know that no man will marry her because of me."

He walked slowly forward as he spoke. She couldn't help but shiver at the heat in his gaze.

He stopped in front of her, close enough that his stomach rubbed against hers. "And because I have wanted you from the moment I saw you."

"You have no right to claim me," she whispered.

"I have stolen the right to claim you," he told her before bending down to capture her mouth with his own.

He tasted of apple juice and lightly spiced chicken, and his mouth was boldly demanding. She knew she should fight, but instead gave herself up to it and kissed him back. Reveling in the feel of her body pressed against his. He was hard and hot, pressed against her softness. He backed her towards the bed and her excitement level rose. The mattress hit the backs of her knees and she took him with her as she tumbled back on the bed. Their combined weight hit the mass of blankets and a loud shriek filled the quietness.

"What the fuck was that?" he asked, pushing up off of her.

She reached under her body and came up with a pink, stuffed monkey. "Mr. Pickles. Ellen will-"

They both heard the cry from outside of the room followed by, "Mommy? Daddy?"

"Well shit. Shit!" He pushed himself fully from the bed.

She smiled sweetly at him. "You're on duty tonight, Daddy."

The big man sighed, adjusted himself, and then leaned down and kissed her on the top of her head. She held him and guided his mouth to hers for a longer kiss. A re-energized wail finally broke them apart.

"Care to try Captive Maiden again tomorrow night?" she asked him.

"It's a date." He kissed her again, grabbed the monkey and opened the door. Their daughter was already in the hallway, the baby still crying in his room.

"By the way," she said as he started out of the room.

"Yeah?"

"I'm telling my sister you called her a bitch."

Take that Chance

by Trisha McKee

Pennsylvania

Darcy simply wanted to go home, watch some mindless television, eat some crazily fattening ice cream, and crash into bed once she was so exhausted there was little chance of lying down and staring up at the ceiling as all of the stresses crashed through her mind.

But she was stuck in line at the grocery store where only two checkout lanes were open, and she had unwittingly chosen the one with the talkative, slow-moving cashier. Usually, she appreciated the banter, but after a day full of hyper children and a call from her flaky ex asking for money, she was in no mood for public places, for strangers invading her space.

"Never fails."

Darcy turned to the guy behind her, frowning when he grinned. "Excuse me?"

"The line. I always go in the shorter line, only to have it move slower than any other line. Every time."

She nodded and turned back around, not bothering to offer up a smile. That would encourage more conversation, and if there was one thing she dreaded more at that moment than striking up a conversation with the annoyingly chipper cashier, it was conversing with the irritatingly handsome guy.

"I don't really have anywhere to be though. So I don't mind." When she did not turn around, he continued, "I'm Caleb." After another pause, he observed, "You look familiar. Any chance you're a teacher?"

This got her attention. Because no matter what, Darcy had to be civil to parents. Even if the parent was a persistent man that had the most mesmerizing hazel eyes. So she forced a smile and turned back to him.

He looked to be around her age, 24 years old, maybe a few years older, with light brown hair cut short, an unshaven face that made him look his age despite the smooth face, and those hazel eyes framed by long lashes.

"Yes, I am a teacher. Abner Elementary."

"Right. Second grade." She confirmed with a nod, and his grin widened. "My nephew was in your class last year. I picked him up a couple of times. Robby Sinclair."

A sincere smile blossomed on her face. “Aw, Robby. Yes, no way I can forget him.”

Caleb ducked his head with a grin. “Yes, he is a bit rambunctious.”

“He is a great kid. Really, he is. So smart. And yes, lots of energy. Please tell him Ms. Heights says hello.”

“I will do that.”

She flashed a polite smile and then greeted the cashier who had started to move her items across the scanner and bag them. The cashier started a running commentary on the items Darcy was buying, so she was too busy to notice Caleb any further.

But as she made her way across the parking lot, she heard, “Ms. Heights! Wait, please!”

She groaned but stopped where she was, bracing herself. A moment later, he was in front of her, that smile meant to dazzle, but it simply put her on guard.

“I was wondering if you’d like to go grab a cup of coffee.”

Lifting a bag, Darcy shrugged. “Sorry. Don’t want to ice cream to melt.”

“Then tomorrow.”

“Caleb.” She spoke his name with a sigh. “I don’t think so.”

“You’re married?”

“No.”

“Boyfriend?”

“Believe it or not, a woman can turn you down for reasons other than being involved with someone else.”

Her words caused him to draw back in surprise. “I- I am sorry. I didn’t mean- I just would never disrespect someone’s relationship. That’s why I asked. But... sure, I mean, if you don’t want to then...”

“Again, give my best to Robby. Have a great day.”

Darcy had to rush to her friend Amy’s house to pick up her daughter Janie. Her four-year-old was the light of an otherwise dark life, and she was immediately cheered at the thought of seeing her after a longish day.

“Amy, I’m sorry. The store was packed and -”

Amy flashed that perfect smile. If she had not known her as the wonderful, funny woman she was, Darcy would be jealous and intimidated by her. Blond hair that was always perfectly styled, the latest fashions that framed her figure perfectly, and a confidence that radiated from her like a glowing crown. But Amy was her biggest support and best confidante. There was no envy between the friends.

"Please stop, Darcy. Janie was a perfect angel. She helps out with Otis." Otis was Amy's one year old son. "She said she had to do naptime at school today. Again." The women laughed.

And then Janie ran into the room, all blond curls and dimples. "Mommy, Frankie threw up at school today!"

"Oh no! I hope he feels better soon!" She picked her daughter up and hugged her before letting her loose. She was a ball of energy and as soon as her tiny feet hit the ground, she was gone. "Hey, Janie, get your coat! We have to go." She sighed. "Great, sick kids at school. I hope she doesn't get it. Hey, so Ryan called me."

"And?" Because Amy knew as well as Darcy that Ryan called when he wanted something.

"He needs money."

"Right. Like you don't need money for Janie? He's unbelievable. Please tell me you told him no."

"I did. I have to worry about my own situation. I just keep hoping someday he will grow up."

Darcy and Ryan had been high school sweethearts and continued dating while Darcy attended community college. But when she became pregnant with Janie unexpectedly, Ryan had begged her to leave town with him. He was still immature, unable to commit to anything, let alone supporting a family. And she realized she did not love him in that way. He was her best friend, but she wanted more for herself and for the baby.

So Ryan left when Janie was only a few months old. He had visited a handful of times and sent money sporadically, but more often than not, he asked for money. Or he begged her to follow him on whatever scheme he was chasing. His interest was more invested in her than their child, and that broke her heart.

But all thoughts of Ryan and the disappointments in his fathering skills faded once she was home with Janie. Her daughter was brilliant and while most mothers thought that of their offspring, it was true with Janie. She had started speaking well before a year old, and her vocabulary was off the charts for her age.

Darcy had her daughter tested and then had educators come in to help her handle her daughter's extraordinary gifts. They taught her how to communicate with the tiny genius, how to handle her when she became overwhelmed, how to best nurture that amazing ability. They also helped her make an informed decision to not place Janie in a higher grade in school at this time. She had her in preschool, and she felt it was the best decision to get her daughter acquainted with the routine and to focus on social interactions.

"May I be excused?"

"Eat some green beans, please, Janie."

Janie sighed, swinging her legs and poking at the green beans with her fork. "Mom, I got enough nutrition at lunch. I ate all of my apple and carrots. Please." When Darcy gave her a look, she sighed and took a bite of green beans.

"Good girl."

Darcy read her a couple of stories, and then Janie read a story out loud, almost bored with it as she flipped through the pages and quickly spouted off the words, and Darcy reminded herself to buy new books so she could see if Janie was actually that good at reading or was simply great at memorizing.

And then Darcy was alone, her daughter fast asleep. It was in these late hours that she found herself feeling lonely, missing that connection. But it had been almost four years since she had been with a man, since Ryan. She had been raised by a single mother that drank away her problems and brought a parade of unsavory men through, and she had sworn she would never do that. So dating was not an option. Her job was to raise that brilliant little girl. Nothing else. There was no room for anything else.

There was nothing routine about a teacher's day except the timeline of classes and activities. But Darcy knew better than anyone that each day with young children was different, an adventure. Some days it was a great adventure and other days, it was a scary, tiring adventure. But she loved it. She adored her students and loved seeing them light up when something she taught resonated with them. At this young age, they were already leaning toward strengths. Some were great with numbers, some were amazing with words.

That day was a great adventure, and she got lost in the magic of it, in the schedule running smoothly and the children focused and happy. These were the days that time did not just fly, it ceased to exist. There was no glancing at the clock or counting away the minutes.

When she finally had a free period, Darcy used it to get caught up in future lessons looking over the math worksheets. She made a mental note to work with Susan on adding and subtracting three digit numbers and to tell Sean's parents that he might need to be bumped up a level.

"Hey, Darcy?" Rosie, the office secretary leaned into the room. "I've been looking for you. There's someone here to see you. He's kind of cute."

Darcy was still in the excellent day daze as she entered the office, and it took her a few moments to recognize the man standing at the counter, grinning at her. Then it hit her. Caleb. The guy from the grocery store.

"Oh! Caleb, how can I - how can I help you?"

"So I told Robby about running into you, and he wanted me to come in and give you this." He stepped forward and handed her a paper with a drawing of her in front of a classroom. "I miss you, Ms. Heights," it read.

"That's sweet. Although I see him in the hallways every day. He is still in the same building." She stared up at Caleb, her gaze unwavering. "Let me walk you out, Caleb."

Once they were in the empty hallway, she turned to him. "Look, I'm not sure what you're trying to pull, but I would appreciate it if you don't interrupt my day at work. This is so inappropriate."

He lowered his gaze, running a hand through his thick hair. "I'm sorry. I - I -"

"And using your nephew as an excuse to execute this scheme is -"

"Now wait right there! I told Robby about running into you, and he was excited. I understand you know your students better than most, but he is a nine-year-old boy. I don't think he would be very comfortable walking up to you in front of his friends and handing you this picture." He paused and then asked, "What is it about me?"

She sighed. "I don't date."

"Okay. But when you turned and saw me at the grocery store, there was something in your expression. Have we met before?"

"I don't care for your type."

He choked on a laugh. "My type? You don't even know me."

"Ripped Tendons."

Realization lit up his eyes. "Oh. My band. You knew me ... back then?"

"I saw you play once. I was like eighteen. You came up to me after the show. You were arrogant and pushy. Sleazy."

She expected him to argue, but instead his cheeks flushed and he slowly nodded. "I was an ass back then. That was like, what, five, six years ago? I was just a stupid, insecure guy. I was shy most of my life. Bullied in school. Then I get this band, and women were all over me. I ... it went to my head. I'm sorry you saw that side of me. It isn't who I am. And when I saw you in the grocery store... I don't do this. I don't. It isn't who I am. I just wanted a chance to ask you again out for coffee. Just coffee."

Darcy did not want to be swayed. She had her life rules. She averted her gaze. "I don't date. I just don't."

"So not a date. Just coffee."

"I can't."

"Can't is different than won't. Why can't you?"

She made the mistake of looking up, right into Caleb's eyes, and she melted just a little bit. She was attracted to this stranger, and it was dangerous territory. "I have a daughter. A four year old."

He waited as if he expected more, but then tilted his head. "And... does she not allow you to socialize?"

"I have to focus on her. I can't bring men in and out of her life. No."

"Of course. Absolutely. But ... I'm asking for just a cup of coffee."

"I hate coffee."

He ducked his head and grinned, and Darcy found herself melting just a little more. "Then tea. Or milk. Anything you want."

And Darcy did something she had not considered doing in years. She agreed to a date. "Okay, fine. We can meet somewhere for a soda. Maybe a light lunch."

Caleb beamed, and she tried not to consciously notice how good-looking he was when he smiled. "Okay, great."

"But wait. On one condition."

"Of course. Anything."

"After that, you leave me alone. No more of this.... This showing up at my place of work. Creepy."

"Agreed. So creepy. If you decide after lunch that you want nothing further to do with me, then I'm out. I promise."

Darcy might not have been as head-turning as Amy, but she had plenty of guys trying to get her attention. With dark blonde hair with light blond streaks and large green eyes, even downplaying her looks with no makeup and ponytails could not dim her beauty. She was not skinny, but she had curves in the right places. Darcy was self-conscious about her body, so she usually donned on oversized shirts to cover the extra pounds. But while many men leered, Caleb seemed to see her, to compliment her in a respectful, sincere way. She even found herself wearing a not-so-loose shirt and a skirt that showed off her legs. She was comfortable with herself around him.

It was how two weeks later, Darcy found herself on the phone with Caleb in the late hours of the night, giggling like the schoolgirl she had never been. "Well, you seemed to enjoy the movie."

She had gotten to know him, to know his humor and charm. She knew that he worked as a graphic designer for an up and coming software company, that he fixed up older homes in his spare time with his father and sold them for profit. She knew he loved barbeque chips and grape juice, and he hated olives and slow drivers. She knew that when he got quiet and stared at her lips, he was about to kiss her, and she knew she loved those moments.

"No." His voice was low, smooth as it caressed her ear, and she shivered. "It was horrible. So it doesn't count. We have to try again."

And a laugh bubbled up from deep inside, spilling out of her mouth. "Just like lunch was gross. And the walk we took just wasn't scenic enough. Right?"

"Exactly. You get it. We have to try again."

"Mommy."

Darcy spun around to see Janie standing there rubbing her eyes. "Give me one second," she whispered into the phone before setting it down and sinking to her haunches. "Hey, sweetheart, did you have a bad dream?"

"No. My throat needs a drink."

Janie had a habit of resorting to baby talk when she was tired or overwhelmed. The therapist assured Darcy it was normal. "Okay. Let's get you some water. Then back to bed."

After taking a few sips, Janie spied the phone and pointed. "Is that Aunt Amy?"

"No, sweetie."

“Gamma Harris?” Ryan’s mother called weekly to get updates on her only grandchild.

“No. It is a friend of mom’s. Are you done? Okay, good. Let’s get you tucked in.”

“I can tuck myself in. Too tired for goodnights.”

Darcy waited until Janie was out of the room before picking up the phone. “Sorry about that. We were talking about trying again.”

“Darcy, she sounds adorable.”

And Darcy bristled. Because this did not concern her daughter. Whatever this was with Caleb, Janie would not be a part of. “So back to trying to get this right. What’s your suggestion for our next try?”

For the next month, Darcy saw Caleb several times a week. They were coming up on two months of dating, and Darcy could not deny she was falling for this charming, considerate man. She had never realized there could be such electricity between two people, that she could feel so alive, tingly.

They were on a rare evening date, as Darcy rarely liked to leave Janie with a sitter, but Amy had volunteered. And Caleb had made reservations at a particularly nice restaurant Darcy had never had the pleasure of patronizing. It was out of her price range, and with Janie, any restaurant they went to had crayons and coloring menus available. But even that was a treat.

“You look beautiful,” Caleb murmured in her ear as he pulled out her chair for her. And for the first time in a long time, she felt beautiful. He had a way of making her believe his words, his eyes never leaving her, as if he could not get enough.

“Thank you.” She tried to keep the color from heating her face. “You look nice too.”

“So... next week will be two months since our first disastrous date.” They both laughed. Then he reached out for her hand. “I know you’re hesitant. But I am hoping we can continue this... I’m always thinking of you, counting the minutes until I can see you or talk to you.”

“Wait.” Panic coursed through her as Darcy realized this was quickly snowballing out of her control. That loss of control caused her to lose her breath. She withdrew her hand. “Just... no. I can’t... this is really fast-”

“Darcy. Two months.” But he studied her expression and

leaned back. “Okay.” His tone was softer. “I’m sorry. I won’t overwhelm you.”

She appreciated his understanding, but the damage was done. Darcy knew Caleb was looking for more, and she had nothing more to give. They ate their meals in silence, Caleb whispering her name every now and then to try to get her attention.

As he walked her to her car, he reached out to grasp her fingers in a move so gentle, she did not jump. “Wait. Darcy. Just hear me out. Please.” She turned to him, raising her eyes to meet his, knowing as she did so that it was a mistake. She got lost in those eyes. “I know you’re scared. I don’t know what happened to you. Or who hurt you. But I just want to get to know you better. I think I’ve shown you I don’t have ulterior motives. I have not pushed you in any way. I’m not that guy you knew all those years ago. Please. Just a chance to continue this. Your speed. You want to slow down? We can. Just don’t say goodbye. Please.”

She spoke his name under her breath. “Just give me time. Because this is overwhelming.”

“Hey. Don’t cry. No. I don’t want to be the reason for that. This is a lot. I’ll give you all the time you need. I’m here. I’m not going anywhere.”

Caleb kept his word. He called and texted but did not push her. He did not demand answers or beg for another date. Instead, he called and they talked about their days, about their jobs and anything else that merely skimmed the surface. Darcy could hear in his voice that urge to push more, to ask what she was thinking or when he could see her next, but he resisted. For that, she was both grateful and disappointed.

Because the longer she went without seeing him, the more she missed him. After years of being resigned to never dating, she was now craving his company, desiring his touch, dreaming of his lips...

“Mom?”

Darcy broke out of her thoughts to see Janie staring up at her with similar round green eyes. She resembled a doll, beautiful features and adorable curls, and strangers often came up to them to get a better look. But Janie did not warm up to strangers easily, and she was uncomfortable with the attention. Darcy wondered if she got that by watching her, mimicking her behavior. “What is it, sweetheart?”

Janie reached up and touched her mother's cheek. "You look sad."

The observation caught her off guard. "What? No. No, honey. I'm not sad."

"You've been sad all week. I'll be talking to you, and you just get this look on your face. Don't be sad."

"No. I won't be sad. Do you want to color?" It was the one activity that could get her daughter's mind off of things. "Get the crayons and coloring books. We'll color."

But she realized that her daughter knew the difference. She could tell something was going on, and it was then that Darcy knew she had to see what there was with Caleb. Because she missed him.

Caleb did not gloat or demand when she admitted to missing him. He simply suggested he bring her lunch at the school the next day. It was casual, and she appreciated that.

The next day, Amy's husband William stopped at the school to get her house keys. She had a leaky faucet he was going to look at. She had a small, modest house, but it was still a lot to keep up with, and William was nice enough to help whenever he could.

She met him outside the front doors, and as they chatted about the faucet and a drafty window, Caleb walked around the corner, slowing when he saw them. He gave them a hesitant smile and approached them slowly.

"Caleb, hi! Caleb, this is William. William, this is my friend Caleb."

The men shook hands, and then William gave her a friendly hug, something he did often. "I'll get your keys back to you. Shouldn't take me long to fix the faucet. I'll look at the window too."

Once he left, Darcy smiled up at Caleb. "My classroom is empty. We can just have lunch there."

Caleb was quiet as they settled in, but after taking a bite of his sandwich, he set it down. "So that was... your brother?"

"I told you I don't have any brothers."

"Then... cousin?"

"No. I don't have contact with my family. Not a good childhood. Mom was a drunk. Dad was not there. So ...." With a start, she laughed. "Oh wait. You're wondering why ... oh, I'm sorry. William is my best friend's husband. He helps me out with the house. With repairs and stuff like that."

Relief flooded his face. “Oh.” He gave her a sheepish grin and laughed. “I have to admit, I felt a little spark of jealousy when I saw him hug you.”

“No, he and Amy are my dearest friends. They are my daughter’s godparents.”

He took another bite and then said, “Aw, Janie. How old is Janie? Four, right?”

Darcy took her time opening the bag of chips before sighing. “I don’t - I don’t want to talk about my daughter. She’s off limits.”

Caleb nodded. “I noticed you change the subject when I ask anything about her.”

“She’s just... not a part of this... whatever this is.”

“Whatever this is?” He looked pained. “I thought this was dating.”

“It is.”

He sighed, and she noticed how young he looked. Much younger than she felt. “So dating... it is about getting to know each other. The main part of your life is being a mother. You have a child. We can’t just ignore that.”

“She isn’t a part of this.”

“How can you say that? She’s a part of you. And I’m ... I’m absolutely head over heels for you. I know you don’t want to hear that, but I am. I’m not asking to meet her tonight but eventually-”

“No. Not eventually. Look, we can date. But that part of my life is off limits. I’m not going to parade men in and out of her life. No. I had that happen when I was a child. It was a nightmare.”

He studied her, his hazel eyes intent but softening. “Honey, your mom was not a good mom. I’m sure she did not have the best judgement when it came to men. But me, you’re getting to know me. I-”

“Caleb. No. This won’t get to that point. I’m sorry.”

“So what are we doing? Huh?”

“We’re dating. You said it would be at my pace.”

“Right.” He wrapped his sandwich up and scooted his chair back. “That’s when I thought it was going forward. I didn’t realize this had no future.”

“You should be happy. Isn’t this what men want? No commitment.”

She squirmed under his stare. Finally, he responded, “No. That isn’t what all men want. It isn’t what I want. I’m crazy about you, and I want a chance at a future with you. A chance. Get to know me more, do a background check, whatever you have to do, but don't tell me there is no future in this. I can't do that."

He waited and when it was clear she would not assure him, he got up. "I'm falling for you, Darcy. I fell for you the moment I laid eyes on you. I notice that you don't jump as much when I reach for you. You've lost that scared look in your eyes. I know there is a lot in your past that has you terrified of this, of us. I wish you'd talk to me about that. But I can't... don't ask me to just be some guy you think of occasionally. I want more."

Darcy wanted to simply let him walk away. She reminded herself of the promise to never let a man close to her again. Never let a man near her daughter who wasn't Ryan. But as he reached for the door, she found herself standing and calling out his name.

He stood, his back to her. "What, Darcy?"

"Caleb."

"No, I want you to talk. Talk to me, tell me what you're thinking and feeling. I want to go at your pace, but I have to know where you stand."

"I'm scared."

This time he turned, his expression softening. "I know you are."

"And this is just ... it's new to me. My mom brought men into the house that ... I had some bad experiences. Scary experiences. And my goal as a mother has been to protect my daughter. Her father- we were high school sweethearts, but he bailed on Janie because I didn't love him. And I don't want to hurt her by a relationship that might not work out."

He stepped closer to her but stopped when she trembled. "Darcy, honey, I understand. I do. We can take this slow. When you're as sure as I am that we are meant to be, then you choose when I meet your daughter. I'm just asking that you don't close that off as a possibility. I never want to hurt you. I will never purposely hurt you or your daughter."

"She's... not like most kids."

He grinned. "That's okay. I'm not really familiar with kids, so I won't know the difference."

"No, you will. She's ... she is only four years old, but she is a genius. A literal genius, and that intimidates a lot of people."

"Perfect," Caleb quipped. "I'm sort of smart myself."

She laughed through her tears and nodded when he motioned toward her. That was all it took for him to cross the remaining distance between them and take her into his arms.

A month later, when Darcy was unable to deny her feelings for Caleb, she took him to meet her daughter. She had prepared Janie in the weeks beforehand, explaining that she had a friend she wanted her to meet. Janie was curious but cautious, and when Caleb arrived, Darcy took her daughter by the hand and led her out to the living room, where the man she loved waited.

"Janie," he said with a wide grin. "I've heard so much about you. I heard that you love pizza."

"Everyone loves pizza," Janie growled, and his grin never wavered. Darcy had warned him that her daughter could be a bit abrasive with strangers.

"You're right. So I thought I'd take you and your mom out for pizza." He was careful not to get too close, remembering Darcy's warning of Janie's need for personal space.

And that evening once they were back home, Janie invited him into her room to color. It was the ultimate sign of approval from her daughter. She lingered in the hallway, listening to ensure her daughter was not overly rude.

"So," Caleb started, sitting in a too small chair, coloring in the book Janie had given him. "I had fun with you today."

Janie continued coloring. "I don't like to talk while I'm coloring."

"Oh, of course." He colored in silence until he was finished. Then he glanced over at Janie's picture. "Wow. That is great!"

"Thank you." Janie made a show of standing and staring at his picture. "Oh. Well, don't worry," she sang out. "You'll get better."

When Caleb threw his head back and laughed, Darcy knew it would all be okay. He was not fazed by her daughter's unique personality, and Janie seemed to take to him. This was still scary, and Darcy guessed there would be more obstacles to overcome, but the difference was that she was ready to face them. She was ready to take that chance.

Love is Love - *A Romance*

by Ms. Agnes C Chawadi

Missouri

Richard was a thirty-something IT professional with meddling relatives. As a young man from India, he knew that his family worried he was drifting in life and perhaps even late to launch into the stages that most people seemed to find normal: finding a partner, getting married, and starting a family.

It had been a long and somewhat boring night at the school fundraiser. Richard's cousin, who worked at the school, had encouraged him to attend, with the unspoken goal of setting him up with a mutual acquaintance, Vanessa, an attractive, available and young high school teacher whom he had quietly admired for many years. He had resolved to be pleasant and encouraging. And he knew he was attracted to Vanessa.

"Hi, Vanessa, you look awesome! I have been watching you the whole evening, and I just could not take my eyes off you. Congratulations for organizing such a lovely evening of entertainment."

"Thanks! Have we met before?" asked the lovely young woman.

"Oh, I am Richard Patel," he replied. "My cousin Rita invited me to attend the program tonight."

"Wow! I didn't know that Rita had such a handsome cousin." Richard almost couldn't believe his good luck, and he decided to go all the way with flattery.

"Well, *you* are pretty beautiful," he teased back, as she smiled nervously.

As the two generously exchanged words of polite praise and appreciation for one another, each quietly wondered whether there might be more going on beneath their spoken words. Richard had been sincere in his interest in finding a prospective love interest. He was pleased when they exchanged contact numbers and departed for the evening.

For her part, as the teacher who had been chosen by the school's board from more than 150 other teachers to organize the fundraiser, Vanessa was grateful for and proud of the event's success. She was only 25 and had been at the school for only two years. The fundraiser—nothing less than a huge state festival--had been an overwhelming success. Over a thousand students, along with their parents, participated in the event and had enjoyed the opportunity to present their creative thinking skills, leadership talents, and stage and theatrical abilities.

*

Rita had been teaching at the school for more than a decade. She had been quite taken with the newer young teacher, Vanessa, and cultivated a friendship with her. Upon learning that Vanessa was single, the well-meaning Rita, with an interested extended family, appointed herself as a matchmaker. *My introverted cousin needs someone just like Vanessa who can complement him to walk through life*, she thought.

India is well known for arranged marriages, and the country's divorce rate is the lowest in the world. While not all marriages are happy, most remain married with support of extended families. And Rita was not embarrassed to try to be the one who arranged for Richard and Vanessa to come together.

Rita could not wait to get home and inquire more about the meeting. She called Richard on his cell. "Hey, Rich, how did it go?" *Tell me more.*

"Oh! She's really an amazing young woman," Richard replied. "I had a good feeling and think it would be worth pursuing her."

"I hope you know what to do next?" inquired the helpful cousin.

"Yeah, I will let the week go by and then give her a call," he said.

Rita, ever the busybody, had more advice. "She loves chatting on the phone. Try giving her a lot of compliments. And don't forget to keep in the loop."

Rita took seriously her solemn duty to serve as a helpful relative. Primary and extended family members in India do not need reminders to fulfill their responsibility to help young people find suitable life partners. They not only help them find one, they also help them keep them through thick and thin, the ups and downs, of life.

*

Richard, for his part, took seriously his intention to pursue

Vanessa, and so he decided to make use of her phone number.

"Hi, Van, it's Richard!" he said, wondering if she could tell that he felt nervous.

"Oh, hi, Richard. What a surprise!"

"How are you doing?" he said, realizing he wasn't sure what else to say.

"I am doing well...how about you?"

"I am good and have been thinking about you ever since the fundraiser!" he replied.

"Thinking about me?" she responded.

"Yeah, I am."

"I am feeling a bit embarrassed about that. What makes you think about me?" Vanessa said, both excited and embarrassed.

"I can't stop thinking about you," Richard said, too enthusiastic to be anything less than sincere.

But for her part, Vanessa was a bit overwhelmed. "I don't know what to say. Don't think too much about me. Tell me something about you."

"What do you want to know about me?" Richard replied, curious that anyone else would be curious about him.

"Just about anything. Like where you work, your hobbies and a little bit about your family and so on," said Vanessa.

"Well, we can talk about that," said Richard. But he was undeterred by his primary objective. "But I am simply fascinated by you."

"Okay, but I have to go now," said Vanessa, a bit overwhelmed, but also happy that a seemingly kind and handsome young man had expressed an interest in her. "We will talk sometime soon."

Vanessa had enjoyed receiving Richard's interest and a phone call from him. In fact, she had made some inquiries about him from his cousin, Rita, at the school. She had asked if had a stable job, an apartment of his own, a good family. Was he a good man, and did he have good habits? Once satisfied by this basic information, there was more to know. Did she like him? Did they click? Did they have common interests or senses of humor? She felt quite satisfied about the preliminary information she had extracted from Rita, but Indian cultural expectations require that even if a woman is interested in a man, it is not polite to make the first move. And so, Vanessa waited to hear from Richard once again.

As she went about her usual chores and activities, it was difficult to conceal that something was different from her family. She hummed and sang little songs as she graded papers, chopped the vegetables and ironed the clothes. She tried not to let them see her glancing at the phone. It seemed an eternity, but it was only three days before Richard called again.

*

Vanessa answered the phone on the first ring. She hoped she did not seem too eager.

"Hi, Van, it's Richard!" he greeted her.

"Oh, hi! How are you doing?" she said.

"I'm well, and how about you?"

"Well, also. I was just thinking about you," she said, wondering if that seemed too forward.

"Really? Thanks!" he said. "I wanted to call you just as soon as we ended our other phone call, but I didn't know if you would appreciate that."

"Hmmm, I would have minded at all," she said, smiling.

"How's school going?" Richard asked.

"All is going pretty well," she said. "We are getting back to our regular classroom lessons after the excitement of the fundraiser. Our board and all of the parents were very pleased with the annual function, and they threw a party for me in appreciation of my work!"

"That's great," said Richard. "I would like to take you for a treat, too."

"Really?" she asked. "Oh, wow, thanks!"

"When are you free?" Richard asked.

"Hummm, well...I need to think about that," she said. "I can't get away without my parents' permission," Vanessa said, apprehensively.

"Let me know, I will be waiting to hear from you," he said, undeterred.

Vanessa pondered the situation. It had been a long month since they had first met at the school event, and it was clear that Richard and Vanessa had an undeniable attraction to one another. They were not only thinking about one another, but also looking forward to speaking on the phone. She decided to meet with

Richard secretly at a local mall. Their clandestine meetings grew from once a month to once a week. As they met, they realized how much each enjoyed being with the other, and their affection grew.

Vanessa had grown up in a traditional family and in close relationship with the members of her extended family including dozens of cousins, some of whom had seen them together at the mall and made discreet inquiries about the secret friend. Vanessa had brushed off their queries and asserted that there was nothing serious between herself and Richard, who was "just a friend." But in her heart of hearts, she was enjoying her newfound love but was not assertive enough to acknowledge it. The adult in her family were totally unaware of this behind-the-scenes love story.

For his part, Richard had no time to waste. He would soon be 31, and he wanted to propose to Vanessa. Unlike in the U.S. or other countries, the traditional proposal does not happen simply between two young people but between two prospective families. Vanessa was not prepared to bring the topic to her parents. Richard's family had had some inkling about the affair, and they were hoping that he would move ahead. After careful consideration, Vanessa suggested that his family come to her family through the local pastor. Thus, the drama of proposal was set up by the two young people who felt culturally bound to have their union approved through their respective families.

The local pastor whom they approached noted that he was privileged to offer a personal touch to his ministry by bringing Richard's bio data to Vanessa's family members, who were very regular churchgoers and active church members. They knew the pastor on a personal basis and were sure to honor his visit and act of service. Thus, the discussion of potential suitors for Vanessa began for the first time in her family. Her parents carefully looked at Richard's bio data, the young man himself, his job status, and the educational status and marriage stability of his parents. They found these were all positive points to be considered in his favor. These were, after all, factors parents consider in helping their daughter have a happy and stable married life, while they can still remain somewhat clueless about the mutual attraction between two young people. In arranged marriages, the valuable contribution adults make is to help a couple look seriously beyond mutual attraction and consider essentials of family life requirements.

*

Vanessa's parents did their homework and had, through family and friends, diligently worked to acquire more information about their prospective son-in-law and his family. Once they were satisfied with all the information they had gathered, they found a suitable day and time to introduce the topic to their daughter.

"Vanessa, please read through this paper," said her father, handing over a sheet of information provided by the pastor. "What do you think?"

"I think I am interested in him," she said, smiling.

"Well, if you are interested in this matter, I will follow it up with the other party's family," he said. "I have made inquiries, and they seem to be a good family," he concluded.

Vanessa, half smiling and half embarrassed, didn't know how to act. She later confided to her mother that she had met and knew Richard already. She cautioned that her father was not to know this.

Richard and Vanessa had met in October at the school event, and by December their families were meeting to get a sense of one another. After careful scanning of information and people, the young man's family felt confident to present an official proposal to the young woman's family asking for their daughter's hand in marriage and setting a date for the wedding. In mid-January, Richard visited Vanessa's family. The two joyful families shared some pleasantries. The parents deemed it opportune to meet separately in the family room while the boy and girl had some privacy to spend time separately in the other part of the house–with dozens of cousins who were quite happy to join the young couple on their first expedition together!

*

Vanessa had done some thinking and had prepared a list of twenty-odd questions for Richard to answer. Empowered by the presence of her cousins, she began her rapid-fire round of questions:

"Did you propose to any other girl before me?" she interrogated him.

"No."

"Why did you wait for thirty years to propose to a girl?" she continued.

"I was waiting for the most ideal woman that I could find, and that was you," he said.

"If we get married, are you planning to live separately from your parents?" she pursued.

"I would like to treat both your parents and mine respectfully," he replied patiently.

"You said we would live separately on our own. You liar!"

"Well, I would like that initially we live with them," he responded.

"But you said you have an apartment of your own and we would live separately!" she exclaimed.

"Yes, I do have an apartment of my own in the same building as my parents. We can initially live with them and slowly move out on our own."

Vanessa was not satisfied. "That's not what you said to me when we met by ourselves."

She continued her interrogation. "How much do you earn?"

"I earn about $1000 every month," he said.

"What investments do you have?" she persisted.

"I have two properties and a few investments in the market," he told her.

"What if I wanted to settle down with you in some other country?"

"Yeah, we can do that," he allowed.

"How about you going to Canada and then we can get married and move?" she asked him.

"I can do that," he said.

"That's good. I wanted you to settle down in another country!" she said. "Will you allow me to pursue my career and higher education after marriage?"

"Yes, I certainly will," Richard said.

"I wanted to do my doctorate in education."

"Oh! That's great," he said.

Now Vanessa was all in. "I don't know to cook. How will you manage your food?"

"Well, if we stay initially with my parents, you will have a chance to learn from my Mom."

"What if I don't learn from your Mom?"

"Not a problem, my Dad cooks every now and then. I should not have a problem with that,"

"Will you let me buy another piece of property in my hometown?" she queried.

"Absolutely, I will be with you in all of your pursuits," he assured her.

"When do you think you can make it to Canada?"

"Maybe six months from now," he said.

"Do I have to ask permission from you for everything?" she asked.

"No, you don't have to," he said.

"What if I don't like to live with your parents?"

"We need to learn to love and honor each other's parents," he insisted.

"Well, I don't know about that. First, you go to Canada and then we will see what the next thing to do will be," she said.

The cousins observed that Richard seemed uncomfortable and sweaty. He had tried his best to satisfy her with his answers. The cousins felt empathetic towards Richard and suggested to Vanessa not to push her agenda on him. The contents of the meeting eventually got reported to one of the paternal aunts, Aunt Rene, a matronly figure who felt it was her bound duty to put some sense into her young niece's head. The aunt had noticed some red flags across the whole conversation and made her own assessment of the two without knowing them in person. She was sure that the questions Vanessa posed were more about what she was looking for in a committed relationship than about Richard.

*

The concerned Aunt Rene wondered about her niece's inner dynamics and what they meant to the future success of married life. Why would Vanessa want her spouse to settle outside her own country when both of them were doing well locally? Why is the young man submitting to all these questions and not asking any himself? Is he so desperately focused upon getting her that he is not showing his true self? Or is he so dumb that he had no questions and is totally infatuated with her? Why is Vanessa not treating him with the respect that another human being deserves? Why is

Richard allowing her to mistreat him? Doesn't he know the difference between true love and hidden inner baggage?

Aunt Rene took it upon herself to reach out to the young couple, meeting each separately and engaging them in some hard conversation. Vanessa felt intruded upon by Aunt Rene. She thought that, at the age of 27, she was capable enough to make her own decisions and choices. She was enjoying all the attention, phone calls, visits, gifts and outings with Richard, and she was confident that she had her man in her control.

Richard acknowledged to Aunt Rene the feeling of being pushed and talked about his efforts to migrate to Canada. He was realistic about the difficulties he would face in marrying Vanessa. He did not want to move away from his hometown and from the people he loved, but he would do so for her. Now in his early thirties, he was beginning to feel he was too old for the marriage market, and he wanted to get married to Vanessa by hook or by crook. He also felt that if he did not agree to go to Canada, she might turn him down.

The cousins contributed their own viewpoint. There were many hidden dynamics among the cousins that Vanessa and Richard were not aware of. They thought that Vanessa wanted to be superior to the rest of her cousins living in India. Since some had settled outside the country and she could not emigrate on her own, they believed she was pursuing her desire through her potential husband. Being young themselves, the cousins did not see the need to seek help from the older adults in the primary and extended family.

*

About fifteen months after they first met, Richard appeared for various exams and pursued the move to Canada. As soon as they had solid plans for Richard to emigrate to Canada, they decided to get engaged. Engagement is typically a family affair in India. The two families make an official and public declaration that their children are engaged to one another. Official engagement allows young people an opportunity to meet and do outdoor activities together. Unfortunately, Richard's emigration plan fell through after two weeks of engagement.

Richard and Vanessa continued to meet and pursue romantic activities, but there was more discord between them over the issue of Canada. The family, meanwhile, prayed that they would be able to move through this phase and learn to discover and share true love hidden in their hearts.

*

Vanessa cut Aunt Rene off for intruding into her love relationship and simply stopped communicating with her, but Aunt Rene was one of those individuals who would not take "NO" for an easy answer. She decided to approach the pastor for help. A pastor is the leader of a Christian community who also gives advice and counsel to people under his jurisdiction. One of the duties of pastors is caring for the flock by teaching them. The pastor was more than happy to exercise his pastoral ministry in such a personal way. Since the pastor knew both the families, he had no difficulty inviting Richard and Vanessa for a personal meeting with him.

The pastor personally came to the door to welcome Richard and Vanessa into his office. The pastor's office was, in effect, a small chapel and a sacred space for him to pursue activities of holiness. His office was neatly organized and depicted his choices and beliefs in the Catholic Church. On the left side of the table was a huge book of canon law and Vatican II documents. Right above his head, behind the chair, hung a huge crucifix on the wall. To the left side, in the corner of the room, was a statue of the Virgin Mary with a little lamp at her feet. Richard and Vanessa felt recognized and grateful to be personally meeting a man of importance in the community. He was kind and welcoming.

"Look at the two of you. Aren't you awesome together?" said the excited pastor.

The two young people shyly exchanged subtle smiles as they sat.

"How are the two of you doing?" the pastor asked.

"Very well, Father," they replied in unison.

"It's been four months since your engagement, uhhh...." he continued.

"Yeah, the time simply flies," Vanessa replied.

"What are your plans for the wedding? Have you decided on the dates?" he continued.

Richard looked at the floor and gave Vanessa a chance to

handle the questions. "No, Father, not yet," she said. "Our families have been making some suggestions, but we haven't finalized anything."

"How sure you are about wanting to get married to each other? Uhhh..." he queried, knowing full well all the background information he'd been given by Aunt Rene, but he didn't want to disclose this to the couple.

Vanessa looked at Richard and passed off the question with a smile, waiting for him to respond to the awkward question.

"Yeah, Father, want to get married soon," said Richard.

"Have you looked at the dates for marriage preparation courses?" he asked them.

"Not yet, Father," said Richard, unable to meet his eyes.

"Is there something or anything I can do? I am here to help. Let me know...ummm," said the pastor.

Vanessa cut in. "No, Father, there's nothing," she said quickly. Vanessa continued to believe the issues between them were solely their own personal responsibility.

"We will, Father. Sure, if we need anything..." added Richard.

"Well, both of you have had some time to get to know each other," the pastor said. "I hope you did spend some time together? Do you think you have fallen in love with each other?"

Both Richard and Vanessa looked at each other and smiled at this. There were a few moments of silence before Vanessa dared to take the question.

"Sometimes we feel we are and sometimes we feel we are not," she said.

The pastor was curious. "Will you explain that to me? When do you feel you are in love?"

"When we go out for dinner, movies or an outing ...it all looks good and full of love," she said.

"And when do you think you are not in love...uhhh," he continued.

"When we talk about our life plans, jobs and other issues like that," she said.

"That's serious stuff...uhh," the pastor said. He was sober and continued, "Let's get to some serious issues now. Are you looking to one another to love you or are you looking to share the love you have in your heart for the other?"

"I didn't understand that, Father," said Vanessa.

"Let me explain," he said. "It's very important. Are you looking for Richard to love you the way you want him to, or are you here to share the love you have in your heart for Richard?"

"I don't know, Father," said Vanessa.

"Good, that's a good place to start," he said. "If you don't know, you need to find out, right?"

There was silence.

"Well," the pastor continued, "Let's make a list of things we need to find out before we get into the serious matter of marriage." The pastor pulled out a clean sheet of A4 size paper and a pen. He got a thick book to use underneath as a writing board.

"Let's brainstorm together and come up with a worksheet that will help both of you to do some soul searching and to know if you are ready to transform your initial attraction into love and love into marital commitment," he said.

Richard and Vanessa looked at the wall, floor and at the pastor's desk. For the first time since the conversation began, they did not look at one another.

After a few scratches and sketches on the paper, the three were ready with the initial worksheet draft. The pastor made two copies of the worksheet and handed them over to the young man and woman sitting in front of him. He allowed a few moments of silence to help them read through the worksheet, which listed the following questions:

- What does love mean to me?
- How and when do I feel loved by someone?
- What will I do when I feel unloved?
- What do I do to express my love towards the other?
- Do I think I have enough love to share with the other one?
- How do I generate and maintain my capacity to love self and others?
- How will love look different in our 20s, 30s and 40s?
- In changing experiences of life, what will I hold onto in myself and the other one?
- What elements of love can never be taken away from me, no matter what?
- Am I open to evolving love as life unfolds, or do I have a

- fixed idea about how love should look all throughout my life?

"Uhhh...How do you feel?" he asked the couple.

"Fearful, Father," said Richard.

"You've taken away all the romance from love and it looks nothing but scary—and hard work," replied Vanessa.

Well, I think that's enough for today," said the pastor. "Take the questions to your heart. Search for answers within you. If you feel like talking together, do it. If you want to talk to a trusted friend or family member, do it. If you want to come back to me, do it. Umm..."

"Yes, Father, thank you!" they replied together. Richard dropped Vanessa off at her home and went his own way.

*

Vanessa placed the worksheet on her desk. She did not want to look at it, nor at the difficult questions in it. She was afraid of the answers she would have to find within. As soon as she worked up the courage to read through the questions, she remembered the phone calls she needed to make, or the chores she needed to complete. It had been two weeks since the visit with the pastor, and since then, she had refused to go out with Richard.

Richard carried the folded worksheet in his pocket for two weeks. At work or leisure, he glanced through the questions and tried to scribble a word or phrase next to one or more questions. He realized that love is serious work and was afraid of losing Vanessa. He had hoped marriage would solve their problems and that after marriage, Vanessa would settle down and accept him and life situations as they arise. He was not happy about their meeting with the pastor. Secretly he blamed the meeting and the pastor for Vanessa's refusal to see him since.

Feelings of fear and doubt have invaded their minds. They are both trying to deal with their personal feelings. They feel vulnerable and reluctant to open up to one another, to a friend or to a family member. They respectively hold some guilt and blame in their hearts for having come so far, and yet not far enough--to still be questioning the future or their love and marriage. What if they are not capable of happily married life? What will others think of their failed engagement? Will they be able to use their relationship to grow in love and freedom that comes from true love? The seeking has begun

Pardon Me

by P.A. O'Neil
Washington

"Pardon me, but I believe you dropped this?"

Marta jumped at the sound of the man with the German accent seeking her attention. She pulled her nose out of the book she was reading, remembering to place her hand in-between the pages so as not to lose her place.

"Oh, I'm sorry. I didn't mean to frighten you. I just wanted to know if this glove was yours."

She peered at the piece of blue-gray suede held level with her eyes by the tall, slender man with a pencil-thin mustache standing in front of her. He smiled with closed lips, eyebrows raised as he waited for an acknowledgement.

"Oh," she said as she lifted the hardback book to confirm the glove did indeed match the one in her lap, "Yes, it is mine. I must have dropped it while I was reading." She took the limp piece of leather from his hand, and with a demure smile, thanked him for the return of her lost article.

"I walked past here about ten minutes ago. It was lying on the ground then. When I returned and found it still at your feet, I knew you would probably be missing it. My name is Hans, by the way, Hans Nikol." He tipped his fedora and extended his right hand.

Marta's lips moved as if to speak, but no sound emerged. She blushed when she took his hand and stammered, "M-Marta Dowling." She gave a small giggle, but quickly followed with a firmer tone, "My name is Marta Dowling. It is nice to make your acquaintance, Mr. Nikol. I guess I was deeply engrossed in my book."

"It's what I thought when I saw you the first time, I mean, you were still reading when I returned on the path. Not that I was staring at you or anything like that," he added. "If you don't mind, I'd like to know what has your attention so rapt."

"It's called *Gone with the Wind*, by an American woman named Mitchell." She turned the book over so he could see the writing on the spine. Marta looked up into his face, hoping to see a like appreciation for the story.

"Oh, yes, they made a motion picture from this book. In fact, I believe it is playing at the cinema on Diamond Street." Hans put his hands in his pockets and turned slightly as if to leave, but stopped and spoke as if it were an afterthought, “I have been meaning to see that film. I might even go tonight.” He returned his gaze to her face and inquired, “Have you seen it yet?”

Again, she parted her lips as if to speak, but closed them to offer a soft smile instead. Marta hoped his question meant he might want to spend more time with her. She had to be sure, “No, I haven’t seen it yet, but I think I would like to—maybe even tonight.”

“The film is a long one, so it starts earlier than usual movies.”

She frowned not understanding his implication. “Oh, that doesn’t leave much time for me to go home and prepare.”

Hans smiled as he removed his hat and extended his hand. “I think you look wonderful just the way you are. If we leave now, we can take a small supper at the bistro across the street from the theatre.”

Marta picked up her book and clutch to cradle them in one arm. She placed her free hand on his open palm and rose to stand close enough to catch a whiff of his cologne. “Magnificent idea. Shall we go?”

He replaced his hat, cocked at a slight angle, and repositioned her hand into his crooked arm. “Yes, shall we, indeed.

“You know, I have to admit that I wanted to talk to you the first time I walked through the park. Your glove still lying on the ground, when I returned, gave me the perfect excuse to open a conversation.”

Together they strolled out of the park, chatting about trivial things, enjoying each other’s company when Marta abruptly stopped, pulling his arm back, her smile turning to shock.

“What is it? Did I offend you with my confession?”

“No—my gloves!”

He patted her hand. “Don’t worry, my dear, I’ll buy you a new pair,”

A Play

by Timothy Naslund
Florida

An utterance, that's all it was. An utterance, a spark, a flicker of flame on parched kindle. Dried to the edge of combustion – fire upon contact, the outcome of your prolonged absence. The utterance of your name being enough of a catalyst to induce a burn; a stranger sharing your name spoken in conversation I overhear, and I'm jarred from contentment, feeling trapped in my seat, my gaze lost in the heated dance of flame, affixed until its inexorable extinguishment.

It was a lady in white who shared your name. Gold prisms dangled from each lobe, her cheeks blushed a scarlet tone, her lips reddened, looking up from the familiar call to her company of friends on what seemed a night-out in the direction where the shrieking subway car roared nearer, she shared your name in all of her suppleness. But to compare you two would be to compare the midday sun to the lambent end of a candlelight shielded by the soft radiance in the wake of its battle with encompassing darkness, the ever-looming presence of an exasperated breath from a lonely man being a threat to the latter and inconsequential to the other. Be it as it may, her tendency to bite with her two front teeth her bottom lip in earnest attentiveness toward her brunette friend in a devil's red dress, the loose, strands of hair falling from behind her ears and into her face, and the cocked imbalance of weight she put on one side of her hip echoed to the branded image I have of you in my mind that seems frivolous to believe it would ever fade.

How long has it been – almost two years since our divorce? Yes, the date was nearing toward that woeful memory remembered in vague and painful stabs to the sternum, puncturing my lungs and heart, every attempt at a breath being drowned by the overbearing effects of both my desire for rectification and the burden of self-loathing, heartbroken sorrow. (Why did I have to be on this subway car, out of them all, to hear that piercing name, to render me such a pitiful state of perfervid pieces?)

Fate: the most elusive yet trifling temptress.

The night, now scorched from a passing moment, astray from its expectance, diverted away from what was once assumed to be just a blissful evening spent watching a show at a newly renovated playhouse to now a subway ride – filled with brooding animosity toward my own sudden restless state of fervent, reminiscent thoughts – becoming all the more unbearable with each passing second. With every word the young lady in white spoke, most likely the same age as when you and I first thought of tying the colloquial knot, I had to restrain myself from getting up and moving to the next car over, to avoid hearing that poly-syllabic name uttered one more time. Truth be told however, beyond the stricken pain I felt unearth itself with every memory coming to life behind my affixed pupils, I reveled in the undulating nature of fate's pendulum swinging you back into my life.

As I stepped off the subway, I imagined I would see you standing there, heading to the theatre as I was, alone, where our focus would undoubtedly be ushered to one another, a beacon guiding our eyes to meet, and for all I care the world could then cease its incessant spinning (leave me there, trapped in that moment, with all of its glorious ambiguity). You weren't there, however, and at that moment I knew the night and however many nights after would be plagued. The subway jerked forward, taking the genesis of such an infection along with it. The claws of the cold night air intruded down into the depths of the terminal, chilling the metal handrail leading to the numbered exits that would lead me to the playhouse, only a walking distance away from where I was. I fastened the buttons to my coat, pushed through the cold metal of the subway's turnstile, and removed a pair of wool gloves from each of my coat's pockets, anticipating the late evening's frigid embrace, bitter from the sun's nightly absence.

The wind was dead, so the cold air was not so torturous, yet it was still reassuring to know I only had to walk a couple of blocks before I was once again surrounded by the warmth of walls and moving bodies. Upon the sight of the busying streets illuminated by storefronts, street lamps overhead, and the alternating of white and red car lights, an orchestra of light that embodied the city's emblazoned nature, mirroring our starry spectators up above, I thought about the time we spent the weekend at your father in law's farmhouse upstate. We sat facing the remaining ember of a fire, your legs curled between mine, your head pressed against my collar-bone, remarking on how well of a job the stars lit up the night sky on their own. Most of your family members were asleep and the ones that were still awake took refuge from the persistent mosquitoes inside the screened in porch, where we occasionally heard one of your uncles or cousins yell in victory as they hugged a pile of multicolored chips toward their burning cigarette and half empty glass of rye. This was in our second act, a few months succeeding our first reencounter and eventual recommitment to one another – a phoenix reborn in flames, the aftereffects now smoldering in the fire pit a foot away while we spoke into each other's eyes, letting our lips form the words before our minds could guard them with any pretense. It was in these moments where I felt like my life belonged to you, not out of any force belonging to me, but from an ominous decree of something I felt compelled to abide to, intoxicating me with the desire for your ardor and the reciprocation of such desires. You asked me if I could name one of the stars what I would name it and I was unable to find a name worthy for such a question, and it was left at that.

My mind wandered back to the present just in time to notice I was in front of the luxurious building faced with a giant billboard of the featured play: a tragedy set in romanticized times of dressing gowns and rapiers hilted at the side of feverish men, the autonomous churning of my legs bringing me to my destination while my infected mind carelessly indulged in the tortuous stimulant that is nostalgic reminiscence. I remembered I was meeting colleagues, and a friend of old fashion who preferred waiting outside rather than going in alone greeted me, walked up to me wrapped in her familiar double-breasted wool coat and a velvet, modern styled cloche I hadn't seen on her before. We were still waiting for three more to complete our party, but she assured me that they should be arriving at any moment now; they had informed her they were in a taxi currently on their way.

"How are things with you?" Joselyn asked. The crowd of people forming around the entrance of the theatre steadily increased.

Before I had a chance to answer, however, a silver taxicab opened its doors and out stepped Brian, Guillermo, and Viviane. Brian paid the driver the fare and Viviane waved charismatically toward Joselyn and me, her bare legs exposed to the cold air underneath a black lace tapered dress ending just short of her knees. She trotted toward us in thin heels, Joselyn closing the gap by meeting her halfway and embracing her in a warm-felt hug. I followed behind, smiling and extending my hand out to Guillermo, walking behind Viviane, who pulled me in for a more cordial embrace. Guillermo and Brian wore matching black ties, but Guillermo wore a cornflower blue shirt, buttoned up to where the collar closely hugged to his neck, while Brian wore a more somber, less energetic blue.

The five of us exchanged pleasantries and after remarking on the wind picking up, we decided to migrate into the theatre to claim our reserved seats. The vestibule to the theatre was lavishly adorned with ornate drapes bordering the translucent windows at each of the entrance door's sides. A thick slab of marble laid smoothen out horizontally, cut in a squared partial toroid, where two employees sporting matching tuxedos stood behind the counter recording names and handing out the reserved tickets to the elegantly dressed patrons. We all walked up to the reception, and Joselyn gave the younger of the two men her name. After finding her name, the man handed Joselyn five tickets, which she promptly passed out along to the rest of us as to not be responsible for losing such valuable pieces of flimsy paper.

We went to go see our seat and were delighted to see our orientation to the stage at a perfect distance. People were still shuffling into the theatre and most people wouldn't be sitting for at least another half hour, so everyone decided it would be best to enjoy a little time at the inside bar toward the west side of the playhouse.

I thought a drink would do me good, perhaps rejuvenate my spirit after the subway ride. How your essence lingered, every bit clinging to anything passing my eyes that could remotely invoke a modicum of a memory of you. Fortunately for us, a large enough table was empty and within the time it took for us to sit down, remove out coats, place them on the backs of our chairs, and check our watches to make sure we knew just how long we could indulge in becoming inebriated, a waitress greeted us and took our drink orders, leaving with the same jubilant smile she approached with. Our drinks came shortly after. Not a fan of liquor as it has the tendency to lie dormant and upon a later time in the night awaken in either drowsiness or worse, nausea without much if any forewarning, I was the only one who ordered a pilsner, its head foaming just beyond the mouth of the curvaceous glass. Joselyn and Viviane ordered red and white wine respectively, and both Brian and Guillermo ordered whiskey sodas, donned with two oversized ice cubes and a wedge of orange clinging onto the rim of the drink.

We were all around the same age, Guillermo being the youngest by two years and Joselyn being our eldest. We all worked in the same office, five of around two dozen brokers for stocks and foreign exchange, first becoming friends based on the proximity of our ages and desks to one another. We've all been working together for almost a year now, Brian and I being the longest tenure of the five of us. Viviane followed shortly after, then came Joselyn, and finally Guillermo, a newly graduate from the university which Brian was an alumnus to.

Naturally, after spending so much time together, Brian and Viviane began becoming intimate, first hiding it from everyone, grabbing at each other in short bursts of time of solidarity throughout the office, whether it alone in the break room, stair well, or the parking lot after they believed everyone had left for home, but by the time Guillermo was hired, their love interest surfaced to the open public and the thrill to hide their affair faded, leaving a mutual interest in one another that blossomed into their current, stable relationship.

I thought them to be a good match, too. Even now, sitting here, finishing our first round of drinks hastily to sneak in a second and hopefully a third before we were ushered to our seats, I caught glimpses of the two sitting to my right stealing little glances at one another, their enthusiasm not able to be restrained and held at bay without these moments of tottering discipline, both pairs of eyes communicating passion in frequencies they both were all too familiar with from the time they've spent investing into one another. Brain blindly reached and held Viviane's hand as he continued talking about an agitated client who kept calling him all afternoon, which he had to try his best to calm down and eventually averted his attention in another potential avenue for his investments. They both were outspoken, always wanting to steer the table's conversation which they did a fine job volleying the duty back and forth most nights we were all together.

Joselyn sat across from me, tipping the wine glass up to her nose until the last bit of the savory liquid met her lips. Already painted a dark hue, the wine stained her top lip further, accentuating the whiteness in her teeth whenever she bared them in moments of uninhibited laughter. Unbeknownst to the others, we had recently shared in a spell consisting of an inebriated exchange of a series of silent blinks leading to a complete lapse of any sense of consequence. On the night that this spell was casted upon us, it was originally planned as an outing for the five of us, yet only Joselyn and I were able to make it, and seeing how we had already made the trek to the restaurant, we decided to spend the night together, leading to a morning of waking up to the unfamiliar heat of another's body pressed up against one's own and a thrown-about bed sheet, barely covering her and my own bare chest.

The clarity of realizing I had woken up in a different bed than the one I originally planned to retire that night always violently struck me in the morning as the feeling of separating myself from the situation grew paramount in my desires, but waking up and seeing Joselyn's messy nest of hair and makeup-less face brought on a different, new sensation I was unaccustomed to feeling and had only ever felt for you. Discomfort still manifested itself between us underneath the bed sheets, but not from the outcome of the night spent tangled in one another's legs and musk, but rather from the unknown of what was to occur when both parties were awake and if there would be a mutual outlook on such an unexpected morning. I sat up in the bed, and within seconds of such thoughts lapping around my head, she turned over to her side, reaching towards me, and told me to get back under the covers – she wasn't ready to start the day, and so, without any reluctance, I followed her orders.

After dozing in and out of sleep, changing positions within the bed whenever we felt the need to explore each other in a different way, feeling different parts of our skin rub against one another, and occasionally indulging in our intimacy both vocally and physically, we stayed in her bed long until the afternoon, where eventually her mother's repeated phoning managed to make Joselyn reluctantly respond to the consistent vibrating buzz from the nightstand, marking the ending to our morning affair. She peeled herself from my arms and the bed covers, and paced back and forth in front of a dresser centered with a semi-circular mirror overlooking where I laid, a naked spectator to Joselyn holding the phone to her ear, aimlessly teetering from one end of the mirror to the next, looking more beautiful than I had ever saw her before. In her purest form, not bothering to pick up even one of the articles of clothing strewn about on the floor, marking a path from the doorway where we ravaged the clothes off each other's bodies, she carelessly played in her messy hair, curling frizzled strands around her finger only to let them go and have them fall straight. She hung up the phone and caught me staring at her. With a playful turn of her head she walked toward her bathroom, her hips bouncing from side to side in an emphasized manner. She then turned around before entering the brightly lit, linoleum tiled room and asked if I was going to sit in bed all day or was I going to come take a shower.

Reminiscent of the persistent steam lingering throughout the shower and even after as it clung to the bathroom's mirror, I left her apartment with a dopamine induced smile stuck between nose and chin along with the uncertainty of the next day. Nothing else was spoken besides friendly goodbyes and a slightly awkward departing kiss – our engagement too forceful, but not from the anticipated departure, but more of an excuse for our ardor to once again collide between overzealous lips – still not enough, however, to stagger the elation I was enveloped in until I reached my car, feeling the heat absorbed in by the black steering wheel bite back at my palms as I autonomously placed my hands on it. It soon began to melt away.

Fast forward to the present, she caught me staring again, this gaze not resembling the look from that night, however, and like clockwork, evoked from a peripheral sound of a phrase spoken by an adjacent table, you pierced through the barricade of suppressed emotions and clouded my attention and thoughts with the aspiration of your presence. How devastating, just the conception of a thought with a smudge of your blemish can be; this crippling power you possess while being so distant, so unknowing, seems like an enigma I will keep strenuously trying to solve in jest – torturous, poetic jest. She smiled at me, crashing me back down from my tortuous thoughts to the present, and I meagerly responded with a cheap smile. I hoped she couldn't read the distress in my eyes and perhaps interpret it toward herself. The fact is, on the drive from Joselyn's, the magic surrounding me seemed to dissipate the further I drove away from her apartment complex, onto the highway, and toward my lonely apartment. It was nothing she did, nothing that was provoked by some minute detail that can send the precious image of a lover into a spiral of eventual reluctance and doubt. And even though you weren't in the forefront of my thoughts as you currently are as we all polished away at our drinks, silently and modestly racing to the bottom of each glass, I can only surmise that it is you who erased the magical aura surrounding me, replacing it with stale air, poisonous afterthoughts that billow into a hovering cloud of doubt and pessimism (selfishly, you left her with no chance). The culprit, the fire starter, you always did like to meddle.

At work, Joselyn and I agreed without speaking that it would be best to keep our affair out of view from anyone's eyes, and perhaps, it seemed, even our own. I remember halfway through the week following that lovely morning, Joselyn invited me over, just me. We talked, drank some wine, slept together, and on the surface, everything seemed resolved – this was only for us and for now it would stay within these walls – but I did feel guilty every time I checked my phone for the time, or looked over at Joselyn lying next to me to see if she were already asleep. It was not that I wanted the day to end any sooner, but rather I was afraid my disposition toward Joselyn would take a turn for the worst from some irrational correlation to an action or subtle behavior belonging to you that I would have inevitably perceived as detrimental to my feelings for her. I was on edge, terrified of the unknown workings of my mind and wished I could redirect the ardent bliss I gambled all on you to her, yet I was at your mercy, unrelenting as it was.

I need to stay in the present, I thought to myself. No more tremulous thoughts that can spoil this night shall be provoked, I've mulled on it long enough. Helpless words, I sadly admit.

Halfway through our third round, we all agreed we would have to finish our drinks off quickly if we were to make sure we were seated once the show began. I went to go pay the bill (we had an alternating payment system for our alcohol filled nights and I was up to bat tonight). Joselyn casually waited for me to finish signing the bill and walked alongside me out of the amber lit bar and into the overbearing brilliance of the vestibule. The others went on ahead (I vaguely caught a glimpse of the back of Brian's head as they were being ushered into their seats) and Joselyn and I walked toward the curtained entrance at a slow pace, either to not make the other feel any anxiety to depart their moment alone or to enjoy one's company before eventually reuniting with our party. I was unsure which reason was slowing my walk to a crawl and I was unsure of Joselyn's reason, though she did privately embrace my hand hanging intimately close to her own as our steps fell in unison, dancing her fingers along my open palm, softly pinching my thumb's nail, provoking a smile and a reciprocation of my own groping at her turquoise nails and supple appendages. Upon entering the theater area, we both stopped our childlike courtship and caught eyes with Viviane and saw two seats to her left, dark and empty. Joselyn and I were fortunate our friends didn't separate our clandestine desire for sharing our warmth (unexpectedly, she valiantly stole this moment from you, my dear).

It was one of tragedy, soaked in melodrama – a saturation point I found quite extreme, yet eerily familiar – where the lead male character's love interest gets torn from his ardent grip and he himself faces a tragic death, the ending not in the least bit ambiguous, but still entertaining theatrical fodder to chew on during a cold evening. The play went on and captured our attention for most of its duration (towards the descent into the third act the play started to lose its footing, but it was able to regain itself after a much anticipated confrontation between the protagonist and his lover's father, utterly despondent to their impassioned romance). Around that time, Joselyn felt comfortable enough, shrouded by the blanket of darkness covering the audience to casually lean her shoulder into mine, a small physical interaction that I knew sufficed neither of our desires but was enough to temper our fires to not engulf us in our seats in robust fashion.

I felt Viviane's head turn over towards us, her senses picking up on Joselyn's and my magnetic fields intertwining, but unable to confront Joselyn in private with enough evidence, she stole glances, her eyes taking into account the little details of Joselyn's hands in relation to mine, the orientation of our shoulders and heads, any syncopated mannerisms we displayed. I paid the glances no mind. I didn't concern myself with her intrusive manners in our affair, I was not being secretive for everyone else not to know our interest in one another, but rather to protect ourselves, considering, in a moment of honest reflection, how fragile my sense of loving is as I am crippled by the parasitic memory of you burning my flesh every time my hands run down another woman's soft, convex ribcage to her waist, burning my eyes upon each woman that falls underneath my biased gaze, waning in the radiance that emits from every fresh and faded memory I have of you, burning and burning me until the day I am simply ash to be blown away at the will of your prevailing winds.

That day was on the first day of a cold front, marking the seasonal change in temperature, the air crisp with the freshness of the chilling wind, the leaves rustling in the trees louder than usual, applauding their vigilance through the sweltering summer and their transition to a more festive color that they were now sporting. I was poking at a fire kindling in the pit behind my parent's house when you came up behind me and first spoke about wanting a divorce. Your words became muttered, crashing into one another due to my inability to process the meaning they were trying to convey. There seemed to be a roadblock of incomprehension protecting me from breaking down at that moment, and I kept poking at the fire as you spoke to me, coolly. All the nights where we fell asleep, resting our heads on pillows of animosity toward one another, waking up with stiff necks and shortened conversations over breakfast, I thought our quarrels were one's of passing and not little tears that would eventually lead to our permanent disconnection. The love you had for me seemed to be no more, a monument crumbled to the ground, it's rubble recycled and used for other building purposes, the ground it once laid on repaved, the memory of the monument long forgotten, yet the statue I built of you seemed impenetrable to such drastic renovations – the destruction of it seemed to lead to ramifications too painful to endure. I remember I stayed outside that entire night, even after you told me to not act this way and to come to bed, I stayed even long after the fire was extinguished, only moving when my father came out to me the next morning, telling me that you had left, packed your bags, the only trace of you left being the engagement ring and wedding band I gave you lying on the bathroom counter along with a broken, snapped hair band.

An ending soaked in blood, the protagonist laid in a pool of some thick, unidentifiable darkened liquid that appeared too sticky to be real blood, his life leaving him with each passing syllable gasped in his final soliloquy. And then, both fortunately and coincidently death came at the end of his monologue. The last scene: the reprieve of the father's initial iniquitous disposition of the ill-fated protagonist, crying to the heavens for the life of his beloved daughter and future son-in-law. The audience was insufferable. The tiresome sound of people rifling through purses and pockets for tissues to wipe away tears reverberated throughout the play hall, sniffles to stifle their body's reaction to the poor pair of lovers on stage dying for the will to love, in vain.

After the applause of the audience clamored throughout the theater, soft lights along the edges of the walls emitted just enough light for everyone to find their way to the swung open curtains opposite of the stage, and the vestibule's light billowed in and stretched as far as it could into where darkness resided for the performance's duration. We walked out, everyone discussing what we enjoyed and how we were impressed with the stage effects and the acting, especially the beloved female lead. While I found certain qualities of it lackluster and the protagonist an insufferable heartthrob, I did enjoy the play and did my part chiming in on the scenes that stood out in my memory, all of us, for the most part agreeing on the execution of the story being exemplary.

Brian and Viviane declined the invitation of going to a nearby bar for an overture of clinking mugs of beer and the battle of conversations over the speakers of music pumping out overhead and insisted they must get home and have an early night. Guillermo followed suit, remarking on how tired the play left him and how he didn't wish to take a cab alone, seeing how he lived on the way to Brian and Viviane's. Leaving Joselyn and I outside the evacuated theater, we said our goodbyes and watched our friends crawl into a nearby parked cab, merging into the myriad of blinking lights heading westbound. We were once again alone, and I looked over to Joselyn and asked if she had taken the subway as well.

"I took a cab. Would you like to get one?" She said, holding onto my arm.

I do not wish to indulge further on what had transpired after accepting such a passive invitation. My mind, just as it was in that moment and for the entire night, masked with all my efforts by claiming that the play left me pensive – an excuse to cover up my evident disconnect from the blissful atmosphere that previously enveloped us, was elsewhere. On the surface, we had a lovely evening and culminated it with an equally loving night. As consistent as your treacherous infliction to my soul, I was utterly bemused and beside myself that what I wanted most when lying next to Joselyn, a band of sweat evaporating off my forehead and along the small of her back, my fingers walking up and down her spine as she laid on top of me, her head nuzzled into my chest, was to know where you were in that moment, and if I was even a passing thought in a single moment – a breath – in your days. Lapses in my shielded state exposed my wandering mind, and on two separate occasions Joselyn voiced her concern, prompting me to assure her that it was just the play, all that blood and the unfortunate fates of the young man and woman, that was the reason, and she seemed to either believe me or consolidate her worrying inwardly. Meekly, I hadn't even the strength to warn her, for in my weakness, this exchange of emotional investment, diluted and tainted as it was on my end, came as a temporary relief. And I was aware that my intimate transgressions would eventually be exposed by my insincerity (I do wish it simply weren't the case), opening new wounds for me to mend at a later, more crippled time, but for now, the temporary relief was enough.

Glimpses of the Future

by Archit Joshi
India

The humongous line of readers spilled out of the hall. All those faces waiting eagerly to get their copies signed, waiting to interact with the author of the book they'd enjoyed so much... it all seemed unrealistic. Vivaan sat beside Aarushi, mechanically repeating his motions of smiling, signing copies, beckoning to the next person. The event had turned out to be everything they could've ever hoped for and more. And yet, something was amiss. He'd definitely woken up on the wrong side of the bed today.

The book had been a real struggle. Titled 'A Visit Inside', it tackled the trite notion that the answers you seek are always hidden inside you, unlocked only through experience and certain heartbreak; shrouded underneath years and years of wrong decisions, fears and hopes. She had been worried all her sweetheart's gusto would be crushed under the critics' reproach that the plot was derivative. But he'd come through with an avant-garde style that made the book his own. Vivaan's viewpoint was plausibly unique, his prose, startlingly fresh.

Frankly, Aarushi thought the storyline was a lot like The Alchemist, in which Santiago the shepherd travels thousands of kilometers to the Pyramids in search of a treasure. Towards the denouement, he finds out that it was buried after all underneath the tree in the backyard of the church where he lived. But she didn't point that out. For in The Alchemist itself, Paulo Coelho has written: 'All things are one thing only.'

She was a painter herself. She knew she was in control only for the first twenty odd minutes. Then, the brush came alive and did its own work. What resulted was a painting that had her soul poured in it. But the symbolisms for love, anger, fear and all other emotions were pretty much the same everywhere. Originality is over-hyped. What distinguishes artistic endeavors is how much love the artist has for her art. That's what reflects in the work. That's what makes art compelling.

A young boy hardly fourteen years old came forth shyly and held out his copy of the book.

"Thank you, Vivaan," he said, as Vivaan signed his copy. Vivaan smiled at him.

"Hello young lad!" Aarushi said. "Tell me, what did you find

most interesting in the book?" She was intrigued by how such a deep, philosophical work could interest a mere fourteen- year-old.

"I liked how he hasn't named his hero. Always referring to him by 'The Boy' or 'He'... I felt I was the one going through the adventures. I always find names to make the hero feel different from me. But in this book, I was the hero!" The boy gave a toothy grin and pranced away, hugging his copy of the book tightly to his chest.

Aarushi smiled at Vivaan, only to be met with an exasperated gaze.

"Don't go on asking questions now, Aarushi!" Vivaan snapped, "My readers will keep me here until midnight if they see me entertaining them personally!"

The smile on her face faded. She averted her gaze.

Under the table, she moved her hand closer to his, tried to clasp it. But he brushed it away. She gave a long sigh. She was slowly slipping out of his life. She didn't know why. But it had been rocky for the last couple of weeks. Some stress she attributed to the jitters of his book launch. But apart from that, Vivaan's erratic behavior upset her.

A young woman with a curvaceous physique approached. She held out her book and smiled a charming smile. Vivaan smiled back and signed her copy. She held out her hand. He shook it, holding it just a mite longer. When the woman left, Vivaan's gaze followed her to the door. For the rest of the evening, Aarushi maintained a diplomatic smile on her face, but inside, her heart wept.

A smothering silence hung in the car as they rode back home. No words were exchanged in the elevator until they reached Vivaan's apartment. There, Vivaan all but kicked his door open, and slammed it shut behind her. An ugly glare colored his face.

"What the hell is wrong with you?"

She tried to get closer to him. She wanted to whisper sweet nothings in his ear, calm him down. But he pushed her away.

"Today was an important day for me! Why would you ruin it?"

"Whatever have I done?" Tears brimmed in her eyes, ready to tumble down her face.

"What's gotten into you lately? You're... very unlike yourself. You've become pushy, obsessive. I don't even have my own life anymore! You're just everywhere." Vivaan's face grew redder, his voice louder.

"I feel I'm losing you, Vivaan! I don't feel like I belong in your

space anymore!" she cried out, surrendering to the tears she had been holding back.

"So I've been a little into my work lately. So I'm focused on honing in my skills. Does that bother you? Don't you want me to improve? Realize my dream?"

"When have I ever come between you and your dreams?" She clutched at his shirt. "Answer me. I've put up with so much just so you could complete that idiotic book of yours!"

"IDIOTIC?"

"It's not even an original plot, Vivaan. You're a plagiarizing fraud!" Instantly, she wished she could take her words back. But they were words. They stung.

"I don't see long lines of people waiting to gaze upon your shitty paintings."

She deserved that. She took a deep breath and tried to control her sobbing. With her tone as calm as she could make it, she said, "This is getting ugly. Maybe we should get out of each other's sights for now." She looked searchingly in his eyes for a hint of the love he had for her. She found none.

"Maybe we should get out of each other's sights for good," said Vivaan, and stormed off into his bedroom.

* * *

After a particularly long shower, Aarushi came to her bedroom to find her phone flashing.

"Good night hon!" Vivaan's texts always oozed cheerful energy.

"We need to talk, Vivaan." A pause, then backspace.

"Something's bothering me, Vivaan." Backspace.

"Good night sweetie. Sleep tight!" Send.

Aarushi threw her phone on the bed, and went to dry her hair in front of a full-length mirror in her bedroom.

She unwound the towel around her head, and let her long, dark curls fall. Began drying her hair with the towel, staring into the mirror. Two concerned, green eyes bore back into hers. Her gaze went to the scar above her shoulder, along her neck.

She could remember the accident as if it had happened yesterday. It had thrown her life into a blizzard of unforeseen problems and changes.

* * *

The seven-year-old self of Aarushi was gobbling up breakfast, excited for the show the local circus was going to put up that day. It was a bright summer morning, and she couldn't finish her bowl of cereals fast enough.

Every year, *Pune Circus Company* organized their antics near her house. They would travel all the way from Pune to Hadapsar, where she lived in a small locality they didn't even mention on the map. Every year, she would visit with her Granny. She enjoyed the theatrics, yelling and screaming as the rope walkers daringly made their frightening walks. What she told no-one was that she was rather afraid of Bobo the Clown. Something about him scared her, though exactly what she couldn't pinpoint.

But that particular year, poor Granny was bedridden with the flu. Aarushi had begged and begged her father to take a leave from work to take her to the circus, but in vain. Her mother had to visit her sister in another town, and couldn't take Aarushi to the circus herself. Adamantly, Aarushi had declared she would go alone.

Kissing Granny goodbye, she ran out the house and was at the circus in no time. The next hour passed joyfully. Tez the Knife Thrower had come up with a new act, which made her sit at the very edge of her seat. The final act was that of Bobo.

Aarushi's cheer vanished as she shrank back into her seat, realizing for the first time that there was no Granny to comfort her this time. Bobo presented his antics, making people double down in laughter. Were those people idiots? Who could find this scary clown entertaining?

The clown turned to Aarushi. He saw her cowering in her chair.

"Oh, little darling, don't be scared! Come on up. Be a guest in my new act," Bobo said, bringing out a long sword from a chest in which he kept all his props.

Of course, the sword was made of plastic and bent in clever ways to make illusions more realistic. It was a classic magic trick! And around two hundred other people would've disagreed, but Aarushi thought she could see a wicked grin on the clown's face. She shook her head and pressed harder into her seat.

"Come child, come! Don't be scared," Bobo urged, moving towards her, sword pointed at her.

Leaving all thoughts of public humiliation aside, Aarushi let out a loud shriek. People laughed. A few seated behind her encouraged her to go up on the stage. The clown kept coming towards her, almost at the end of the podium now. The sword was dangerously close to her; she was seated in the very first row.

And then the lights went out.

Aarushi let out another scream and ran towards the exit. Seeing sunlight streak through the folds of the circus tent, she dashed towards it. Only when she was safely away did she slow her run to a trot. She looked back at the circus and gave a sigh.

"What a scare that cruel clown gave me!" she thought.

Then, a car came swerving around the corner and crashed into her.

For the next few weeks, nothing happened. Her heavily bandaged frame lay unmoving on the hospital bed. The worried faces of her family kept her company. Her mother, Prafula, would read to her by night if Aarushi was awake. Darsh Solanki was a distraught man, but he did his best to put his worry aside and be the gentle father he always had been. He would play Aarushi's favourite songs on the mouth-organ he was so adept at playing. Granny hadn't fully recovered yet, and refrained from visiting her dear granddaughter in her ward, lest Aarushi contract her flu and complicate things further. She'd called the hospital ward couple of times, but Aarushi had been sedated at the time.

The doctor's report declared multiple fractures to the legs, damage to the thoracic spine, bruises all over the body. And damage to the frontal lobe of the brain.

"The fractures will take about three months to fully heal," the doctor explained to Mr. and Mrs. Solanki. "Her spinal cord needs a little support for now, but it will get better with time. The primary concern for now is for her to come out of the shock. She needs very delicate handling, both mentally and physically. As for the damage to the brain..." his voice trailed off.

"What about it, Doctor?" Darsh asked, his face going pale.

"Well, the frontal and pre-frontal lobe of the brain is responsible for perceptions, imagination, motor control and other functions that aid us in routine activities. I cannot guess at the severity of the damage until a more thorough examination is conducted. But I'm afraid, even after recovery, there will be repercussions."

"Like what?!" Prafula demanded.

"Well, she may grow a little slow in her learning capabilities. Her hand-eye coordination could be hampered. Sometimes, she may behave erratically. Just support her, and don't point out to her that she's being strange. Let time do its trick. I'm not saying it's bound to happen. I'm simply stating my observations of her injuries."

With that, the doctor left them to themselves. Doubtless, he felt rather important having so much knowledge in his tiny little important brain. Aarushi's mother threw the doctor's leaving figure a sour look, and began sobbing into her husband's embrace.

Aarushi, who was under heavy sedation at the time, was oblivious to all this raucous. She didn't know the accident had changed her life forever; at least, not then.

After weeks passed, she had recovered enough to be discharged. Once home, she spent most of the time in bed, reading, eating and taking pills. So many pills! She wanted to roam free, see the world outside. She wanted to jump, to run, and watch the things that happened beyond what see could through her bedroom windows.

When all else fails, there is always art.

Confined to her bedroom, she asked her mother for some paper and crayons. At first, she began drawing mindlessly. The same old scene with the birds, the mountains, the sun.

But little by little, her paintings began to tantalize her. She began to paint intuitively, worrying not how it looked on the paper. She found she had a lot to say, and the drawings could help her express. Her pencil strokes became more and more precise, the colors deciding for themselves when and where to show up on the page.

Within two weeks, she moved from paper and pastels to canvas and oils. She asked her mother to set up the canvas near the bed so as not to strain her weak legs too much. She found herself blissfully lost in her world, skipping meals and losing sleep. She grew irritated when anyone disturbed her when she was painting. She even asked her Granny, who had gotten better from her ailment, to please leave her alone whenever she came into Aarushi's room. After a while her family let her be, content at least that their little Aarushi had diverted her attention from her tragedy.

One day, she decided she was well enough to do some running. She needed fresh air and a little exercise.

"You're *not* going outside," Prafula warned. "Do whatever you want in the backyard where I can keep an eye on you."

Sullenly, Aarushi went out in her backyard and started jogging in circles. The movement felt weird, alien. The body forgets. She kept at it, feeling the life come back to her legs.

On her third round, she felt a sharp pain creeping behind her temples. She stopped abruptly in her tracks and clutched at her head. The world around her whirled and the scene of her garden disoriented. And then, she could see herself from up above, as if she'd floated right out of her own body.

She was at the well which was located near the marketplace of her town. She was somewhere above, someone different from Aarushi. She saw two boys running towards the well, caught in a frantic game of catch. She recognized neither of the boys, but she recognized the place. She was not Aarushi, but she knew what Aarushi knew.

One of the boys, in his excitement, tripped over a rock and lost his balance. He tried to regain it by clutching at the cement wall around the well. But it was strewn with moss. The boy slipped and fell headfirst into the well.

The last thing Aarushi remembered before passing out were the boy's cries for help. When she came to, she was in her bed, burning with fever. It took a few seconds for her to register her surroundings and clear out the fog in her mind. Her mother and Granny were hunched over her, worried sick.

Then she remembered her visions.

"Mum! The poor boy! Somebody help him!"

"What boy?" Granny asked.

"He fell into the well! Send someone to help," Aarushi replied.

Right about then, Aarushi's father came into her bedroom. Bending over, he kissed her on the forehead.

"Are you alright, poor baby?" His soothing voice was a fresh change over the frightened demeanors of the other two.

"Daddy! There's a little boy in trouble near the well. Please send someone to look out for him!"

"But sweetheart, when did you ever go up to the well?"

"I... I..." Aarushi's retort remained unfinished.

When *had* she gone near the well?

But her intuition was buzzing. It was worth checking out. At the worst, it would mean a wasted trip down four blocks. She said she couldn't quite explain, that she was still a little groggy. It must have been the urgency in her tone, the angst on her face that convinced her father. He immediately went outside and set off for the well.

He returned a while later and reported there was no boy in trouble by the well.

"You're just scared, Aarushi," her mother said, tousling her hair affectionately. Aarushi was convinced, and thought no more of the matter. Another month passed. The incident never happened again. She got better with the passage of time. Everything healed, but the scar above her shoulder. That would stay; a crimson reminder of her ill-fortune.

On Tuesday mornings, Aarushi would go along with her mother to shop for groceries. She had a secret pact with an elderly vegetable seller at the market. The old lady would ply her with fresh green peas, and in exchange Aarushi would flash her cheeriest smile.

It was there that Aarushi went along with her mother three months after her accident. After the covert handover of peas with the old lady, she ran after her mother, who was bargaining for some juicy tomatoes. It was at the tomato vendor's stall that she saw two kids playing. She'd seen them somewhere but couldn't place where.

"Bye, Dad!" one of the boys shouted in glee.

"We're going near the well!" the other yelled.

The well.

On an impulse, Aarushi cried out after the two boys. They paused in their stride and turned around.

"Don't go near the well, please," Aarushi said.

"Aarushi!" Prafula scolded her. Turning to the boys, she said, "I'm awfully sorry. Don't mind her. Scoot along!"

The boys stared at the strange little girl with dark hair and green eyes for a second, then went off to play.

All through the trip home, Aarushi and her mother bickered. Aarushi maintained that she could sense trouble. Her mother remained staunch that it was all her imagination. Of course, her mother knew what Aarushi didn't: poor Aarushi had incurred damage to the brain and this was exactly the sort of behavior her doctor had warned about.

The locality where Aarushi lived was a small one. And in small communities, news spreads like wildfire. The next day, as neighbors gathered at Aarushi's house for tea and biscuits, a man started telling animatedly about an incident that had happened the day before: one of the vegetable vendor's sons had slipped and fell into the well, and had been dragged out with much heaving and chaos.

That summer, two things became very clear to Aarushi. First, she wanted to become a painter when she grew up.

Second, she was a clairvoyant.

* * *

Aarushi snapped back from her reverie to find herself standing awkwardly in front of the mirror, towel in hand. She slumped back on her bed mindlessly.

The early days had been tough. Soon after the incident of the well, her family had been struck with disbelief. For a while, the elders tried to plain ignore the elephant in the room. But that couldn't hold down Aarushi for long. She was just seven, for crying out loud! A child's curiosity never rests.

On her repeated questions and requests, they had decided to talk about it. Aarushi's father gently told her what the doctor had said in the hospital. She was horrified to learn about the damage to her brain. Why hadn't anybody told her, she wanted to know?

After years of arguments, heated discussions, grief, dissuasion on her family's part – *why can't you just forget about it all and be more normal?* – and then finally pride, Aarushi grew up a confident woman. A woman who knew what impact she could have, if she so willed. The visions became more and more frequent when she focused on them. Her town was skeptical about it. She took on the bullets of their criticism bravely.

After moving to Pune, a bigger city, she had met Vivaan in an Arts fair.

A grumpy, untidy young man with a shock of shabby hair and eyes that darted all over the place... She couldn't understand what had made her fall for him. And she didn't need to. When it's meant to be, love finds a way.

"Your paintings... They capture emotions so perfectly. I can only marvel about the hand that drew them. Just amazing!"

"Thank you," she had replied, "Do *you* paint?"

"I paint with words."

Vivaan didn't need powers of clairvoyance to know he had met The One. The blush on her face had been enough.

After a month, on a dinner date, she finally found the courage to tell him about her condition. There was no disbelief on his part. Believing in the extraordinary is a prerequisite for being a writer. He had taken her very seriously, without any hint of incredulity.

He helped her explore her condition, gave her the moral support that was crucial when she was wallowing in self-doubt. But they had survived, and she was now fully in control of the gift entrusted to her.

"A lot of good that did," she muttered to herself presently, rising from the bed. Her most recent vision at the book signing had rattled her. She needed to paint. Setting the canvas on the easel, she dipped the brush in black. It was a night to set her hand free. So, she started with the first thing that came to mind.

It was a question mark.

She began painting aimlessly. By the next half hour, she had painted two hands clasped together over the question mark.

"Yes, I must hold on," she affirmed to herself.

She decided to take a long walk. Setting the painting to dry in a corner of her room, she threw on a hoodie over her clothes and slipped into her sandals. It was getting late and the air outside was chilly. Locking the door behind her, she set off for no specific destination, arms tucked in tight around her body. After about forty minutes, she came to a park bench. She sat at the edge of the bench, lost in thought, next to a restless young man who was fiddling with something.

Could the visions have lied? They never had until now, so no reason why they should this time. Another reason she wished for them to be true was the completed, rapidly selling book Vivaan had managed to complete. Presently, Vivaan was struggling with the idea, and didn't quite know how to pursue it further. She at least knew now that he would pull through.

To disrespect her gift was unfair to Fate, which had so lovingly taken the time to intervene in her life.

The stranger next to her had his own problems to deal with. He had little mind to pay to her. But had he paid attention to her, he would've seen her eyes go terrifyingly blank, her head stoop and her body tighten.

After a while, Aarushi suddenly straightened up and turned towards him.

"Hey! You should go for it. She's going to say yes."

The man couldn't have known the stranger on the park bench was a clairvoyant. But he needed the boost and encouragement. Hearing what she had to say, his face shone brighter than the ring that was cushioned in the box he held in his hands.

* * *

They were seated in a café. Vivaan ordered coffee. Always the coffee. She couldn't for the life of her figure out what the connection was, but writers had an unhealthy affair with coffee.

"I was inspired this morning!" Vivaan gushed over his cappuccino. "Wrote ten pages. Ten! The words just flowed. The plot moved along great. The MC comes home to yet another quarrel between his parents. But he's bursting with frustration; he wants to shout, express himself, lest he explode. So, he finally finds the courage to break out of his shell and speak up. He says their constant fighting is taking toll on him; that kids in class are making fun of him; that he's become lonely. I think I've captured the emotions perfectly."

Aarushi gave a chuckle.

"What's so funny?"

"You don't remember? The first conversation we ever had, you had said these exact words. 'You've captured the emotions perfectly.' Ha!"

Vivaan didn't even make the effort to remember. He wanted to talk about his book. He was making progress. Not so tactfully, he steered the subject back to his story.

"I have named the main character 'Ronit'. Not a lot of thought went into it. I'll probably use global replace to change it later. But what do I name him?" He spun his half-empty cup absent-mindedly against the table. "Gosh! Why do Indian names carry so much meaning to their names? It puts such a pressure on us writers."

"Vivaan, here's a suggestion. Don't name him."

"What? Who doesn't name protagonists?" He retorted. "How will people connect with him?"

"Refer to him simply as 'the boy' in noun form and use simple pronouns later! *The Milkman* has this weird style of referring to characters. Perhaps you should give it a go." Aarushi knew full well it was going to work wonderfully.

Vivaan seemed uncertain at the prospect but agreed. It was better than 'Ronit' anyway.

"So, what's up with you?" he asked at length.

"Well, I'm feeling inspired as well. I painted yesterday. Our hands, fingers clasped together."

Vivaan gave a smile.

"They will stay that way, won't they Vivaan?" Aarushi asked.

He gave her a quizzical look.

"What's wrong, Aaru?"

"Answer me!"

"Of course, they will! We get each other. We're perfect for each other. Nothing can go wrong with our relationship."

His smile felt reassuring. She felt glad.

"You're so weird." He chuckled. "I love you."

* * *

It was a damp September morning. They were on their usual hike along the cliffs. It had rained the previous night, making the cliffs look lush green and refreshing.

He'd declined the hike at first. He wanted to tackle a bad case of writer's block. The protagonist simply wouldn't listen to him. The book wasn't going well.

He'd consented for the hike later- her idea for not naming his protagonist seemed to give a nice effect. Might be a stroll with her could spark something new.

But something about his girlfriend bugged him, although what he couldn't exactly say. She'd grown more obsessive, asking him irritating questions all the time. They had become inseparable, like those hopeless romantics in movies that pissed him off. 'Baby this', 'Baby that'. 'You love me, don't you?', 'Promise me you won't leave'... that kind of stuff.

Immediately after setting off for their usual path, she took his hand in hers. Man, where was the sense of boundary? But he let it be that way. He did love her after all. She seemed needier than usual, but that could be his imagination. Maybe it was the book that was giving him the creeps.

Intertwining his fingers with hers, he said, "I'm blocked."

"What's happening in the story?"

"My MC has started placing it all together. He's got it all now, his parent's pride, all the attention he didn't get in his childhood, good friends, and clear goals."

"And that bothers you because...?"

"There's no conflict! Plots don't move forward without conflicts."

"What if he realized he was made for something else? That all this success wouldn't keep him happy for long, because it was all taking him away from his identity?"

“I’ve showed his struggle for the things he wants now all through the book. How do I show this complete turn in his internal monologue?”

“Diary entries,” Aarushi replied knowingly. “Let him write his most private thoughts into a diary. Let him have some doubts from the very beginning.”

That sounded plausible.

“That’s a great idea!” What he didn’t know was that she had already seen a few diary entries in the story in one of her visions.

“Maybe add an unattainable quest for him to take on, a girl perhaps. That could set him off his path. But that’s a good sign. We often find what we need, while in pursuit of things we only think we need. That way, you could write about a revelation...” She broke off mid-sentence and rushed to the edge of the cliff. The ground there had become muddy and dangerous due to the showers the previous night. She caught an elderly woman by the arm and pushed her in the opposite direction.

“Hey! Watch it!” The woman yelled in indignation.

“Don’t go down this trail. You will fall and get hurt.”

“I was being careful.”

“You will get hurt.”

“None of your business.” The haughty woman continued defiantly down the same trail. Aarushi shrugged and returned to Vivaan and they set off to complete their walk.

As they were returning from their walk, they heard a concerned din of voices. A few people were gathered in a circle, around the elderly woman, who was whimpering in pain.

She had lost her footing and crashed to the ground.

* * *

All Aarushi could manage to paint was circles. In about twenty minutes, she had mindlessly painted about thirteen circles. After having had enough of it, she threw the brush on the floor and started pacing her room.

In alchemy, the circle is a symbol of entrapment. Draw a circle in sand, and put a wiggling snake in it. It will lay deathly still. Whether it does so out of respect or because it feels bound and captivated, Aarushi couldn’t know. She didn’t care. She certainly felt the latter. She was a wild, free creature, who had to stay still because she was caught in this circular cycle.

Vivaan was behaving irrationally, but his feelings reflected the progress of his book. The progress of his book changed course because of the insights she'd gleaned from the future. She felt neglected because all he seemed to care about was his damn book. But to not guide him just so he could pay more attention to her... would be selfish.

She chose to be selfish.

Vivaan pecked away at her cheeks as they sat lazily in his living room. They had chosen staying in and browsing Netflix, over a crowded restaurant. Aarushi said she didn't want to share him with other restaurant-going strangers.

After the movie, they sat idly on his couch. Vivaan started talking about his book. He had finally decided on a title: 'Of Hopes and Dreams, Memoirs of a Boy.'

That was rather long. 'A Visit Inside' was concise and more symbolic. But Aarushi reminded herself of her promise not to meddle.

"That sounds amazing, babe!" She lied through her teeth.

Vivaan was happy. He cooed on about how he wanted his protagonist to travel off to the unknown on a spontaneous road trip, and serendipitously realize a few hidden secrets. That, he said, would start the ball rolling and change the course of the book.

In the version she had read, the boy finds a mentor in his college who helps him find himself when he's feeling lost. She gave a sigh. Maybe he would learn it wouldn't work later. All she was interested in was preventing the fight from happening.

They spent another hour together. Then Vivaan decided he needed to get back to his writing.

* * *

Three months passed. Aarushi felt like a content, pampered kitten. She got all the attention she needed. Vivaan was making good progress, almost nearing the end of his book. To her surprise, his viewpoint worked along well, made his story more compelling than the one she'd read.

"Have you lied to me?" she asked no-one in particular, glancing up at the sky, on one of her morning walks.

She couldn't know if her visions had lied. But it had been

liberating to let things run their natural course.

She came across two women at a donut vendor's stall nearby. One of them asked the other rather pointedly why she was eating donuts, after her long sprint.

"Haven't you heard of cheat meals?" Aarushi overheard the other woman's reply. The one who had reprimanded her asked, "But won't that hamper your progress? Reset your weight charts back to square one?"

"Sometimes it's important to put yourself first, Aditi!" the 'sinner' replied.

That did it for Aarushi.

She had had her cheat meal, and it seemed to have saved her relationship. There was no reason for any gift-granting deity to be angered.

The month after that, Vivaan finished tidying up his completed manuscript and sent it off to a publisher. It came back with a little pink slip saying, 'Not quite right for us.'

"It will be published," Aarushi tried to reassure him, worried he would lose heart.

"Will be or might be?" Vivaan asked with a playful grin on his face.

"It *will* be. Not because some vision told me, but because I believe in you."

"Eh! To hell with this rejection. There are lots of publishers."

"That's the spirit. Keep on trying! I'm with you." She messed up his already unkempt hair, something he told her he hated, but secretly enjoyed.

The sixth publisher said they had loved it, and would represent him. It was slated for a winter release, that December.

December couldn't come fast enough.

"I have ignored you, haven't I?" Vivaan said on a date night.

"It's perfectly fine, Vivaan. It's important to put yourself first sometimes."

December came. The book launch went off in a grand fashion. A few months later came the call from the publisher. The one which bore details of a book signing Vivaan would have to handle, for publicity. Soon, the fateful day dawned on a nervous Aarushi and an excited Vivaan.

There were posters everywhere, displaying a beaming Vivaan holding his book titled, 'Of Hopes and Dreams, Memoirs of a Boy'.

The humongous line of readers spilled out of the hall. All those faces waiting eagerly to get their copies signed, waiting to interact with the author of the book they'd enjoyed so much... it all seemed unrealistic. Vivaan sat beside her, not allowing his repetitive motions of smiling, signing copies, and beckoning to the next person, to become mechanical. There was sincere gratitude in his eyes and he greeted every person in line with genuine warmth.

As if on cue, the young boy arrived.

"Thank you, Vivaan," he said, as Vivaan signed his copy. Vivaan smiled at him.

"Hello young lad," Aarushi said automatically. "Tell me, what did you find most interesting in the book?"

"I liked how he hasn't named his hero. Always referring to him by 'The Boy' or 'He'... I felt I was the one going through the adventures. I always find names to make the hero feel different from me. But in this book, I was the hero!" The boy gave a toothy grin and disappeared. Aarushi's heart sank.

As the boy was going, Aarushi smiled uncertainly at Vivaan, who grinned back.

"It's amazing, these observations. Maybe he'll grow up to be a writer herself," he said.

A young woman with a curvaceous physique approached. She held out her book and smiled a charming smile. Vivaan smiled back and signed her copy. She held out her hand. Vivaan barely shook it, calling out 'Next' rather curtly. The woman's disappointment was evident on her face, as she left.

"Your readers are going to make you wait until midnight, it seems." Aarushi tittered nervously.

"I won't mind! Not in the least..."

* * *

Once they were home, and it really was midnight by that time, Vivaan called for a celebration.

He went into his kitchen to bring back a bottle of champagne. Aarushi noticed one of her paintings framed beautifully on his mantel. A few spiteful words from a distant memory came to her mind:

I don't see long lines of people waiting to gaze upon your shitty paintings!

Aarushi's heart clenched. Her throat ran dry. As Vivaan came back with champagne, she threw herself into his arms and began weeping.

Vivaan held her delicately, asked her what was wrong. Aarushi narrated the events of her visions in between sobs.

"My love, you have something special in you," he whispered, kissing the top of her head. "Be reverend of it. Try your best to become an instrument of service, use your gifts to help those who feel lost. But, also pay heed to the words of my favourite professor," Vivaan said and paused like he did when he was about to make a dramatic statement.

Aarushi knew him well enough to know a lot of his favourite people were fictional characters. His 'favourite professor' was a wise old wizard, with a flowing white beard, and blue eyes adorned by horn-rimmed glasses. Vivaan echoed the wizard's words:

"It doesn't do to dwell on dreams, and forget to live."

Aarushi kissed Vivaan ardently on the lips. In his embrace, she asked herself a very important question.

Between the past, the present, and the future, which was the true place to live in?

The Lost Shoes of Paris

by Simon Clarke
United Kindom

At the main entrance to the Parc Monceau in Paris is a magnificent rotunda. Up the steps and through the columns is a set of railings. On these railings hang the lost shoes of Paris. There are children's shoes, adults' too, but never a pair. How does one shoe get left behind? At what point does someone notice they have only one shoe on? Sometimes people find their lost shoes, and sometimes the shoes find lost people...

* * *

"Marie, no! Just sit still for a few more minutes. Please." said Bernard.

Although it was only mid-morning, Marie had already had a long day, getting up at 5am for the 20 kilometre trek from her tiny bed-sit in Sarcelles north of Paris to Parc Monceau. On the metro she had noticed a man sitting across from her. His lined face looked worn and exhausted. Is that how my dad would look if he had stayed, she thought, is that why he left, to save himself from us? Marie's mother had died when she was 11. Her Grandmother had passed away a year ago and Marie still missed her. It was the only place she had felt looked after, and safe ...

"Marie, stop moaning my little cabbage," said her grandmother, whenever Marie protested doing chores. She had been sent to get a calf's foot to add to the pot. "We must have one Marie," said her grandmother. "Off you go." Time spent cooking with her grandmother had been a great comfort after her mother died.

The train jolted round a bend and shook her back to the present. She looked at her reflection and smiled at the memory. Her grandmother used to tell her she had been found in a cabbage as a baby.

"Poor little cabbage," she said to her reflection as the darkness blurred past...

Marie did not want to sit, she wanted to parade, walk elegantly and adopt sophisticated poses. She had read about such poses being adopted in Marie Claire last week. Not her own copy, of course, she couldn't afford it. She had picked it up on the Metro and spent a glorious afternoon devouring all the articles. For a short while it helped her escape the reality of struggling to make her way in Paris, alone. Oh, there were guys who would chat her up, spend time with her, but she knew it wasn't real. Her mother had taught her that.

"Look at yourself Marie," she would say. "The only reason a man is going to be interested in you is because of what you can give him, the one thing they're all after. It'll not be because you're pretty, because you're not."

"OK, Bernard, but I need to stretch my legs first."

At least he doesn't leer at me or pretend to like me, she thought, the only thing he's after is a photo.

"Come on. Just a few more minutes,' said Bernard. "The pose and the background are perfect."

Here we go again, thought Bernard. He exhaled and rubbed his face, vaguely aware his attempts to maintain fashionable stubble had failed. She seemed to be translating his ideas into really good pictures, so he would be patient. In fact, for some reason, he wanted to be patient.

"I can't. My leg hurts," said Marie.

They glared at each other. She couldn't hold his gaze. Suddenly she didn't want to be defiant, independent. Her shoulders dropped. She was tired of fighting. Her sense of security died with her gran a year ago.

"I just want to stop," she said.

"What do you mean, stop?" said Bernard. "We're nearly done."

"Oh, I don't know," said Marie, embarrassed by her outburst. Help me... she thought.

"You read too many magazines," said Bernard. "This is reality."

Marie stood up and pushed her long dark hair back from her face, "I know magazine-world is unreal Bernard. Beauty gets you all you need, troubles are cured with talking, and love conquers all. Pouf! I think beauty is how worthwhile you feel, scars will always be there and love is selfish, it decides when to come and when to go. It's not something we can just have and keep."

At this Bernard looked closely at Marie. I have scars I'm spending my life trying to mend, he wanted to say. A jogger ran past disturbing a group of pigeons nearby who clattered into the trees.

Suddenly the spell burst and the day collapsed back into focus.

"Look," he said, "Just wait and... and you can keep the shoes we have for the next shot".

Marie loved shoes. She would love to have different shoes for every day of the week. In reality Marie only had one pair of shoes she might describe as 'not bad', and certainly nothing that was in any way stylish or beautiful. She wished she was stylish and beautiful.

"Ok, but where are they from?"

"My sister Therese manages a repair shop, she gave them to me. We were talking about the photo shoot and she assured me they go with the short trousers you are wearing. They were returned because the soles were too scratched."

"By the way Bernard," said Marie, "They are not short trousers, they are cropped pants!"

Some fashion photographer, thought Marie, frowning at Bernard. Marie decided free shoes, whatever they were like, would be worth a little discomfort even if they didn't quite fit.

"Alright," said Marie.

The photo taken, Marie stood and stretched her legs. She was as tall as Bernard, taller when wearing heels. As she did so Bernard couldn't help but notice Marie's legs, and come to that, the rest of Marie. She really is quite stunning he thought and caught himself imagining how soft her cheek would feel against his lips.

"What are you staring at Bernard?" said Marie.

"Oh, err..., sorry Marie," said Bernard. "Justine, did you remember to bring those shoes with your make-up stuff?"

Make-up stuff, thought Marie, Justine won't like that. He's such a bloke. But she had to admit he had something about him.

"Yes, I have the shoes," said Justine. "Here Marie, you can try them on."

Marie walked over to Justine as she pulled the shoe bag Bernard had given her from her holdall, opened it and lifted out a shoe. The sun glinted on gold glitter cut-outs in a velvet ankle strap above the sweeping lines of a cream-lined black velvet peep-toe shoe with a red leather sole. It was the most beautiful shoe Marie had ever seen. Inside was written 'Christian Louboutin'.

Oh My God, she thought, What if they don't fit me? I hope they fit me. Are they really mine?

"Are they really mine, Bernard?" said Marie.

"Yes, I said so didn't I?" said Bernard. "What's up?"

"She can't believe it," said Justine. "If I'd have known what they were I would never have just stuffed them in my bag like that."

"What? What are you both going on about?" said Bernard. "What is she doing now?"

"Marie is crying Bernard," said Justine.

"But I thought it was a good thing to give her some shoes." Bernard realised that he really did want do something good for Marie. "My sister thought it might be a good thing to give you Marie. I described the clothes for today. And talked about you, come to think of it.'

"What did you say about me?" asked Marie.

That you are beautiful, he thought. "That you were tall, a good face, and err... eyes."

"You said I had eyes," said Marie.

"No. I mean yes," said Bernard, "and good at your job. Which you are, you know."

He's such an idiot, thought Justine. "It is a good thing," said Justine. "Don't you know what you have given her?"

"Just some posh shoes," said Bernard. "Therese works in quite a posh shop, I think."

"Yes, posh shoes. Shoes none of us could ever hope to buy, ever," said Justine.

"So... still a good thing then?" said Bernard, blushing.

Bernard, now doubly confused, appeared to Marie transformed into a lost, rather scruffy, teddy bear and an old hope surfaced, to be held, to feel safe, protected, even for a few minutes. She was shocked to realise she was feeling this. Wishing for something she could never have, to be able to let go and just be held. Tears appeared and blurred her day. Why does he make me think like this? She thought.

"Oh, shut up you two. I need to get her ready for the next shots," demanded Justine.

Marie sat on a nearby park bench and turned her attention to the elegant shoes. She picked up one shoe and carefully placed her foot into it. She felt the velvet leather tenderly wrapping her bare foot. She quickly put on the other one. They fitted.

"Oh My God, they fit. Bernard, Justine, they fit! Bernard, I love you, I love your sister, and I love everyone. Quick, let's get some photos."

"I thought you were stiff and needed a break," said Bernard. "You need to look after yourself."

"Well now I'm cured," replied Marie. "Come on you two."

So Marie, all discomfort gone, posed with sophistication. How could she not with such shoes?

* * *

The sun is setting and the park closing. Bernard had waited for some softly-lit shots before they finished. Marie is tired, but not exhausted, just relaxed, and happy. She takes off her beautiful new shoes and takes her time carefully putting them into her bag. Justine and Marie had reached the Park Gates so, quickly swinging the bag onto her shoulder she rushes to the main exit to catch up. Marie only notices that one of the shoes has fallen out of her bag when she reaches the Metro.

* * *

It is the next morning. Marie rushes up the park keeper, just emerging from his rooms in the rotunda.

"Monsieur, monsieur, please help me! I lost my shoe here yesterday evening. It's beautiful and it's lost."

"And it's here, I think, mademoiselle." Says the park keeper.

"Oh, yes, thank you monsieur, thank you."

"Merci, mademoiselle, but this young man is the one to thank. He found your shoe this morning. He said he was here to go jogging, and was already waiting when I opened the gates. Though I am not sure he is really dressed for jogging, are you monsieur?"

Marie was staring, "Bernard, what are you doing here?"

"I... I had to come and find your shoe Marie. You were so upset yesterday after the Park closed, and I... I thought about you all last night and, do... you think we might..."

Marie smiled, "Oh, come on Bernard, let's get a drink and celebrate. I've been thinking about you as well, you know."

"Oh," said Bernard, smiling back.

The End

A Quiet Love

by M. A. Thea
Kansas

The noise was intolerable.

His doctors called it tinnitus, and asked him questions like was he ever dizzy, was there any pressure, and did it sound louder in one ear than the other.

He didn't, there wasn't, and he tried to explain that the noise wasn't in his head. It was like hearing one of those loud cars, that someone had tuned to be obnoxiously loud when it was running. He could hear it moving across the fields and the woods, and around his house. The doctors simply nodded, and called it bilateral. They told him to avoid stress, salt, caffeine, and loud noises. They suggested massage and meditation, and taught him mental exercises for focus. When that didn't work, they tried to match the tones he would hear.

But the tones changed. Sometimes he heard bells, a thousand bells, ringing merrily. Other times it was a roar, or a swarm of bees. But always it was moving, moving; through the sky, across the trees, circling his house. The doctors eventually gave up. They told him tinnitus often had no cause, and there was no cure. But that he should continue to avoid stress and loud noise, and try to listen to pink noise every day. Not white, not brown, nor any other shade but pink. They wrote in his file that ototoxic medications should be avoided. He wondered why sounds were described by color.

And always there were questions. Endless questions. Did he feel suicidal or ever think of suicide? Was there a source of joy in his life? Were there people who cared about him? Every week they would ask, and tell him there were numbers he could call, people he could talk to. He told them the only thing that made him want to kill himself was having to answer these questions over and over and over, but they simply laughed, or looked concerned, and kept on asking. He wondered why they didn't listen.

His gram always told him not to listen to them, that he heard the *gaoithe sidhe.* She'd hammered nails into the window frames, circled their house with lines of salt, and hung herbal wreathes. Once, she'd given him a horseshoe and told him to keep it in his pocket. She'd told him stories, endless stories of hunts and abductions, tricks and favors, and insisted he never invite anyone in unless he knew who they were. His mother sighed, pulled out the nails, and refused to plant any rowan trees.

None of it did any good, but he preferred his gram's explanations. Never trust a *sluagh* or love a *sidhe*, she had often said while kneading dough for her baking, although she'd never told him why. Never swear an oath by the moon, she's once said while untangling a long mess of yarn his mother's cat had gotten to. He'd asked her why, and she'd simply shaken her head.

He was lost when she died. She'd breathed her last alone, in her bed. The doctors told him she'd gone quietly, peacefully. They gave him Diazepam and reminded him to avoid stress, to avoid worry. He left it unopened.

He stood at her funeral, staring into her coffin, listening to everyone proclaiming that she was in a better place now, and she looked so beautiful. They said they couldn't believe she was gone, and that they expected her to jump out of the coffin at any moment. He disagreed – she never wore green, or painted her eyes in that shade. But he simply thanked them for coming, accepted their food, and their condolences. He rarely carried the horseshoe she'd given him, but he did that day.

He snuck out the night she was buried.

It might have been madness or despair that had him running through the woods, chasing after the rapidly moving sound. It was bells that night, endless bells, ringing almost sorrowfully as though whatever caused the sound was grieving along with him. When he'd run as fast and as far as he could, until his breath gave out and his chest was heaving with unfamiliar exertion, he collapsed against a tree and gave in to the sobs that had been threatening to fall for as long as he could remember.

He cried for his gram, and for himself. He cried for the stories he'd never hear again, for the cookies she'd snuck him when the noise was at its worst, circling around and around the house until he was going mad. He shook with sorrow, swelling with it until he felt he would burst. When his last tear fell, his fist was torn and bloody from being slammed into the tree, and he sunk down to the ground in a heap. He didn't know the hour, or how long it'd been. The stars and moon were bright, and the insects that had fallen silent during his mournful wails were picking up again to join the warbling of the nearby brook.

"Surely it is not as bad as all that, now?"

He spun around, but there was only a tiny whirlwind beneath an old alder, full of circling leaves, twigs, and a single torn and empty candy wrapper. It faded out even as he saw it, and the world was quiet, save for a joyful laugh.

"My gram is gone," he replied, sinking down to the ground again. Something brought his gaze up and up, from the whirling wrapper to the highest branch of the tree. There was a man in the boughs, with milk-white skin, eyes as pale as the moon, and hair so fair it nearly glowed into the night. He thought it was long, but perhaps that was merely the tendrils of thin leaf-covered branches.

"The trees took her?"

That had him gaping. "What? Trees? No!" He looked away, "They said she had a heart attack."

There was the sound of scraping wood and movement. He looked up; the stranger had dropped down a limb and pressed his hands flat against the trunk. "Then why are you punishing it?"

"I'm not! I'm-" But his hands are raw, the knuckles cut and bleeding. He became aware of the pain, then, and winced away. "I'm sorry," he said softly.

"Do not tell *me*," came the reply.

His gaze lifted, the stranger had dropped down to another, closer branch. He nodded, and pressed his hands against the trunk. He leaned forward, closer still, and let his forehead rest upon the bark, above his hands. "I am sorry," he whispered to the alder. He wondered that he did not question this task, of speaking to the tree. There might have been a murmur in reply, a soft susurrus of sound that was felt more than it was heard. He laughed, wonder bringing him from his sorrow, and he lifted his eyes again.

The stranger had moved lower still, and their eyes met, his own blue catching pale. They were bright, so bright; his breath caught, his heart sounded so loudly it was all he could hear. "I'm Kevin," he whispered, fearing louder speech.

"Cefin," came the soft reply. There was heat in those pale eyes, a heat that was reflected in the intimate shifting of his name to its more ancient roots. "I am Lleu."

They met frequently after that; Lleu in the trees, Kevin beneath. They spoke of dreams and fancies, of wants and of fears. Kevin's heart pounded every time Lleu dropped down to a lower limb, bringing them closer and closer. Spring heated into summer, then began cooling into fall and further into winter. Kevin's grief never left him, but it did fade, slowly. And with it, his aversion to the sounds he heard. It was the bells he learned to like the most. Always he went running after them, through the fields and woods, until finally he would lay panting, and that laughter he'd begun to love would sound through the night.

It was one year later, after his gram's funeral and their first meeting, when Kevin reached for more. All day he agonized over what to wear, and what to say. He finally chose a dark blue t-shirt that he'd been told sang to his eyes, black jeans, and a black jacket to ward off the night's chill. He slipped his gram's horseshoe once more into his pocket for luck.

The night began as it always did, with Kevin settled beneath the alder, and Lleu swinging in the branches above. Few of them remained.

"I do love the way you say my name," Kevin said, looking up into the branches toward Lleu.

"Cefin," came the soft reply. "It is like you, a gentle name."

"It was my gram's.." Kevin's voice wobbled briefly before he continued on. "I was told my gram bullied my mum to get me this name. She'd wanted to call me Michael."

Laughter floated down, "Your gram sounds wise. You are far more a Cefin than Meical."

"Did your mother name you?"

Lleu was quiet for a time, before he spoke in a tone Kevin had never heard before, "Yes, she did. But it was my uncle who raised me."

Kevin longed to ask more. Lleu rarely spoke of his family, as Kevin rarely spoke of his. But he wanted to know more about the man, and hungered for every morsel that was dropped. He dared to ask, "What is he like?"

"My uncle?" Lleu seemed surprised.

Kevin nodded, certain that Lleu would somehow see or know it in the dark.

"He is difficult to know." Lleu chuckled, "Never far from a joke or pointed observation. But uncle Gwy is kind. I know he will be there if I need him."

"I would-" Kevin drew in a breath. He trembled, then said softly, "I would, too." He looked up, their eyes met. He knew his betrayed him, shining with everything he'd wanted to say. "If you wanted me. I would."

The night seemed to quiet, as though it held its breath along with Kevin as Lleu prompted him to finish, "You would?"

"I would be there for you."

Lleu's eyes widened. He dropped nimbly, his gaze never leaving Kevin's. When Kevin reached out, Lleu stepped forward. Their hands met. Instead of the heat that he'd expected, the warmth of touch, there was instead a roar of sound. A scream that echoed on and on, blasting beyond the ringing pain he'd spent his life knowing and into agony. Kevin recoiled, dropping to his knees, hands flying uselessly to his ears.

"Haearn," Lleu hissed. A vortex blew up from nowhere, then another and another, until all sights and sounds were obscured with their whipping winds. It was but moments before they vanished. And with them, Lleu.

He walked home in what might have been heavy silence to others. He had never before heard the wind in the trees, the rustle of grass, his breath, or his own footsteps. Always, the ringing had obscured such sounds. But he heard them now. His breath was loud and ragged, his every footfall might have been a clang of thunder, and the trees screamed in the wind. But there was no joy in it, this granting of what had been his greatest wish, haunted as he was by the image of those pale, bright eyes. By the time he made it home, the noise had returned, but rather than bells or bees, it was now a discordant, high frequency wail.

His true pain struck the next morning.

His clothing was rumpled, abused by the fitful sleep, and felt heavy as he stripped. When he tossed his jacket, it fell with a thud. Kevin stared, then inched closer, step by step, and reached down. When he straightened, he held the horseshoe he'd slipped into his pocket in memory of his gram. Her words as she'd given it to him rang through his mind.

"It will protect you."

It will protect you, protect you, protect you...

But from what?

He dropped the curved bit of iron and sank to the floor.

He spent three days in misery, clutching his head in the dark, curled over the discarded horseshoe. The phone rang, people pounded on his door, but he heard none of it over the incessant shrieking, buzzing, clamoring in his head. A life of medical appointments and struggles to simply live had left him largely alone.

But on the fourth day, Ivarr dropped by. He didn't bother to knock, he simply leaned in just the right way against the ancient cottage's doorframe and let himself in. He found Kevin on the floor. After a moment of consideration, he went into the kitchen, filled a pot with cold water and dumped it on his friend.

Kevin recoiled, spluttering and cursing.

Ivarr threw a towel at Kevin, then leaned casually against the wall. "What the bloody hell are you about, lagging on like a wolf that's lost its mate? Buck up, you arse, and get your baffies on. We're going out."

"Sod off," Kevin muttered.

Ivarr squatted down, peering at Kevin. "Lost yer fairy love, then?"

Kevin's eyes widened and he jerked around to stare at Ivarr. "How'd you-"

Ivarr chuckled. "Think I've got bollocks for brains? Ye've been chuffed all year, but I've not seen you about." He poked Kevin in the chest, "Auntie wants to see you."

Kevin blanched, and held up his hands as though to ward Ivarr away. "I don't think-"

"No, you don't," Ivarr replied cheerily. "Lucky you've got me, eh? Now get up, you arse. Quit yer lollygagging and let's go."

Auntie lived in her own cottage across the village. It was close enough to walk, so they did, although Kevin's steps grew heavy as they grew closer. The air smelled sweet and crisp, heavy with the scent of herbs and flowers, and wreaths were hung beneath the windows. There were likely birds in the gardens, chirping their enjoyment of the day, but Kevin couldn't hear them. He stopped before her door, unable to bring himself to enter. Ivarr lifted his hand to bang on the door, but it opened before his fist made contact.

"Ivarr Alwyn Thomas," said the diminutive old woman as she appeared. "Surely you weren't about to pound down my door like a rampaging barbarian?"

"Surely not," grinned and unrepentant Ivarr, undeterred. "I've brung him."

Her eyes swung to Kevin, and locked on shrewdly. "Poor lad." She stepped back, opened wide her door, "You are welcome here, come in."

The scent of herbs replaced the floral as they stepped inside. Kevin had been here before, visiting Ivarr, but it felt as though he were viewing the place with new eyes. Things stood out that he'd not noticed before; oddly shaped stones, bits of glass and wrapped herbs, an iron teapot. A lump formed in his throat as he caught sight of a crooked nail jutting out of the window sill and thought of his gram.

"Sit," commanded the old lady, and Kevin and Ivarr did. She bustled about, making tea and piling a tray with sweets.

"Now then," she said with a smile. "Drink up and tell us about it, there's a good lad."

Kevin stared down into his tea, wishing he could divine ... something ... in its depths. He recalled the look in Lleu's eyes as he'd dropped down in front of him. The heat curling into his belly as he dared to touch. The agony of that cry, that was only mildly echoed in his head. Ripples formed in the water as his hands shook. "What is there to tell? I hurt him. He left. That I did not know does not negate injury."

There was a rich chuckle from behind him. Kevin started, nearly spilling his tea. Auntie Thomas narrowed her eyes and started to rise, but the voice spoke, "Peace, woman. I bear no ill-will to you or yours. I would aid you." He faded into view, a tall and slender man, fair of hair and eye. Kevin caught a familiarity in the line of his jaw and brow and his eyes widened. The man winked.

"You are not welcome here," she said calmly.

"You did invite me in," he leaned back, smiling broadly.

"I did no such." her voice trailed off uncertainly, and she frowned.

His smile widened. "'You are welcome here, please come in.'" He held his hands wide, "You did not exclude poor Guidgen, and so I, believing myself a part of this troupe, came in too."

"'Poor Guidgen' indeed." Auntie Thomas snorted. "What do you want, Gwyddien fab Dôn?"

In answer, Gwyddien looked down at Kevin. There was a sudden screaming pressure in head as the ever-present whine intensified, grew louder. The teacup shattered in his hands, but he refused to look away. He kept his gaze locked to Gwyddien's, even as the ceramic shards dug into his hands and tears of pain leaked down his cheeks. He faintly sensed Ivarr and Auntie Thomas rising, shouting, but none of it mattered. The only thought that he clung to was of Lleu.

Then, abruptly, he could breath again. He gasped, and let the shards fall.

"Be at ease, *Cefin Ddifâr,*" murmured Gwyddien, and Kevin somehow knew these words were only for him to hear. "My nephew argued well on your behalf." Then he stood straight and tall, and seemed almost to radiate power. His voice rung clear and melodic as a bell. He spoke to Kevin, although his words resounded with the power of a decree, "Hear now that Lleu Llaw Gyffes, so named by the Silver Arianrhod, has sought the ancient right to claim his Consort. He would claim the one he names *Cefin Ddifâr,* known to men as Kevin Eirin Price. If you would permit his claim, seek the ring of stones atop Bryn y Goed as the sun sets. Should you be embraced by any other than Lleu before the sun rises, their claim shall overwrite his. If you would refuse, avoid the stones, and we will none of us bother you again."

"You believe yourself cursed, Kevin Eirin Price. But it is a gift, if you listen." Gwyddien gave Kevin one last wink, and faded from view. As he did, the loud screaming whine in Kevin's head quieted to a more tolerable level.

Chaos erupted. Kevin turned to find Ivarr on his feet with an entirely shocked look upon his face, and his aunt looking on firm-mouthed and pensive.

"*Lleu Llaw Gyffes*?" Ivarr exclaimed. "I saw you running toward the rivers, and thought you'd found yourself a *gwraig annwn* and were wooing yourself a bride. But all this time, you've been sneaking out to meet *Lleu Llaw Gyffes*?"

"He told me his name was Lleu," Kevin mumbled. He turned his hands over and about as he realized they were unwounded, then noticed the teacup was unbroken and stared.

Auntie Thomas gently took the teacup and replaced it with a towel. "Your gram always believed the Twyleth Teg had their eyes upon you."

Kevin looked up, eyes moist. He nodded, "It was.. her horseshoe-"

She smiled gently and patted his hand. "I do not envy you your choice."

"Choice?" Ivarr burst out. "What choice?! Of course he must refuse!"

" Ivarr Alwyn Thomas," the old woman began.

“Don't Ivarr me!” Ivarr shouted. “It's one thing to have a fairy wife! But Lleu Llaw Gyffes! He'll take him away! He'll-” Ivarr stood there, jaw working, then he spun around and ran from the cottage.

“Ivarr, wait!” Kevin stood to chase after him, but Auntie Thomas shook her head and reached out to stop him.

“Just give him some time, lovey,” she said.

“But-”

“You go on home, have yourself a think,” the old woman said. “I'll see to Ivarr.”

There was nothing else to do, no matter how troubled he was, so Kevin went. But instead of home, he set his steps out to the fields. Claimed as a consort? What did that even mean? He kicked a stone, watched it fly out and then fall to disappear into the heather. It had never even occurred to him that Lleu might be anything other than simply Lleu. Marvelous, breath-taking, exhilarating Lleu, with his voice of smokey whiskey and eyes that flashed a wicked humor. Consort by any definition he knew conjured forth images that made his heart pound. He wondered what it would be like to be held in Lleu's arms, to taste and touch and explore that pale skin. But Gwyddien had made it sound like some sort of title. Lost and troubled, he simply wandered the fields. He heard the ringing of bells and the buzzing of bees, the discordant whine, but none of it called to him enough to follow.

* * *

Lleu waited.

He knew now what made the bards sing, what prompted tales of love and loss, what formed madness in the hearts of the impassioned. This uncertainty, this fear that twined around his heart. What if his love did not return? And if he did, would he hold out his arms in welcome? If he could only see – but he could not, eyes bound as they were.

Gwyddien had brought the veil to him, his eyes fair sparkling with guile. “You are not to see him until the trial, *cenau.* But never were the other senses forbidden.”

And so, blinded, he waited, at his beloved's door.

The sun had sunk nearly to the horizon, sending shadows

stretching out into the distance, Cefin finally returned. Lleu had walked across a thousand battlefields and slain so many foes he'd been called the Red Ravager, yet never before had his heart trembled as it did now when Cefin's steps paused.

Without his sight, sound and scent took on increased proportions. He heard an uncertainty that matched his own in the hastened steps as Cefin resumed his approach. "Lleu?" came the hesitant query.

Lleu turned, letting his hood fall. He could not gaze upon his beloved with his covered eyes, but he could face the man. His heart beat, and he thought he could defeat a thousand men to claim this one.

Cefin stopped in front of him. "Are you.. are you hurt?"

Lleu's laugh was pure mischief. His uncle was by far the cannier, but he, too, enjoyed practicing his wiles. "Do not be concerned. I am merely not to see you, until.." He could not bring himself to say it. He had thrown Cefin to the hounds by seeking this claim, and done so without permission. By what rights might he expect acceptance?

He heard movement, the rustling of fabric. Then, an unexpected touch. He drew in a breath, his Cefin was warm, so very warm. He leaned into the touch, craving more. "Forgive me, cariad," Lleu murmured. "For so burdening you with no warning."

"Forgive *you?*" Cefin pulled back, but did not let go, and Lleu dared begin to hope. "I'm the one who injured you with iron."

"Injuries heal," Lleu replied. "Vows remain."

"Right then. This isn't a conversation for the stoop, now is it. Will you come in?"

More poignant than the moment a conquered enemy fell, this feeling as his hopes grew. "You are inviting me in?"

Cefin stepped closer still, and Lleu smelled the heather from the fields and the early evening wind in his hair. "Unless you'd rather not?"

"I would be honored," Lleu felt himself tugged toward the front door. He followed Cefin's guiding hands, through the entryway, across what felt like wood and flagstone floors beneath his feet, and finally settled into some large, soft chair. Cefin's hands left him then, and he felt bereft. Three days was nothing in the span of his life, but he stifled the urge to laugh at the thought that he was already impatient for them to be done.

"So," Cefin's voice came from a short distance away. There were clinks, small thumps, and little hisses of impatience as he struggled with nervousness and whatever task he'd taken on. "Auntie Thomas, she's Ivarr's auntie not mine but I've always called her auntie, called him Gwyddien fab Dôn. He said, um, he said.."

Lleu heard something small go flying. He merely waited, sensing his beloved had not finished what he'd been wanting to say. There was an odd pull of power, as though some sorcery was being cast. Alarm had him half-rising before he realized it had the flavor of Cefin to it. But nothing more happened, and how he wished that he could *see.*

"What did he mean. What does it mean, that you want to claim me as your consort?"

Lleu sucked in a breath. This fear that he would lose his Cefin if he spoke in error was like nothing he'd felt before. Injuries of the flesh would heal, but of the heart? Wars had been fought for less. "They would have killed you, if I had not called for the claiming rite."

Cefin's voice when he replied was somehow flat and distant. "So you did this, to save me."

Lleu's heart trembled. He nodded. He'd miss-spoke, but his tongue lay heavy in his mouth, knotted and thick. "There are ancient laws that bind us," he said softly. "That not even we might break. When you struck me with iron-" He somehow felt Cefin flinch at those words. "Through willful intent or no, I had to leave you. The more vengeful among us sought retribution."

"Fuck this," Cefin muttered. His steps as he stalked toward Lleu were quick with fury. "Did your balls get bound along with your eyes? Tell me why I shouldn't just refuse. Tell me why I should risk everything for you."

Lleu laughed, passion blazing at the direct demand. He surged to his feet and reached for Cefin as he drew near enough. He could not see the heat that often glimmered in the man's gaze, but he knew it was there. "*Fy annwyl,*" he murmured, knowing his voice was rough. He rubbed his thumb over Cefin's mouth, reveling in the way his lips part and the slow indrawn breath. "I bare my soul for you. By the sun's light, I love you. By the moon's embrace, I yearn for you. You shine brighter than the stars themselves."

Cefin gave him a shove, pushing him back down onto the overstuffed chair, and then climbed on to straddle his hips. Lleu groaned as cock ground against cock, and he heard the wicked grin in Cefin's voice, "That blindfold is hot."

Lleu answered by sinking his fingers into Cefin's hair and plundering his mouth. Each searing kiss melted into another, leaving Lleu groaning and arching as Cefin traced a blazing trail across his jaw and down to the hollow of his neck. "Ah, *cariad*, what you do to me..."

Cefin slid his hands beneath the hem of Lleu's shirt, and pushed it up and up until it tangled around Lleu's wrists. He circled each nipple with his tongue, and asked huskily between kisses, "What does that mean, what you call me..."

"My love, my heart... my beloved..." Lleu's words faded into moans as Cefin's hands quested lower. The leather of his breeches seemed to magnify the heat of Cefin's touches, leaving Lleu writhing and rocking as his flesh was bared. He tugged at the t-shirt Cefin wore, beginning his own explorations as the fabric ripped open.

Clothing flew in every direction. Lleu found himself dragged to the edge of the seat, one leg sprawled across the chair's arm, the other draped over Cefin's shoulder. He felt Cefin's breath, warm against his thighs. "You make a compelling argument," murmured his beloved.

Then there were only the sounds of pleasure as Cefin's tongue circled his entrance, and teased inside.

* * *

The standing stones atop Bryn y Goed cast dark shadows down the slope of the hill. The moon was full, and Kevin shivered as he realized the shadows were unblemished despite the weathered and broken stones. Some had fallen completely and vanished into the brush, but still, long shadows where they would have stood stretched into the evening dark. There was a clamor in his mind, of bells and bees, whispers, screeches and winds that grew stronger the closer he approached.

He breached the circle just as the last rays of light vanished behind the horizon.

He'd heard of Lleu Llaw Gyffes and Gwyddien, of Pwyll and Arawn, the Wild Hunt and the antics of the Twyleth Teg. He'd lived for such tales that his gram told; the *gwragedd annwn* who dwelled in the lakes and sometimes took men as husbands, the *bwbachod* who if pleased might help with household tasks, the *gaoithe sidhe* that heralded the arrival of the *sidhe,* and the *ellyllon* who haunt groves and valleys. He'd heard the term the fairy host, but had never understood its true meaning.

He understood it now.

What else could one call an endless array of unimaginable faces? He saw faces that were pale and faces that were dark, lips and beaks, feathers and fur; claws, hands, hooves and twigs. And every one of them focused on *him.* The collective din was overwhelming, and he *knew* as he stood facing them that had he not spent the length and breadth of his life fighting alone against an enemy that no one could see and only he could hear he would had fled.

Then Lleu stepped into the circle of stones and Kevin was no longer alone. Lleu turned his shining smile on Kevin, and Kevin thought perhaps he would not have fled after all.

A single melodic tone began, and drown out all other sounds. The Host around them stilled, and a figure stepped forward. The note grew louder, and louder still, overwhelming all else. Kevin dropped to his knees beneath that note, and somehow knew all others did as well.

"..Mathonwy."

The whispered name carried through the gathering, as though the moon herself gave it reverence. And then Mathonwy spoke, his words carried with that ringing sound.

"Lleu Llaw Gyffes. You have the right of Vengeance, against the touch of iron that was forced upon you. Yet you have sought the rights of Claiming in its stead. Is this your will?"

"It is."

Kevin knew the figure turned its attention to him. That note stretched on and on, somehow ringing to him as Mathonwy continued.

"Kevin Eirin Price. In lieu of Retribution, you have been offered the chance to prove your worth and claim the name of Cefin Ddifâr, Consort of Lleu Llaw Gyffes. Is this your will?"

With a sense of wonder, Kevin heard a second note, winding its way through Mathonwy's overpowering one. He heard Lleu's laughter in it, and recalled his words of love. Was this his will? He had no doubts at all. "It is."

There was a sudden scream of fury and a brilliant flash of silver. Kevin caught a glimpse of long, fair hair like Lleu's, and flashing eyes, but the silver light remained too bright to see more. "By what rights do you grant him this! He is not to wed!"

Kevin flinched at the escalation of noise. There was a rumbling murmur, as though many voices were whispering amongst themselves.

"Your *tynged* stands unbroken, Arianrhod," came Mathonwy's calm reply. "It is no wife that Lleu Llaw Gyffes is seeking."

"And him! This human! This-" Arianrhod's eyes flashed and sparked with such fury it shone through the silver light that surrounded her as she spun around to point at Kevin. Her eyes narrowed. "I know you."

"We all know him, *mum*," Lleu's voice was insolent, almost goading. "He is the boy who begged for silence."

"Silence?" Arianrhod stared at Kevin. He felt the urge to step back, but resisted. She stalked him, moving furiously. Her lips curled, "Well, I shall lay a destiny upon this boy. Never will he gain the silence he seeks. He shall live until he hears it, and on that moment, that moment only, he will perish."

The glow around her lit up, as though the moon stood before Kevin. A chill enveloped him, as though his soul had been plunged into ice. His vision went white as the glow went brighter still. And then it vanished. When he was able to look up again, Arianrhod had vanished. Lleu was gazing at him with wonder on his face.

And then there came laughter. Gwyddien stepped forward, grinning. "How nicely done!" Then he turned to Mathonwy, "She did not deny his address."

"She did not," Mathonwy inclined his head, then turned to Lleu. "We welcome you to the House of Dôn, Lleu Llaw Gyffes ap Gwyddien."

There was a murmur of sound again, as though the entire Host had drawn in its breath, then a roar. When it had faded, Mathonwy encompassed both Lleu and Kevin in his gaze. "Have your wills changed?"

"No!" cried both Lleu and Kevin at once.

"So be it."

There was a blinding light, and when it faded, Kevin and Lleu alone upon the hill.

Mathonwy's voice rang out across the night, "You have one

hour before the challengers begin their Hunt. Should any other than Lleu Llaw Gyffes embrace the one he would name Cefin Ddifâr before the sun rises, they may claim him in his stead."

The single note faded, returning the endless clamoring.

"Fuck that," Kevin muttered. He looked to Lleu. "How deep is this shite? I mean, I'm bloody well no prize. There won't be many 'challengers' to worry about, right?"

Lleu smiled and reached out to press his hands against Kevin's cheek. "You are a prize that shines more brightly than the sun. But even were you the foulest of villains, there are those who would seek you simply to deny me."

Kevin froze, staring at Lleu. Right. Of course. He closed his eyes and pressed his cheek against Lleu's palm. "How does one outrun the Fairy Host?" Then his eyes flew open and he stepped back in horror as he processed his own words. "I am being hunted? Is this the *Wild Hunt?*"

Lleu laughed, and gathered Kevin against him, holding tight. "I do not believe Arawn will loose his hounds upon you, f*y annwyl.* No, this is merely a challenge. We shall overcome it, and all will be well."

Kevin chuckled wearily, "If this is what you consider 'merely' a challenge, I have no wish to see serious one." The noises spiked, and he winced, pressing his hands to his head.

Lleu was instantly at attention. He gently stroked Kevin's hair, "What has happened? Are you well?"

Kevin shook his head, "It is just the noise. It makes it difficult to think. Just, just - give me a moment."

He stepped away from Lleu and sat. Closing his eyes, he recalled the exercises he'd been taught. Focus. Each breath in, each breath out. First he focused on the sounds. Each bell, each buzz, every whine and shriek. He found the one that reminded him of Lleu and listened. It was golden, like the sun, and it grew louder as he struggled to ignore all else. He let it fill him, until there was nothing but that golden note. That accomplished, he sought something else, some other sound not of his own making. But the buzzing pressed in, overwhelming. He drew in a breath, felt himself panicking. How could he make it through the night if he couldn't even settle his mind for five minutes? "Sing for me," he begged Lleu. "Anything."

Lleu said nothing for a moment, but then simply started to

sing. "*Ar lan y môr mae rhosys cochion, Ar lan y môr mae lilis gwynion.*"

Kevin breathed in the song like a lifeline, each word crafting a slow spell that let him push back every other sound until there was nothing but Lleu's velvet singing. When the song was done, and he'd obtained the steadiness he needed, he opened his eyes. Lleu stood attentively nearby, his pale skin shining in the moonlight, strands of his long, fair hair floating around him in the night breezes. He seemed almost to glow. Kevin smiled, "I do love you."

"*Cariad,*" Lleu breathed. He flew at Kevin, gathering him up in his embrace. Unlike the fierce passion of the other day, this kiss was slow and thorough, a vow and a promise of love.

"We should go," Kevin said breathlessly when their lips parted.

"Yes," Lleu said, but neither of them moved. Finally he took Kevin's hand and started drawing him away from the stones. "What sorcery did you cast?"

"Sorcery?" Kevin looked at Lleu in bewilderment. Briefly he considered the oddity of accepting that his lover was Lleu Llaw Gyffes, he'd spoken with Gwyddien fab Dôn, and was about to spend the night fleeing faerie pursuers without question, yet finding the question of sorcery surprising.

"I felt you," Lleu explained. "Working some magic when you asked me to sing."

"That? That wasn't sorcery," Kevin held tightly to Lleu's hand as they picked their way across the tangled landscape. If he was captured by anyone else, he wanted to make the most of every moment they had. "That was just an exercise. To keep the noises at bay." He laughed bitterly, "Gwyddien said I had a gift, but I do not feel very gifted."

Lleu stopped short. "My uncle said this? When?"

Kevin tugged Lleu forward into motion again. It didn't seem a good idea to lose any more time. He was belatedly thankful he'd started spending more time out walking since he'd initially met Lleu. If he hadn't, there was no way he'd be able to last the night, no matter what they did. "When he came to deliver the challenge. He said I felt that I was cursed, but I had a gift. Or something like that."

Lleu did start moving again, but he turned to stare at Kevin with wide, unfocused eyes. "What do you hear?"

"I don't know," Kevin muttered. "Just noise. Never-ending

noise."

"Please, *fy annwyl,*" Lleu lifted Kevin's hand and brushed his lips across the knuckles. "My uncle says nothing to no purpose. If he said this, then - We must unravel his meaning."

He sighed, but Kevin did not argue. "Sometimes I hear bells. Sometimes bees. Or wailing. Sometimes it's just a long, loud high frequency note. And it can move."

"Move?"

Kevin nodded. He paused and pulled Lleu to a stop. "Close your eyes."

Lleu did as bid.

Kevin then circled around him, talking. "Like this. Imagine I am just a sound. I'm moving. You can hear I'm moving, right?"

"Oohh... *Ddeallaf...*"

"Gram said I heard the *gaoithe sidhe.*"

"But that makes no sense," Lleu frowned. "Even if you did hear the winds of our arrival, you would not hear it all the time. Nor would it change. You would simply hear the one sound. What do you hear now?"

"It is better now," Kevin admitted. "It was nearly overwhelming before, like I was hearing all of it at once. Back there, with Mathonwy, there was this one ... loud one." He squeezed Lleu's hand. Lleu squeezed back, and Kevin reveled in the feeling of no longer being alone. "But there is one of them that I do not mind." He smiled. "It reminds me of you. It is the loudest sound now."

"Right now?" Lleu abruptly stopped walking again. He grabbed Kevin, one hand holding each shoulder. "*Cariad,* what is it that you hear? Right now? More than this one of me? Do these noises move?"

Kevin shook his head. "Now? No, they do not move. It is just a clamoring of all of it." He pointed back toward Bryn y Goed, and its standing stones.

Lleu's grip slid down Kevin's arms until he squeezed both of Kevin's hands together. His eyes were glimmering brightly. "Close your eyes. Count to ten, and then look toward where you hear that noise of me."

"O.. ok..." Kevin closed his eyes and did as bid. The golden sound of 'Lleu' sped off. When he opened his eyes again, he found himself staring at Lleu himself, who had run several meters away. His mouth dropped in surprise.

Lleu's delighted laughter sounded, and he ran back to Kevin's side. He grabbed Kevin and spun around. "Your gram was right! But she had only parts of it. You hear *us, cariad!* It is not some source-less curse! You will hear our foes approach, and we will know when they come!"

"But we must go," Lleu said. "They will not move until the hour is complete, but they will move faster than you can."

Then they focused on putting distance between themselves and Bryn y Goed. Kevin knew the moment the hour had run its last, for there came a great roar of sound, then it exploded outward, as though the players in an orchestra had begun to run in different directions while still playing. The sounds he heard were no more pleasant, but knowing their source, their reason, lessened their burden. His heart felt light, for he had Lleu by his side, and now, finally now, his curse had a form, and with form came function. He was no longer a mere burden to be carried and guarded through the night, he could aid their flight.

Although Kevin could not understand why anyone was chasing him, let alone so many, he could not deny that there were. The first few groups who broke ahead were easily displaced through Lleu's trickery once Kevin told him where they were approaching.

"You see?" Lleu grinned the first time Kevin steered them around an ambush. "You are without compare. The wonder is not why so many want you – it is why do you want *me.*"

After that the way became more difficult. Their opponents learned, and with every ambush, began to take more care.

It was closer to dawn than midnight when Lleu slowed. He pulled Kevin into a sheltered ravine. A hollow formed between several large boulders that had been left long ago, when the small trickling brook had run with more force was obscured by several brittle willows. "You must rest," he stroked Kevin's cheek.

Kevin sat wearily and nodded. The sounds were softer than their usual, and he pushed aside the though that the shapes of the hills were unfamiliar. He leaned against Lleu. "How much of the stories are true?"

He felt rather than saw Lleu look down at him. "The same as any tales, all of them, and none of them are true."

Kevin laughed. "Spoken like a bard."

Lleu nuzzled into Kevin's hair, and Kevin relaxed against him. "Consider you."

Kevin looked up, "Me?"

"Mmm... you and I..." Lleu murmured. "I could spin a thousand songs of you and I, and paint myself a villain or a hero or something in between without changing any of it."

"A villain?" Kevin couldn't imagine it. "You could never be a villain."

Lleu chuckled, "You say the sweetest things, f*y annwyl.* But am I not the unknown fairy lover, who has stolen you away? Are you not sitting here, exposed to dangers you could have never found on your own?"

"You have no idea.." Kevin frowned deeply, struggling to find his words. He surged to his feet and spun around to glower at Lleu. "Anyone who would say such a thing has *no* idea what you have done. Danger? This? It is but a single night! One!"

"You risk your future-" Lleu began.

"So what!" Kevin roared, forgetting their need to remain concealed. "I *had* no future before you! My entire *life* has been nothing but the passing of time! Every minute of every day, filled with maddening sounds I could not understand! Music is meaningless to me, I cannot hear half of it over this sound! Movies? Conversations? All of it a trial I have to struggle to understand! And there was no end to it, no hope of an end to it!" He floundered, struggling to reign in his control. "Loving you gives me a future, don't you understand? And now," he flung his arms wide, as though attempting to encompass the world. "Now I have *meaning* for it all! I would defy anyone who calls you a villain, I would fight a thousand nights for you! Not once have I ever had a reason to hope that tomorrow might be better. And *you* have given that to me. To call you a villain is to steal away the very essence of what I am!"

"Oh, how very *well* said," came a voice. "I came here to pay a debt, but it seems as though I will gain a prize beyond measure."

A figure stepped into view. Tall and auburn-haired, he was dressed as was Lleu, in leather breeches and a belted tunic. A sword hung at his waist. Kevin spun around in horror, realizing he'd been so caught up in his shouting that he'd missed the increase of buzzing that indicated a group approaching.

"Gronw," spit Lleu. "I killed you."

"As I killed you," Gronw grinned, and dipped into a fluid bow. "It is truly a tale worthy of the bards, is it not? You, spared from death at my hands by your father, and I, spared from death at yours by your mother. And here we are again," his eyes locked on Kevin. "With your cleverly escaped *tynged* between us."

He had asked what of the tales were true, Kevin thought. Here was the proof he'd rather not have that some of them were real. The *tynghedau* of Lleu Llaw Gyffes, at least one of the curses placed upon him by Arianrhod, was standing before them now. Lleu Llaw Gyffes shall never have a wife of any race that walked upon the earth; Kevin certainly was no *wife.* He edged toward Lleu.

"You will never have Cefin!" There was a roar of fury, and Lleu drew a sword from somewhere. He charged Gronw.

"Lleu!" Kevin yelled as Lleu and Gronw fell behind the boulders and out of view. He ran toward them - or tried to. A troupe of *ellyllon* appeared around him. "Lleu!" he yelled again. He had no hope of fighting them off alone.

"The silver bitch took him," came a familiar voice above. Ivarr landed beside him. But this was an Ivarr he had never before seen; tall and shining, with his crimson hair flaring around him like the halo of some avenging angel. He gripped a spear.

"Ivarr?" Kevin gaped at his friend.

"My father had a fairy wife," Ivarr seemed almost apologetic. "Now, go."

"But how can I-"

"Go!" roared Ivarr. "I'd come to take you myself, but then I heard-" He cut himself off, and swung at one of the *ellyll* as it tried to approach. "Your bond has been granted by Mathonwy himself! She'll curse his death if you don't get to him before the sun rises! *Go!'*

With that final *go,* Ivarr charged forward, sweeping with shaft of his spear to clear the way. Kevin went.

He ran blindly for a while before he paused, panting, to lean against a boulder and look up at the starry sky. Find Lleu. He had to find Lleu. His heart pounded in panic - the silver bitch could only be Arianrhod, and how was *he* supposed to do anything about some kind of goddess who could fling curses? But it was Lleu. He refused to do nothing.

He closed his eyes and drew in a long, slow breath. Then another, and another. And he listened. There were sounds everywhere. He marveled at how much less overwhelming it all was, now that it had purpose and meaning. The buzzing behind him must be where Ivarr was fighting the *ellyllon.* There were deep bells to the east, and south of them were lighter more frantic ones. None of it was what he wanted.

Focus. He had to focus, and find one sound, one note, among the many. And then, there it was. That shining, golden note that was Lleu. He began to run. It was surprisingly close. He hadn't run long before he heard the faint murmurs of Lleu's smoky baritone followed by Arianrhod screeching, "Your very existence brings me dishonor!"

Kevin put on a burst of speed and topped the hill where they conversed. Lleu had been confined in a cage of living rowan. Its red berries stood out sharply in the moonlight. Standing by the cage was a tall woman, with hair and skin as fair as Lleu's. Her eyes flashed with rage as she stared at Kevin. He saw now that they were silver.

"You found me, *cariad,"* Lleu seemed delighted at Kevin's appearance, although his stance was stiff with tension.

"I will always find you," Kevin paused, astonished to discover that he not only meant that statement, but he *believed* it as well. He moved toward Lleu.

"I think not," Arianrhod's voice was cold. "I call down the stillness and quiet of the moon. Let no sound be heard."

There came a sudden weight, as though the air had thickened. Kevin drew in a panicked breath, recalling the *tynged* she had thrown at him. But nothing happened, save the roaring of his ever-present noise, rushing in with greater force now that there was nothing else for it to overcome. Kevin saw Arianrhod's mouth moving, but all he heard was Lleu's golden note and the buzzing of bees. He ripped open Lleu's cage, and Lleu held him fiercely as the two of them turned to face the Silver Goddess.

The first rays of the morning sun rose over the horizon, and with it, came the return of sound. Mathonwy's voice rang out over the hill, "It is done. We welcome Lleu Llaw Gyffes ap Gwyddien and his Consort Cefin Ddifâr to the House of Dôn. Let no one move against them this day."

Lleu let out a yell of triumph, and spun Cefin around. He devoured Cefin's mouth, further deepening the kiss as Cefin wrapped his arms tightly around Lleu in return. When they broke apart, breathless and wanting, Arianrhod was nowhere to be seen. Cefin said, "What just happened?"

Lleu framed Cefin's face in his hands, and smiled. "*You never hear silence no matter how quiet the world, do you, fy annwl."*

Cefin gazed at Lleu in wonder, “It was not silence that I needed, only you.”

Desert Roads

by DJ Tyrer
United Kingdom

The thing I love most about driving through the south-western states of America are the long straight roads that cut through the desert and scrub. Some are highways, others nothing more than vague lines of tarmac and heat haze. What I like about them is that their length and straightness, and the general lack of other vehicles, means you can engage your cruise control and let your car just coast along while you relax.

Just lean back and let it do all the work.

Of course, as tempting as it may be, it's never wise to take the opportunity to snooze, nor to completely switch off and admire the stunning scenery, the distant blur of the mountains, the tangle of sagebrush, the pastel shades of red, yellow and orange sand. Even if you have no heart and couldn't care less about the various animals that seem determined to become roadkill on the otherwise-empty highway, having an armadillo lodge itself up inside your wheel arch is just asking for trouble, and there seems also to be a muffler discarded upon the highway every hundred miles, or a rear bumper, for reasons that continue to evade my comprehension, so you need to maintain some vigilance, even as you relax.

Dang, but its hard work, when all you want is a little shut-eye.

It was as I cruised along a road somewhere in New Mexico – I remember seeing signs for a place called Corrales, but it meant nothing to me – that I met Elsa.

She was standing in the shadow of a creosote bush, too blonde and fair to be out in the blazing sun, despite her wide-brimmed, floppy hat. Her white summer dress shone like the sun, and, with a casual motion of her arm, she was thumbing a lift; I pulled over for her.

She raised the brow of her hat to reveal a pair of those heart-shaped sunglasses that look so odd, smiled, and introduced herself.

"Hi," I said. "You want a lift?"

She shrugged the shoulders of her white summer dress. "I don't think so. I was mostly admiring the view. The tumble-weeds passing by. You know how it is."

One pale eyebrow arched above the red frame of her

glasses. Her accent matched her name.

"Really?"

"Of course not. I want a lift." She laughed.

With a smile, I told her to "Hop in, and I'll take you as far as the next town, maybe further, if we're headed the same way."

She slipped into a passenger seat with a lithe grace and smiled as she said, "I was hoping to go all the way."

I looked at her as I put the car back into 'drive'. "Your English is too good not to know that's an innuendo."

Her smile widened and she lowered her glasses to return my gaze, but she didn't reply, just pushed her seat back and kicked her sandals off so that she could recline with her feet up on the dash.

"So, where are you headed?" I asked after a couple of minutes.

Elsa gave a full-bodied shrug. "West."

"Just west, or somewhere in particular? The Old West, perhaps?"

"Old West, New West, Wild West... it doesn't matter to me. I'm on a gap year, just seeing the real America, with no particular aim or destination in mind."

I leaned back and nodded at her.

"You know what I like about these roads?" she asked.

Smiling, I said, "Let me guess: Is it because they're long and straight?"

Elsa laughed. "Exactly. As if they are heading to infinity."

An armadillo was trundling its slow way across the road ahead of us, certainly sick of a cosy life without adventure, if not life altogether.

I restored my control over the car, slowed a little and swerved about it.

"Nice," said Elsa.

"They play havoc with the suspension if they get jammed up in there."

For a moment, as she lowered her glasses once more to give me an appraising stare, I thought my joke had offended, then she smiled and gave a sort of silent laugh that jerked her entire body.

"I can imagine."

The straight road continued ahead, but another curved

away from it into the orangey mountains. It was tempting to just continue coasting along, but the other route did seem to offer interesting scenery.

"Which way do you fancy?"

Elsa gazed ahead. "Well, I do like a good straight line..."

"Me, too."

"But, the mountain road looks fun..."

"The mountain road, then?"

She nodded.

"Very well." I turned the wheel. The engine began to whine just a little as it took on the steepening gradient.

"I think this was the original road," she said. "Probably led to a mining town or something. Then, they built the highway, bypassing it."

She certainly seemed to know a lot about New Mexico and smiled when I said as much.

"I've been travelling here for a while."

"Probably the best way to learn, living it."

"Life *is* learning," she replied, then closed her eyes as if she were going to sleep.

I yawned, as if I might join her.

It definitely wasn't the place to nod off: The straight highways could be treacherous enough, but the road we were on twisted and turned through canyons and along cliff edges, where a moment's distraction could easily result in disaster.

I jerked back to alertness as Elsa elbowed me.

"No sleeping on the job. If you want to snooze, you'd better let me drive."

"Do you even have a licence?"

Elsa gave another of her full-bodied shrugs. "Provisional. But, not here in the States."

"Then," I said, fighting off another yawn, "it's probably best you leave it to me."

I gestured to a roadside sign perched above a sheer drop that appeared scoured by many years of blasting sand. "It said, 'Wilson Springs – 20 miles.'

"I should be able to stay awake long enough to get us there."

I was guessing maybe half-an-hour.

"Okay," she said.

We drove the rest of the way in silence, Elsa relaxing, me with my full attention on the road ahead.

Wilson Springs was the sort of dead town you see out in those parts, dustier than the desert that surrounds it. It might have been called a one-horse town, only there were no horses in sight and only a single pick-up truck parked outside a shuttered general store. The pick-up looked almost as sand-scoured as the road sign.

There was a man, a living stereotype, with a leathery face, seated in a rocking chair on the porch outside the general store. He looked like a cowboy from a 1950s Western and had on a huge hat that, if it couldn't quite muster ten gallons, surely was eight or nine.

The old man jumped out of his chair as we drew up and seemed delighted to see us.

"The town died back when the *guvmint*," he made the word sound like 'varmint', "built the new expressway, bypassing us," he explained as he pumped my hand and eyed Elsa closely.

With a chuckle in her voice, Elsa asked if there was somewhere to stay.

"The motel would be mighty glad of the custom," he drawled and he proceeded to show us the way.

The old lady who ran it did, indeed, seem delighted when I booked two rooms – and, I was even more so when, after supper, it turned out we only actually needed one.

Given her companionable nature, I unsurprisingly entertained thoughts of Elsa joining me in cruising along the long, straight highways of the American south-west. But, when I woke, she was gone and there was a note half-tucked under her pillow.

You may be cross with me, Elsa had written, *and I wouldn't blame you. But, it's not in my nature to be with anyone for long. I travel alone. But, I did enjoy our time together. I hope you did, too.*

Keep following the straight road to your dreams.

Love,

Elsa.

I couldn't bring myself to be angry, although I was curious to know how she escaped the dead little town of Wilson Springs. Maybe our friend in the eight-or-nine gallon hat drove her away in his pick-up, although both he and the vehicle were in place outside the general store when I exited the motel after a very-pleasant breakfast.

If it hadn't been for the note, and the lingering trace of her scent, I might have thought I imagined her... Elsa was just too... perfect? Individual? Unique?

She was certainly something!

I drove back down the twisting mountain road and returned to the highway, putting the car into cruise once more and letting it carry me to who-knew-where.

That was how I met, and lost, Elsa, and, as much as I loved to cruise along that long, straight road, I realised I had loved doing it with her all the more, and I like to imagine she's still out there, somewhere, journeying to infinity on a gap year that never ends.

Ends

Made in the USA
Monee, IL
01 February 2020

21148650R00169